DESTROY UNOPENED

A serial killer is roaming the streets of
Notting Hill...

Alex Tanner, part-time private eye, is shown
a parcel marked DESTROY UNOPENED
by Hilary Lucas. The parcel has been given
to her following her husband's death, and it
proves to contain anonymous love letters
written over many years. When Hilary asks
Alex to find the author of the anonymous
letters, her investigations begin to suggest
that the writer is the mother of the Notting
Hill killer...

DESTROY UNOPENED

DESTROY UNOPENED

by

Anabel Donald

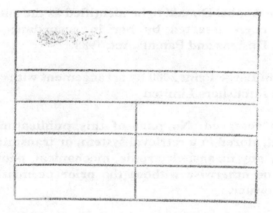

Magna Large Print Books
Long Preston, North Yorkshire,
BD23 4ND, England.

British Library Cataloguing in Publication Data.

Donald, Anabel
    Destroy unopened.

    A catalogue record of this book is
    available from the British Library

    ISBN   0-7505-1540-6

First published in Great Britain by Pan Books
An imprint of Macmillan Publishers Ltd., 1999

Copyright © 1999 by Anabel Donald

Cover photography © Last Resort Picture Library

Published in Large Print 2000 by arrangement with
Macmillan Publishers Limited

Magna Large Print is an imprint of Library Magna Books Ltd.

Printed and bound in Great Britain by
T.J. (International) Ltd., Cornwall, PL28 8RW

Thursday 3 November

Chapter One

DESTROY UNOPENED. Bold printing scrawled in red felt tip on the front of a big, battered, bulging manila envelope. The gummed flap was tacky from being opened and resealed countless times. It lay on the coffee table between us. Ten minutes into the meeting and neither of us had mentioned it yet, though the client's eyes flickered towards it and away so often it was like having a third person in the room. Or perhaps a grenade.

'I don't want to look a fool,' the client said abruptly. 'I'm not a fool. Do I look like a fool to you?'

'No,' I said. I'd have said that anyway, but actually she didn't. She looked like a successful barrister in her fifties, which is what she was. Pink and puffy round the eyes – natural enough, as she was recently widowed – but pleasant faced, with strong once-dark greying hair well cut and springing back from a high forehead. Medium tall tending to stocky, no make-up, untamed eyebrows, short square-cut nails on strong hands. I'm not good on clothes but her trousers and top were a fine silver-grey jersey knit, middle-range expensive. They suited her.

So did the room, a large mostly book-lined living room of a very expensive mansion flat in Kensington. Any wall space not covered by books held paintings, mostly oils or acrylics, all twentieth century, at a guess, and some of the styles were familiar although I couldn't put a name to them. Minor works by major artists, possibly. There were also small sculptures on tables: all head-and-shoulder bronzes of adults and children. One was a younger version of my hostess.

French windows led to a balcony which would have had a view of Kensington Gardens if London hadn't been engulfed in fog. Cream net curtains billowed gently in the sporadic, chilly breeze. 'You'll have to forgive the draught,' she said. 'I always like to have a window open. I like air.'

'So do I.'

Silence.

Her eyes flicked to the envelope. Not a grenade, I thought. A time bomb. She'd mention it eventually, and she was the

10

client. I just wished I knew the timing on the clock. I forced myself to sit back in the well-upholstered armchair. I breathed the acrid fuel-laden air, admired the effectiveness of the central heating, sipped the excellent cup of coffee she'd just made me and waited for her to get to the point. I'd already calculated how often you'd have to wash net curtains in London to keep them cream (once a week), how much the service charge on the flat would be (fifteen thousand a year minimum), and the price of a lease on her flat (start at half a million and the sky's the limit).

'Adrian Trigg recommended you,' she said. 'He's our solicitor.'

'Mm-hmm,' I said, nodding keenly. Trigg is a partner in a top law firm and a contact I want to keep. That's why, though I'd been out of London when he'd rung my office yesterday, I'd rearranged my plans to present myself for this interview prompt at two o'clock, ready to work tirelessly day and night to keep Hilary Lucas from looking a fool. Partly to keep Trigg sweet: partly because, when you're self-employed, day and night is when you work.

'Tell me about yourself,' she said.

I opened my mouth to speak.

'Professionally, I mean,' she added.

I hadn't supposed she wanted a rundown on my star sign and sexual orientation. I didn't sigh though, and said, 'Originally, I was a TV researcher, BBC trained. Self-employed TV research is still about fifty per cent of my work. I do private investigations on the side, and I have no formal training for that. I'm basically a one-woman outfit, but I use assistants as and when they're needed.'

'And what kind of private investigations do you do, mainly?'

'Mostly missing persons. And residential enquiries.'

She lifted a formidable eyebrow. 'Residential enquiries?'

'For prospective buyers of properties round Notting Hill. Mostly media and banking people. Time is money to them, or more valuable than money. They want to buy a particular flat or house, but don't have time to check out what it would actually be like living there. So they pay us to investigate the immediate area for noise and litter and crazy neighbours and other little details of local life. It's a recent venture, growing all the time.'

'Ah,' she said. 'Tell me about your assistants.'

'My chief assistant is Nick Straker. She's young but very bright and committed and currently works full time. The others are employed on an ad-hoc basis.'

'Mmm,' she said. 'Adrian told me you were independent minded. And that you respected confidences.'

'True. It goes with the territory.'

Then I just went on drinking coffee. She didn't strike me as an easy target for gush and empty reassurances.

'You have just come back from Newcastle, you said?'

'Yes. I've been there since Sunday.'

'And what were you doing?'

'Working for Minerva Communications.'

'As a detective?'

'No, as a contestant interviewer.'

I got the raised eyebrow treatment again. I considered leaving the question unanswered. She wasn't hiring me for chat about TV. Or perhaps she was. I'd got up at five that morning – much too early for me – and was beginning to feel stroppy. 'Choosing potential candidates for quiz and game shows,' I said, mildly.

'Is that difficult?'

'Yes. They can't be too stupid or too bright or too ignorant or too well informed or too ugly or too good-looking, and they mustn't babble or dry in front of the cameras.'

'A strange area of expertise.'

'Not un-lucrative,' I said.

'And while you were away in Newcastle, who handled your detective work?'

'Nick.'

'I want you to handle this yourself,' she said. 'If you use assistants, I don't want them to be told the reason for their enquiries, or any of the background. And no record keeping on a computer, please. Can you manage that?'

'Certainly,' I said rather snittily. I don't like being told how to do my job, and so far I'd refrained from giving her helpful pointers on international contract law. Her field, according to Trigg.

She ignored my snittiness and looked at me closely. 'How old are you?'

'Thirty last June.'

'You look younger.'

'People often say that.' It's partly my clothes (jeans, sweatshirt and Doc Martens boots), partly my hair (cropped) and partly my make-up (none).

'You're not very tall, are you?'

That's a sensitive point, with me. I've always wanted to be tall, six foot plus. That's what I feel I am. 'Five feet four,' I said. She looked sceptical. 'On a good day,' I added, repressively. A good day on the rack, perhaps.

'Do you live alone?' she asked.

'Yes,' I said.

'All the time?'

'No. I have a friend who stays sometimes.'

'Often?'

'Often,' I said. My man Barty had been staying more than he hadn't, recently. More than I wanted him to sometimes. While I was in Newcastle he'd left for Zaire, and I was looking forward to having the flat to myself.

'Have you martial arts or self-defence training of any kind?'

'Evening classes in karate,' I said. 'But I don't do criminal or body-guarding work, usually.'

'Forgive me. Your hair – that's not your natural colour?'

The red of my hair is so chemical that, any minute now, environmental protection groups will ban it. I didn't see why it was her business, though. 'No,' I said.

'Do you ever dye it blonde?'

'No,' I said.

'And your eyes are naturally green? Those

aren't tinted contact lenses?'

'My eyes are naturally green,' I said, wondering why she was wandering out where the trams don't run, well at the limit of my patience. Bereavement perhaps.

'And your ambitions? What motivates you?'

My immediate ambition was to spring-clean my flat. I'd been trying to get started on it since the spring and either hadn't had time or Barty had been there. I don't enjoy cleaning round a man: they're too big, their paperwork spreads everywhere, they leave damp towels in odd places and wreck the kitchen when they cook.

I couldn't tell her that. So what ambition could I produce?

'Financial security, mostly,' I said. 'I want to earn as much as I can, doing a job of work I enjoy.'

She half smiled. 'And what are your fees?'

I told her, upping them by a third, what with the flat, Trigg, and her nosiness. Her expression didn't change. Damn, I should have upped them by a half.

'Right, I'd better get to the point, hadn't I,' she said.

Then she started to cry.

I'd already given her my condolences, and

there was a limit to how much sorrow I could express to a very recent acquaintance over the death of a perfect stranger, so I looked seriously at the carpet. She was sad but she wasn't distraught, and she was too self-possessed to welcome hugging or hand patting.

She stretched out her hand to the envelope on the table. The clock on the time bomb had stopped, I thought in the silence, but she withdrew her hand and said, 'Do you mind not answering questions?'

A smile seemed the only possible answer. I gave it.

She smiled back, briefly. 'I'm not being very explicit, am I? What I mean is, I don't want anyone you talk to on my behalf to have the least idea what you are trying to discover.'

As things stood, I'd wouldn't have any difficulty with that, since neither did I. 'I don't mind stonewalling for a client, if that's what you mean. I don't mind lying for a client either, if it's in a good cause. But if you told me what we were talking about, it'd help.'

She took a deep breath. 'As you know, Robbie – my husband – died suddenly, of a heart attack, nearly three months ago.'

'It must have been a shock.'

'Of course,' she said, but absent-mindedly, as if she wasn't thinking about his death.

'And you want me to...?'

Her face went blank, her body stiffened, she snatched up the envelope and clutched it tightly to her silver-grey jersey chest. 'I can't make myself clear,' she said, sounding annoyed with herself, as if lack of clarity was embarrassing. Which I suppose it would be, to a Queen's Counsel whose livelihood depended on articulacy.

What I wanted to do was snatch the envelope and tear it open. What I did was give an encouraging nod. Open-minded Alex. Nothing you say will surprise me.

'I ... I...' She clicked at herself impatiently. 'My husband Robbie is – was – a Professor at NCL, that's New College, London.'

Pause.

She forced herself on. 'He has – had – an office there, naturally.'

'Of course.'

'And they cleared his office last week, and sent me his things. Mostly books, and lecture notes, and research work in progress. And I sorted through them.'

'That must have been hard for you.'

'Sad,' she said briskly. 'Inevitable, though.'

She squared her shoulders and tried to look in control. A naturally independent woman, I thought, when not so recently widowed. I adjusted my expression, phasing out sympathy and leaving intelligent interest.

She cleared her throat. 'Among his things, I found this,' she said, and held the envelope out to me, bottom upwards.

'You want me to destroy it?' I asked.

'Of course not. Not yet. And of course I have looked inside.'

'And what is it?'

'Letters. Love letters. To Robbie.'

Chapter Two

Several questions sprang to mind, but I said nothing. She was as tense as if a dentist was prodding round her infected teeth. I didn't want to hit an unnecessary nerve.

'The earlier ones are typed. The later, word-processed. I didn't see any hand-writing, although there may be some. I don't know. I'm not going to look at them, ever again.'

Very wise, I thought. Wiser still just to chuck them. 'Mrs Lucas, how long had you been married?'

'Thirty years.'

'And he wanted the letters destroyed. Surely he knew you well enough to make the decision for you. Maybe you should respect that.'

She clicked impatiently again, this time at me. 'If he really wanted them destroyed, he'd have made sure the envelope never reached me. He may have been an academic and rather unworldly at times, but he wasn't a complete idiot.'

'He wasn't expecting to die suddenly, either,' I said. 'What exactly is it that you want me to do?'

'Find the woman. Find the woman and tell me who it is. Probably reading the letters should be enough. But perhaps not, since you're an outsider. Ask around at NCL. Chances are she's an academic. Use any cover story you like, but if you need me to back it, make sure I know in advance.'

'Any suggestions?' I said.

'I'm finding difficulty...' She stopped. 'I can't ... think of things at the moment.'

'I could say I was researching a television documentary.'

'What on?' she asked.

'On academics.'

'He wasn't outstanding in any way,' she said uncertainly. 'He was well known in his field, of course.'

'His field being...?'

'Fourteenth-century irrigation and drainage systems. He was a historical geographer.'

'Ah,' I said.

She seemed nettled by my blankness. 'He was the world authority on drainage and irrigation in Flanders, Lombardy, Burgundy and Gascony.'

'Right,' I said. 'Perhaps I should say the

documentary was on heart attacks and lifestyle.'

'If you wish. He wasn't at all dull, you know. It's an important area, historical geography.' Protective affection exuded from her. All their married life, probably, she'd been explaining defensively how fascinating her husband's subject was.

'I'm sure it is,' I said. 'Television is usually concerned with the trivial, though. Let's go with heart attacks, everyone understands those.'

'In that case, you'll need some information,' she said, writing in her organizer, then tearing out the page and giving it to me.

She'd written his age at death – fifty-eight – the name of his GP, the name of the hospital where he'd died, and details of diet, exercise, alcohol and tobacco consumption.

'That's fine. Who was his closest colleague in the department? Who should I start with?'

'His closest friend at work wasn't in the History Department. It was Philip Gein, an English Professor. But he died a week before Robbie.'

'Another heart attack?'

'No, a mugging. A terrible thing. Robbie was devastated. It probably contributed to–' She was remembering, and with the memory came anger, which she turned on me. 'You're not understanding me,' she said. 'I particularly don't want you interfering with Robbie's friends and mine, putting the idea into their heads. I don't want them knowing, I don't want anyone knowing, because I don't think it's true.' She faltered, and stopped. 'I can't believe it's true,' she amended. 'And the fewer people who know about it, the better.'

I didn't say that the chances were that she was the only person who didn't know. 'Fine,' I said placatingly. 'Leave it to me. But you do realize it would be much more efficient – and confidential – for you to read the letters yourself. You'd probably spot the writer in five minutes.'

'I know, but I'm not going to. I'm not going to read another word of – that.' She almost spat it out. 'We were married for nearly thirty years. I thought I knew him. All about him – as much as you can know about another human being. And no, of course it wasn't a perfect marriage, and yes, I think there was at least one other woman, twenty years ago. We had some dull patches, and rocky patches, and fights, and it was hard adjusting to no children, because we both wanted children. But it was thirty years. It's what I did, for thirty years, apart from my work, of course. Do you know what you're left with, when your husband dies, if you don't have children?'

She didn't need my answer so I didn't even formulate one. I cleared my mind of widows' pensions, long leases on huge posh flats, and insurance policies. I just looked enquiring.

'Memories. That's what you're left with. And if I read through that—' she pointed at the envelope 'my memories will be smeared over. I'll have their times and places and chapter and verse, all mixed up with ours. And I won't do it. I won't.'

'I'll take it away and destroy it,' I said. 'Better all round. That's what he wanted. He didn't want you to read them, obviously. He wanted to protect you.'

She laughed, angrily. 'Not enough to destroy them himself,' she said. 'Not enough not to keep them.'

'And you want me to name the woman? Why?'

'Not just name her. Name her quickly. Will a week be long enough?'

'Should be. I can't guarantee it. Why do you want to know?' I repeated. 'And why the urgency?'

Pause. She looked at me, looked away, cleared her throat. She was deciding whether to lie. Perhaps she was inventing the lie.

Finally she spoke. 'Because next Friday is Robbie's memorial service, at NCL. Chances are that woman will be there. I want to know who she is. I told you, I don't want to look a fool.'

I stepped out of Hilary Lucas's warm, well-lit mansion block into the chill of November London and decided to take a bus home because the overnight bag I'd taken to Newcastle was heavy. I'd normally have walked. It's only about a mile and a half north-west through Kensington Gardens.

The bus took half an hour, partly because of the low visibility and greasy roads and partly because Kensington was full of tourists and they milled about in the streets ignoring crossing lights. Until quite recently London was for Londoners, except during the summer. Now tourism was a year-round thing.

Not that I usually minded: tourists are better mannered than Londoners, but they do tend to stand in the middle of the pavement looking hopelessly at maps, and they sometimes ask for shopping advice, which I'm ill equipped to give. I almost never shop for pleasure. When forced to, I go out to buy a specific article.

I was sitting right at the front of the bus. Just behind me were tourists, obviously American, a couple in their sixties. The woman tapped me on the shoulder and after polite preliminaries pointed at a child in the street collecting for his guy and asked me to explain.

'It's a British custom,' I said. 'In the seventeenth century a group of Catholics tried to blow up Parliament. They were all betrayed and executed, and one of them was Guy Fawkes. Every November 5th we have parties, with fireworks and a bonfire to burn Guy Fawkes in effigy. Children make the effigies – we call them "guys" – and collect money for the parties. There's a rhyme that goes with it:

Remember remember the fifth of November, with gunpowder, treason and plot. I see no reason why gunpowder treason should ever be forgot.'

She looked puzzled, understandably. 'A charming custom,' she said valiantly. We nodded and smiled at each other as long as either of us could stand it and then I turned away, reflecting that I'd done my bit for the Tourist Board, and hoping that next time I'd have to explain something that made more sense.

It felt good, being back in town after a few days away up north, and the city looked terrific in the fog. Everything was softened and magical, with haloes of light around street lamps, already switched on though it was only half past three. The ill-assorted, mostly Victorian, buildings of Kensington Church Street blurred to beauty like Norma Desmond through a skilful cameraman's soft filter.

Then an *Evening Standard* placard screamed at me and dented my good humour. NOTTING HILL KILLER SHOCK! Newspaper placards always scream, of course, but this one caught my attention as if it had been my name. Notting Hill is where I live – well, nearly. Notting Hill itself is very smart and exclusive and expensive. My flat, my most precious possession, is on its fringes. When I earn money it's to pay the mortgage and to put enough in the endowment fund finally to pay it off. Preferably before time. And my investment has been soaring up ever since I first chose the shabby flat in the shabby house in the shabby but improving street. I'm proud of it. Proud that I chose wisely, proud that I've managed to keep up the payments, even though in the early years when I was still a badly paid secretary with no access to expenses I'd sometimes lived on bread and bruised remaindered oranges and sardines for days to be able to afford it.

And now I was afraid my investment'd be damaged by a serial killer. If you think I've got my priorities wrong, that isn't true. Of course I was sorry for his victims. Of course I wanted him caught and punished and prevented from doing any further harm. But serial killers are a fact of life, aberrations that can pop up anywhere, and I wished he'd popped up in another district. Usually, Notting Hill was tabloided as *exclusive area, playground of the famous,* or *home to the world-renowned Portobello Market.* Now it was *home to the Butcher of the Bella.* Or *stalking ground of the sadistic killer.*

The man sitting on the other front seat of the bus was reading the *Standard.* I rubbernecked. The SHOCK! turned out to be – yet again – that the killer hadn't kept to his time table. Usually there was a victim every two months. There hadn't been one for getting on for four months. Good news, I'd have thought, but not on planet tabloid.

Firmly, I forced myself to think about something else. After an internal struggle, I focused on the envelope in my bag. I thought about what it would feel like, after his death, to find your husband had a mistress, and I wondered about the callousness, or thoughtlessness, or malice, of a husband who would leave such a time bomb.

But most of all I thought about Hilary Lucas herself, and the deadline she'd set me; the memorial service next week. If there was a memorial service

I'd felt she was lying at the time and it didn't surprise me. Clients nearly always lie, mostly I suppose because, apart from commercial espionage or property research or credit referencing, you only hire a private detective when you're driven to it by intimate and powerful pressures. Not facing the painful issue straight on makes it more tolerable.

Come to that I'd been lying, or at any rate suppressing the truth. I hadn't given Hilary Lucas a full description of my detective agency, a one-woman firm which had taken a growth pill in the form of my assistant

Nick, who had then started hiring casual labourers part time. The Revenue didn't know about those one-off hirings, paid in cash. This temporary expansion would contract next year, I hoped, because Nick was due to start at medical school next September. I'd agreed to let her stay and work her year off with me, to save up some money to live on during her course.

By that time, theoretically, I'd be married. I've sort of agreed to marry Barty because I like him a great deal – more than anyone else I'd ever met. He's quick, competent, intelligent and funny, and he docsn't cling. He's older than me, in his mid-forties: not a bad thing. Men my own age seem puppyish compared to him. He's also better bred and better educated, which I used to resent, but am growing to like, and it'll be useful for our children. And it's well time I had children, if I'm going to.

Chapter Three

Lost in rambling reflections, I nearly missed the Ladbroke Grove bus stop and had to hurl myself down the stairs and bully the driver into opening the doors again for me. From there I had to walk back along the Grove a hundred yards or so to my flat, which took me past my office and the two peevish-looking people – clients? – standing shivering outside, glaring at the CLOSED sign on the door and ignoring Lil, a local character who was standing a few feet away from them, talking loudly. She had to talk loudly to be heard over the barking of her cocker spaniel, and she was using her quotation voice, a well-projected resonant plummy bellow.

'Fog everywhere. Fog up the river, fog down the river, fog on the Scrubs marshes, fog on the Notting Hill heights. Fog creeping into the steamy kitchens of Chinese takeaways, fog lying on the video shops and hovering in the ceilings of banks...'

'Dickens?' I interrupted.

'Of course, my dear, but somewhat adapted. *Bleak House*. You have clients, as you see. Benbow's taken against them, I'm afraid.' She jerked on Benbow's lead and choked his barks, briefly. 'Hadn't you better attend to them?'

I never man the office. Nick does that. It was her idea in the first place. I'd been quite happy working from home. But she'd built up my missing persons business enough to pay her salary, her PAYE tax with the Revenue, and a decent little profit for me which all went straight into my pension fund. So when she showed me we could afford an office and offered to run it, what could I say? It was basically her perk, because she lived there. Illegally, because it wasn't residential. Business purposes only. But she had the office, with a sofa as well as the desk, she had a toilet and washbasin, and that beat the streets, which was where she normally lived, where she'd come to me for work experience from, and now where she didn't live, because she lived in my office.

I fished keys out of the back pocket of my jeans and opened the door.

'So I should hope,' said the peevish man, pushing into the office behind me. 'Do you

34

realize what time it is?'

I disregarded this, and looked round. No Nick. No sign of Nick. No bedclothes on the sofa, a tidy desk.

'On the sign outside, the office hours are given as one thirty to four, or by appointment, Monday to Friday. It is three forty-five now, on a Thursday.'

The windows were closed, the air stagnant, The place felt dead. It wouldn't have been dead long, though, because Nick had rung me from there the day before.

'And the neighbourhood is most unsavoury. We were subjected to the demented ramblings of that old woman for some time.'

'She's not demented. She was quoting Dickens,' I said. 'A fine prose stylist. Educational, really.'

'In the street?'

'She spends a lot of time on the street. Her old people's home doesn't allow dogs, so she had to give him away, but she walks him every day.'

'And the appalling noise that dog makes. All most unsatisfactory. What have you to say for yourself?' demanded the peevish man, peevishly.

'Good afternoon,' I said, dumping my overnight bag and sitting down in the swivel chair behind the desk, deciding against telling him that Lil was one of Nick's most reliable missing person operatives. 'I'm Alex Tanner. And you are?'

'I'm Pauline Eyre,' said the woman. 'This is my husband, Dr Eyre.'

'How do you do,' I said. 'Please sit down.'

The woman sat on the sofa. After a pause, so did the man.

I supposed I owed them an apology. I certainly couldn't provide an explanation. And if they had in fact waited anything approaching two hours, no wonder they were peevish.

'I'm sorry the office was closed,' I said. 'Staffing problems. Have you waited long?'

'Yes,' said the man.

'Half an hour,' said the woman.

'And how can I help you?'

'You can explain exactly what services you are providing for the extortionate sum of money you charged my wife,' said the man.

'Perhaps if we could speak to Nick,' said the woman. She looked about, bewildered, as if expecting Nick to emerge from the walls.

It's a basic office, very bare. Apart from two large radiators which pumped out suffocating heat, it contained a filing cabinet, a desk and a swivel chair, all from a bottom-of-the-market second-hand office supplier, and a sofa from the furniture dealer immediately opposite (house clearances, rubbish carted away). The sofa had certainly been part of the rubbish carted away, though somebody had probably been proud of it once, buying it new when lime green synthetic covers, spindly black metal legs and sharp corners were all the rage. The walls, painted by Nick in white emulsion which hadn't quite covered the previous peacock blue, held only some cork display boards, all of which were occupied by charts, lists and maps. Some of them even related to our business. Others had been scavenged by Nick from nearby skips, and included a map of Cambodia which would doubtless be very useful when Tanner Associates went Far Eastern.

Dr Eyre, looking round, didn't seem convinced by the office. Neither was I.

'I'm afraid Nick's unavailable,' I said. 'When did you speak to her, Mrs Eyre?'

'Monday,' she said. 'And I found her very businesslike and trustworthy' She looked straight at me as she spoke, willing me to do or say, or not to do or say, something.

Chances were that she didn't want her

husband to know that Nick was a half-Asian eighteen-year-old with bald patches on her head where she tugged her hair out in times of stress and who wore a baseball cap to cover them. Looking at Dr Eyre, I thought he might have considered the baseball cap the worse option. I was surprised Mrs Eyre had found Nick acceptable at all.

They were both in their forties and formal dressers. He was average height, but looked taller because he was so thin. His legs were long for his body and planted spider-wide apart. He had short greying sandy-coloured hair, sharp features and pale blue eyes with paler sandy lashes, and he wore a heavy tweed suit, white shirt, anonymous stripy tie and highly polished brogues.

She was also thin, about my height, very carefully made up, with smallish brown eyes and probably dyed dark hair in a feathery cut. She wore a navy-blue Marks and Spencer suit with a shortish skirt which revealed her knobbly knees, a white silk blouse and high-heeled navy-blue shoes. Her long nails were painted a bright coral pink which matched her lipstick, her earrings and her brooch.

Maybe I should pop over to my flat and accessorize, I thought. Then they would both stop staring at my boots.

'Nick's my associate, and she handles missing persons,' I said. 'Her notes on your case will be on the computer, but it'd save time if you tell me what I need to know to answer whatever questions you have.'

'Our girl had been missing for five weeks,' said Mrs Eyre.

'Two months,' said Dr Eyre. 'Samantha's been missing for two months.'

'Actually she hasn't been missing for the last three weeks, because we had the letter, you see. She was missing before that, as far as we were concerned, because we didn't know where she was or what had happened to her.'
'We did receive a letter from her, couched in very vague terms, but she didn't tell us precisely where she is, so she's still missing,' said Dr Eyre.

'She said she was looking forward to the Carnival. The Notting Hill Carnival, you know. She said she'd be very near it. She likes carnivals and fairs,' said Mrs Eyre.

'The Carnival's held in the summer,' I said blankly.

'She likes to plan ahead,' said Mrs Eyre. 'She looks forward to treats.'

'And what I would like to know is, what

the devil do you think you're doing, taking my wife's money?' said Eyre.

They were sitting with a fair old space between them, which took some doing since the sofa's a two-seater. They were both bolt upright, perched on the edge each talking to me as if we were alone.

I was annoyed with Nick for skiving off, wherever it was she'd gone. I didn't like this pair much, and I wanted to get home and get on with Hilary Lucas's job.

'Tell me what you paid and I'll refund it,' I said.

Eyre's pale blue eyes were also sharp, and combative. They flicked at me, and then away again, but not towards his wife. Towards the wall.

'What's all this, Miss Tanner?' he asked the wall. 'Are you, or are you not, the proprietor of a detective agency?'

'I am.'

'Do you, or do you not, undertake missing persons cases?'

'That was why I came to you,' his wife cut across him. 'At the police station, they called Samantha the *misper*.'

'That's what they call them,' I said.

'It sounded final. It sounded...' she paused.

40

'Dismissive,' said Dr Eyre. 'My wife means "dismissive", but she has a limited vocabulary. She was only a secretary before our marriage.'

It was obviously intended as an insult and delivered like a playground taunt. It also sounded well worn, as if the spontaneity of it had gone but the sourness remained. She looked at me, expressionless, and said nothing.

I felt sweat beginning to form on my back. I got up, opened the window and sucked in the foggy air. I wanted to get out of my DMs into a pair of spads. Better still, I wanted to get out of my jeans and into a shower. But most of all, I wanted rid of the Eyres.

The open window, besides air, was letting in Lil's monologue. 'Never can there come fog too thick, never can there come mud and mire too deep, to assort with the groping and floundering condition which this Town Hall of Kensington and Chelsea, most pestilent of hoary sinners, holds, this day, in the sight of heaven and earth.'

'Lay off, Lil,' I said. 'What has the council ever done to you?'

'Put me in an old folks' home. Pee and teeth.'

'Pee and teeth is never Dickens,' I said.

41

'Alan Bennett. "A Cream Cracker under the Settee." Adapted,' said Lil. Benbow barked.

I shut the window and turned back to the Eyres. 'I don't really think...' I started.

'The police aren't doing anything,' said Mrs Eyre urgently. 'I know they're not. She's just another misper, to them. But she's my daughter. Look. Look.' She took a navy-blue leather wallet out of her navy-blue leather handbag with gilt clasps. She flipped it open and showed me a photograph.

A head-and-shoulders snapshot of a pretty, blonde, vacant-blue-eyed girl in her late teens or early twenties.

'Mrs Eyre—'

'She's in danger,' said the woman desperately. 'I know she is. She's – she's—'

'Stupid,' said her father.

'A slow developer,' said her mother. 'She has learning difficulties.'

'She's a moron,' said Eyre bitterly. 'Like her mother.'

Nothing changed in the atmosphere. They didn't look at each other, but only at me. Mrs Eyre didn't change her manner, not by one iota, in response to what I would have taken as a challenge to open battle. Clearly what we had here was a permanent state of declared hostilities. The Hundred Eyres War, I thought uncomfortably.

'So she's definitely at risk,' said the mother. 'It's not like a normal girl leaving home. She can't really – look after herself.'

'She's a better cook and housekeeper than you are,' Eyre told the wall.

'She didn't even go to school. We had her educated at home.'

'We had to hire someone to come in,' said Eyre. 'At considerable expense. But my wife wasn't up to it. Her own education, if you could call it that, having ground to an ignominious halt in her mid-teens.'

'And I'm worried about the – about the Notting Hill serial killer.'

'Having a tabloid mind,' said Eyre to the wall. 'Thinking only in terms of popular stereotypes. Out of the fifty plus million population of our island, if there is a serial killer, he must be focusing his murderous attentions on my daughter, the moron.'

This time she responded to him, but indirectly. 'Miss Tanner, our daughter is nineteen. She is five foot one. She is blonde haired and blue eyed. And she's living here.'

Eyre said nothing. She had a point, of course. Her daughter met the Killer's specifications exactly. Right colouring.

Right age: under twenty-one. Right height: under five two. Right location: the killer's victims disappeared in the Notting Hill area, stayed out of sight for three to five days, and were then dumped on Wormwood Scrubs Common, thoroughly raped and efficiently strangled. And mutilated. But police weren't releasing details of that.

Then it hit me. That was what Hilary Lucas had been getting at, surely, when she'd fretted on at me about my height and age and colouring. Embedded in her exhaustive cross-examination had been exactly that information.

She'd been concerned that I might be a target for the Notting Hill Killer.

I reached for my bag, took out the envelope and put it on the desk in front of me. The bold red printed scrawl had been a come-on. It was still a challenge, but now it was also a threat. DESTROY UN-OPENED.

I looked at it. Just an envelope. Silent. As of course time bombs were, just before they exploded.

Chapter Four

'Miss Tanner? Miss Tanner? Oh really, this is beyond a joke.'

I blinked, looked up from the envelope and focused on fractious Dr Eyre, who sounded as if he'd been trying to attract my attention for a while. I was sure I was right about Hilary Lucas, absolutely sure, but I couldn't see why, or how it fitted in with the job she'd said she wanted me to do.

I needed to talk to her, right away.

Pauline Eyre was talking. 'I just want to know where she is. I want to know that she's safe, that someone's looking after her. Which is why I came to your agency on Monday, having used my secretarial skills, limited as they probably are, to consult the Yellow Pages and make a list of private detectives in the Notting Hill area. And why I was prepared to spend my own money hiring you to find her.'

I looked directly at her. 'You're the client?' I said.

'I'm the client.'

'In that case I'd prefer to discuss the matter with you. Just you. So if Dr Eyre would care to...' I got up.

'Tell her I'm your husband and you want me to stay,' he said to the wall.

'Please, Roland,' she said, looking directly at him for the first time.

'You want me to leave?' he asked, incredulously.

'Please,' she said again, and squeezed his hand.

'Where do you expect me to go?'

'There are some excellent cafes on Kensington Park Road,' I said. 'Up to the traffic lights, turn left, then first right. Have a cup of tea. Watch the world go by.'

'I don't drink tea.' He sounded annoyed, which I'd expected, but also slightly lost, which I hadn't.

'Have a nice cup of coffee and a cake,' said his wife, looking at him for the first time. 'I won't be long.'

'Don't sign anything,' he said. 'Don't sign anything before I've approved it, Pauline. And don't give her any more money.'

'Certainly not, Roland.'

After he'd gone, I gave her the usual warnings. Chances were the girl was no longer in the area. She may have been lying about where she was living. She could be anywhere. And even if we found her, if she didn't want to go home or speak to her mother then we couldn't make her.

'Nick told me all that already,' Pauline Eyre said. She sounded altogether more businesslike and less plaintive, without her husband. 'I'm sorry Roland was so rude. He's upset.' She cleared her throat. 'He doesn't always quite... He's very devoted to Samantha, you see.'

I had no idea what she was getting at. 'Naturally,' I said.

'She isn't always easy to understand. Has her own ways... Did you say there'd be notes about her on the computer? Would you look?'

I booted up the computer and looked, feeling more annoyed with Nick by the minute. Here I was spending time on one of her cases when I needed to get on with something else, urgently. I opened the document: *eyre.1*. Then I felt less annoyed. Nick had done a good deal: a cracking fee, half paid in advance and half at the end of the week and receipt of a detailed report, and if the girl was found before the week was up, we got the week's fee anyway, as a bonus. Plus expenses. A bit of a rip off, actually. Nick's a smart operator.

Then I read the rest of her notes. She'd done what I, would have done, more or less. She'd started in Ladbroke Grove itself and shown the girl's photograph in the local post office, the baker's, the cleaner's, the all-night rip-off grocery store, the off-licence, the video rental place, the two pubs and the five takeaways. Some recognition but no hard information. She'd also set Lil on the case, with the usual deal, twenty quid in cash finder's fee. Nothing from her as of yesterday.

The last entry was much more promising. Possible ID with location, the Golden Kid.

I didn't want to raise Pauline Eyre's hopes too far, but she was watching me so intently that she'd noticed my change of expression. I had to tell her something.

'It seems that Nick had a lead,' I said. 'But it's not clear what.'

'What does it say?'

In a moment, she'd moved round behind me and was reading over my shoulder. I closed the document.

'You'll get a report from Nick when we have something concrete to tell you,' I said.

'I want to see,' she said desperately. 'Let me see.'

'No, Mrs Eyre. We'll be in touch.'

'Soon?'

'As soon as we can,' I said, and got up to show her out, ushering her like a bouncer. Otherwise, I reckoned, she'd stick around all evening.

I closed the door behind her and waited a minute, in case she came back, then I went into the street and looked for Lil. No sign of her. A black drug dealer was leaning against his white BMW, parked on the pavement right outside. I knew him by sight, because he was hard to overlook: six foot plus, wearing only jeans and a singlet, despite the temperature. The singlet was probably to show off his pumped-up muscles which looked as if, at any moment, they'd burst free of his over-stretched skin and writhe around splattering his car.

'Seen Lil?' I asked.

'Loony Lil? She went up the Grove. You all right for the weekend, then? Fixed up?'

'Yeah. Thanks.'

I retreated into the office before he decided I'd dissed him by refusing to buy, and sat down again at the desk. I had wanted to ask Lil if she'd got anywhere on Samantha Eyre and also to ask about Nick, if she'd seen her, if she knew where she'd gone.

First, I'd speak to Hilary Lucas.

Answering machine, of course. It always is when you want a particular human being. I left an urgent ring-back message, giving my home telephone number, then locked up and headed for home.

My flat smelt stuffy and uninhabited. I opened the living-room windows and the fog billowed gently in, dissolving as it came. Last Sunday, when I went to Newcastle, I'd left Barty still packing for his trip. He'd tidied the flat before he left – an effort made for me and not natural to him. The tidiness reminded me of him more than his litter would have. It reminded me of his consideration and his thoroughness and, a little, how irritating his remorseless consideration could be.

I dialled my call-minder. Five messages.

I took my boots off while I listened, expecting something from Nick.

The first three were dates for future TV work, two of which clashed. Always the way. I noted them down.

The fourth was from my friend Polly, who owns the downstairs flat. She's been working in Hong Kong for a while. 'Hi Alex, this is Poll, I'm in England, isn't it great? I'll be back in the flat Friday morning, hope to see you then, lots and lots and scads of kisses.'

I had my usual Polly feeling, that it would indeed be great to see her but not quite yet. Tomorrow morning ... plenty of working hours before tomorrow morning, and she might not be staying long... Then I felt disloyal.

Feeling disloyal meant I hadn't taken in the last message, so I played it again. The call-minder timed it for me: ten thirty this morning. 'Alex, this is Alan. I'd like to see you, please. Any chance you could come over this afternoon? Any time after three, or later this evening. I'm not going out.'

Alan Protheroe is one of my old bosses at the BBC, now an independent producer. He puts plenty of work my way. I looked at the clock. Four twenty. Maybe I'd pop round to get in on the ground floor of whatever he was planning.

But there'd been nothing from Nick. Where *was* the girl? It wasn't like her to miss office hours. She was like a kid with a new toy about the office generally, and she was always going on at me about methodical business practices and building up a client base. And she knew I'd be back in London this afternoon. Usually, she'd have a report waiting for me on the clients she'd taken on while I was away, plus some letters for signing and invoices for approval. She'd also be trying to cadge a free supper and a game of Scrabble, her latest craze. I hate Scrabble. I've only played with her once, but she's stubborn, she keeps trying.

I dialled her mobile phone. A recording told me it was 'unavailable' – presumably switched off. That was really unusual. She carried it everywhere and made incessant location calls: 'I'm in Oxford Street', 'I'm just leaving Paddington Station'. She never, ever turned it off, except for a few hours at night when she charged it. I'd refused to buy her a second battery.

So where the hell was she?

Too late, I wished I'd gone after Lil to ask her about Nick. Lil wasn't on the telephone. Maybe, after I'd spoken to Hilary Lucas, I'd go round to the old people's home and fight my way through the carers whose smiles were as false as their teeth and who resented Lil because she wouldn't sit quietly in front of the television all day and go to bed straight after her seven o'clock cocoa. I opened my overnight bag, fished out the slices of ham and salami I'd pinched from the breakfast buffet in the Newcastle hotel, and bunged them in the fridge. No fresh milk, which I'd asked Nick to get.

I'd been slightly worried before, now I was back to annoyed.

She'd turn up.

I turned on the central heating and the immersion heater – I'd need plenty of hot water later, when I got stuck in to cleaning the flat – then went up to the bathroom and had a quick cold shower. I only just heard the phone ringing, wrapped a towel round my head and another round my body in case Nick came in, and hurled myself down the stairs.

'Hilary Lucas here. You asked me to call.'

'I need some information, please.'

'Have you found something? Do you have the woman's name for me?'

'I haven't looked at the letters yet. I'd like you to tell me why you think the Notting Hill Killer is involved in this case.'

Silence.

I let the silence go on. I was sure I was right, and I hoped she had enough sense to acknowledge it and not go all round the houses.

'Why do you suppose me to think that?' she said.

'Because some of the apparently irrelevant questions you asked me seemed to be slanted in that direction.'

Silence.

I waited again, looking round the living room. I'd been away five days and there was a film of dust on everything, blackish London dust. I took the towel off my head and wiped down the desk with it, then walked through to the kitchen and bunged the towel into the washing machine.

'Mrs Lucas?' I said, groping in the cupboard under the sink for a duster.

'What are you doing?' she said.

'Dusting. I've been away a while and the place is a mess. Are you going to answer me?'

She made an impatient clicking noise. 'I'm thinking,' she said.

She wasn't thinking; she was gathering her courage. I dusted the television and video, then wedged the telephone between my shoulder and my ear, and used my nails inside the duster to scrape out the gunge round the buttons of the remote controls.

'Miss Tanner?'

'Call me Alex.'

'Alex, do you have good contacts in the police?'

54

'Not bad.'

'Would they act on your information if you didn't give a source?'

'Possibly.'

'Have you been following the press reports of the Notting Hill Killer?'

'Pretty much.' I try to skim at least three serious newspapers a day, to keep up, so long as I don't have to buy them.

'Are you interested? Do you have any theories?'

Actually, I wasn't and I hadn't. Somewhere in Notting Hill was a man, probably young, who wanted sex just before, during or after killing his small young blonde partner, which was a problem for the man and an even greater problem for his partner. But I don't find nutters interesting, and tracking serial killers is classic police work: interviews, cross-checking, physical clues. It needs manpower and resources. None of it, to date, had been anything to do with me.

'No,' I said.

Silence again.

I bent down and dusted the underside of the desk.

'I'll come round to see you,' she said abruptly.

This surprised me. I'd have expected her

to get me round there. She was making the effort perhaps as a concession, unless she couldn't stand staying in her flat any longer and wanted to get out and do something.

I agreed and gave her the address, then got dressed and started cleaning. Even if she took a taxi I'd have time to get the living room hoovered.

Chapter Five

I offered her black coffee or Malvern water. She took the water, sat on the sofa and looked about her. I saw my flat through her eyes and silently agreed with her that the street was noisy, that the fitted carpet was cheap and showing its age, and should have been polished floorboards by now anyway, and that the curtains were dated; a faded pastel Florentine print. Plus the woodwork was screaming 'wash me'.

Lucky she couldn't see inside my kitchen cupboards.

'I like it anyway,' I said.

Then she looked straight at me and I saw rage in her eyes and pain. Nothing to do with my flat or me.

'What do you know about 10 Rillington Place?' she said.

'It's been demolished. The whole street has. It used to be round here. It was the house where Christie murdered about five women, including the wife of his retarded lodger, Timothy Evans, plus Evans's child, and buried them in the garden or walled them up in the house. The lodger, a pathological liar, confessed to the murders of his wife and child and was hanged for it. They got Christie later, and hanged him.'

'Exactly,' she said. She'd expected me to know. Pretty well everyone in England did, even though the Christie case was nearly fifty years old. We don't have many multiple sex-killers, possibly because, apart from mild sado-masochism and the apparently inexhaustible male desire to gawp at huge tits, obsessive (or indeed any) sexuality is un-British. Consequently when a juicy sex-killer pops up, we're fascinated. There'd been a Christie documentary every five years or so since I'd started in TV, though I'd never worked on one.

She sipped her water. 'Do you know why Christie killed his victims?'

'He was a necrophiliac, wasn't he?'

'Quite. And the Notting Hill Killer?'

'What about him?'

'He might well be a necrophiliac too. Some reports suggest he is.'

'And some reports in the tabloids suggest he's an alien.' I was beginning to lose patience.

'Alex, if you had a son who told you that

he liked his new flat because it was built on the site of 10 Rillington Place, what would you think?'

'Hilary, I wish you'd get to the point,' I said as gently as I could manage. It wasn't gently enough, because she bristled her eyebrows at me in genuine astonishment. Perhaps nobody had ever told her to get to the point before. Maybe they hadn't needed to.

She was ruffled but not distracted. 'If a son of yours said that, would you think he was the Notting Hill Killer?'

'Not first off. Unless he'd shown other signs. Besides, mothers don't, do they? "My boy's a good boy, he wouldn't hurt a fly." That's what mothers say.'

'That's what they say. I've often wondered if that's what they think ... anyway, that's what was in the letter.' She looked me full in the face, guilty.

'What letter?'

'The last letter in the envelope that I gave you. The most recent one.'

I picked up the envelope, but she said, 'I took it out. It isn't there.'

'Where is it?'

'I – destroyed it.' She looked even more guilty.

'How?'

59

She hesitated, started to speak, hesitated again. Finally she blurted, 'I ate it.'

I didn't even smile, but it cost me. 'All of it?'

'Every scrap.'

'And what exactly did it say?'

'I can't remember the words. But the sense was – the sense was that the woman believed that her son might be the Notting Hill Killer.'

There was plenty I could have said, like you should have warned me, like you may have destroyed evidence, but as that was so obviously what she felt guilty about, I didn't.

'Was the letter dated?'

'Yes. May this year.'

'And she said he lived in a flat on the site where 10 Rillington Place had been?'

'Yes.'

'Then it should be easy to identify him, surely?'

'Not if it's a big block of flats.'

'Did the letter give you any other information? Like how old he was?'

'No. But you should be able to work that out from the other letters. Because...'

This time she didn't look guilty, she looked hurt.

Time to help her out. 'Because it was your husband's son as well as hers?'

'Yes. Which means it was me who couldn't have children, not him.'

'You never had fertility investigations?'

'No. Children just didn't happen. We didn't want to know whose fault it was. I hadn't realized, but I'd always assumed it was his. I suppose I was—'

She was about to launch into a self-examination which she would never normally have done even to a complete stranger, I reckoned, and since I had to work with her I didn't want her feeling bad about it and taking against me, so I stopped her.

'Sure there was no other information in the letter that I should know about?'

She looked taken aback. 'No, apart from what I've told you.'

'And what was the point of the letter? Just to express her anxiety?'

'No. She wanted to meet Robbie, to discuss it, or for him to speak to the young man.'

'And what you want me to do is identify him, tell you and tip off the police?'

'I – suppose so.'

'You'd better let me get on with it, then.'

61

I got up. She didn't. She cleared her throat. I waited.

'I'm not sure I explained,' she said.

'What about?'

'Explained what I wanted you to do. I don't want the process.'

'What process?'

'The process of discovery. I don't want the name of the boy. I don't want you to tell me who the boy is, before you're absolutely sure.'

'Sure?'

'Sure that this affair is real. Sure that there was such a woman and that she had this relationship with Robbie. I don't believe it, you see. He wasn't like that. I'd have known. So I don't want you to keep me informed at all, as you investigate, because I'll hear the names and it'll be just like reading the letters, and that was what I hired you to avoid.'

'So...'

'So, I don't want you to tell me the name of the boy. I don't want to hear from you again until you can tell me if it's true that this woman was having an affair with my husband, and until you can tell me her name. I want you to inform the police as soon as you have the name of the boy referred to in the letters. I want you to leave me out of it, because I won't talk to the police myself, and if you name me I'll deny it, because I can't ... can't... It's too complicated. I should try to untangle it, but–'

'I understand,' I interrupted, determined at all costs to avoid a soul-baring session. 'I'll get right on to it,' I said, and waited.

'And you should probably have this,' she said, taking a piece of paper from her bag and handing it to me.

It was a folded page of A4, blank on one side. I opened it. Half a page of word-processed, ink-jet printed text.

'That's the letter,' she said. 'Her last letter.'

I was utterly taken aback. 'You said you ate it,' I said limply.

'Then I lied.'

Chapter Six

Hilary Lucas left, annoyed with me because I hadn't listened to the secrets she really wouldn't have wanted to tell me.

Neither was I best pleased with her, so her huff didn't worry me. She might have left me trawling through the envelope full of letters, possibly to stumble across a serial killer. The danger didn't worry me so much, mostly because I didn't believe that the identity of the killer lay so easily at the heart of the emotional mess that Robbie Lucas had bequeathed his wife, but I was annoyed by the feeling that Hilary was trying to draw me into her pain, feeding me dribs and drabs of half-information. Didn't she have any friends?

And what did she mean, pissing me about over the letter? Why say she ate it? Seriously odd and out of character. Trying to distract me? Or maybe just a spurt of irritation that came from extreme pressure, which I suppose she was under.

I opened the folded paper and read the

letter. It was dated May and it began without a preamble.

Now I'm really worried. I thought he was pretending, to annoy me. You know he likes to annoy me. He always has. But he really likes that place he's living in – I didn't know why. It was built over that dreadful murderer's house, where he killed those sad women and buried them or bricked them in. 10 Rillington Place. He <u>chose</u> to live there, and he likes it, and he says some women deserve to die. Our own Boy. He was such a beautiful child. I'm now seriously afraid. He talks so oddly about the Notting Hill Killer. Please speak to him, One. He listens to you.

No ending, no signature, not even an initial. More a memo than a love letter, but absolutely confident in its tone, more intimate even than a love letter, perhaps. And why did she call him 'One'?

Anyway, it was time for action. First stop: Rillington Place. I got out my oldest A-Z and looked up the index, just in case. No Rillington Place.

The library, obvious next stop, was closed on Thursday afternoons, and it would take time to go all the way down to the central library in Kensington High Street. A local policeman might know.

Eddy Barstow was my first port of call for anything like this, even though he was based at West End Central, and Rillington Place would be Notting Hill.

I lay on the floor – it was warmer there, near the fire – propped my feet on the desk, and dialled West End Central. Answer. Wait. Same voice, 'Can anyone else help?'

'No thanks.'

Wait wait, then Eddy's voice. 'Alex! Light of my loins!'

'Don't mix your metaphors, Eddy.'

'Real Ripper weather, isn't it? Foggier than a hippo's fart here, and cold with it. Same with you, I reckon.'

Hardly surprising, since we were no more than a mile apart.

'Got the thermal underwear on, have we?' he continued.

'Hardly. What about you?'

'I never feel the cold, you know that. I'm wearing the usual high-fashion garment.' Explosive laugh.

Summer or winter, Eddy wore a polyester suit of the kind of fabric that had never been slapped into breath by a midwife. He'd be red faced, shiny and sweaty: he always was.

'I expect you need help,' he said. 'You only ever call me on the scrounge. So what is it?'

'I need to find Rillington Place,' I said.

'Sorry to have to tell you, Princess, we closed the Christie case a while back.'

'Sorry to have to tell *you*, Eddy, but you hanged the wrong man.'

'Only the first time,' he said breezily.

'You don't mean that,' I said. Eddy was a lot more sensitive than he let on.

'No, I don't, poor half-witted bugger,' he said. 'But that's water under the bridge, right? What's it to you?'

'I just need to know where it was,' I said. 'It's not on my oldest A-Z and it's early closing at the library.'

'OK. I'm pushed at the minute,' he said. 'I'll get back to you, right? Give me an hour.'

I hadn't had my daily run. So I put on joggers and a sweatshirt and my air Nikes, did the warm-up exercises, and set off for the Scrubs by way of Lil's old people's home.

The home was newish, built about five years ago when they'd pulled down the slab-ugly but solid redbrick early-Victorian school on the site. The architect hadn't had his eye on the ball because not only had

68

there been massive cost overruns but he'd forgotten to include any toilets in the original designs, and no one picked up on it until the ceremonial opening: an uncomfortable occasion. It didn't look bad, however, just nondescript postmodern: grey brick with bright-blue window frames, doors and trellis-like metal outcrops.

I talked my way through the security system (two gates and a door) only to be told by a late-middle-aged supervisor that Lil wasn't in yet. 'She's missed her supper.'

'I'll leave a message.'

'We don't take messages for the residents.'

'If you can lend me a pencil and some paper, I'll write a note.'

'We don't lend pencil and paper.'

I opened my mouth to argue and closed it again. Her tone wasn't obstructive, just exhausted.

As I thanked her and turned to leave, she carried on with the task I'd interrupted, spraying air-freshener in the reception area. It wasn't working.

Not far to the Scrubs from there. I was jogging, not running, because I couldn't see a hand's length in front of me and twice I nearly collided with a tree.

The quiet was eerie: once I was on the

open ground, the fog muffled traffic noise and cars were just a slow-moving necklace of haloed lights rimming the space. The massive bulk of the prison loomed out of the dark at me and then away as I circled the perimeter and thought about the Notting Hill Killer and accessibility.

Wormwood Scrubs isn't a park, it's common land. Some of its edges are effectively fenced by buildings like the prison, the hospital, the athletic stadium and the railway depot, but the side bounded by Scrubs Lane is completely open, and I assumed it was on this side where the bodies had been found. It would be very labour intensive to keep a watch here, on the off-chance that the Killer came back. By day Scrubs Lane carries heavy traffic and there are often cars parked on the pavement while their owners walk their dogs or eat their sandwiches or dump rubbish. It's emptier by night, but you still get dog walkers, plus illicit couples.

Dodging an impending tree, I decided an hour's exercise was enough and headed home.

I was in the shower when the phone rang.

Eddy.

'I've got the man for you,' he said. 'Lowly PC doing door-to-door on the Christie case. Did his time as beat copper in Notting Hill. Nothing went on he didn't know. Long time retired. Lives up your way.' Pause. 'This for one of your documentaries, is it?'

Easier to say yes, or he'd fuss.

'Yes,' I said.

'Just asking, because I'm off to Florida tomorrow first thing, won't be around to keep an eye on you. Keep Arthur off the subject of families, right? You don't want to hear about his wife and daughter. Got a pencil?'

I took down the name, address and telephone number he gave me.

'He's expecting you,' he said. 'He owes me a favour or two, OK?'

There wasn't a man, woman, dog or horse in the Metropolitan Police who didn't owe Eddy a favour. That's why he'd survived so long with his unorthodox, policing methods. That was why he was so useful to me. Our long friendship had started with his banging my mother and he'd gone on to incorporate me virtually as part of his family, especially when I went out with his son Peter, youngest of his five sons, when I was eighteen and Peter was twenty. Eddy

71

tried to hit on me every time we spoke, but that wasn't a particular compliment because he tried every woman between sixteen and fifty.

Arthur Fishburn lived about half a mile north of my flat, in a neat little council house in a neat little council street. His front garden was mown lawn, a tiny handkerchief-sized square, littered with leaves in the other houses but spotless in his and a sickly green under the streetlights. The heavy brown curtains across his front window were tightly drawn, but the net curtain covering the square of glass in the top of his door was white, and moved as I went up the flagged path.

I was two minutes after the time fixed and he was waiting for me. He'd have met the height requirement when he joined – still five foot ten then – but time had shrunk him. He carried himself stiffly erect and he wore a crisp blue shirt and dark-blue trousers which still gave the illusion of uniform.

His eyes were bright blue and his face was weathered, clean-shaven and well maintained. 'Arthur Fishburn,' he said briskly, and offered a hand which shook only slightly.

72

'Alex Tanner,' I said. He must be nearer eighty than seventy, I thought, but he didn't look it.

'Come in,' he said. 'Did you come in a car?'

'I walked.'

He tut-tutted. 'Shouldn't walk alone in a fog like this, 'tisn't safe for a young girl like you. There are bad men out there, believe me. Cup of tea? Beer?'

'Beer would be good,' I said.

'Kitchen should do us, if that suits,' he said, ushering me firmly past the door to the front room. 'I don't use the parlour much, and any friend of Eddy's is a friend of mine.'

The back room, where he obviously lived, contained a cooker so clean that I reckoned it had never been used, a sink with one cup standing in it, and a round table with a yellow vinyl cover with a blue pattern of marching elephants. One of everything knife, fork, spoon, plate – was drying on a kitchen towel on the sink drainer, and on the table was a newspaper. A tabloid. He was doing the crossword.

He produced two bottled, room-temperature beers. Not my preference, but we sat on the two kitchen chairs, drank the beer and talked about the weather and Eddy, who

Arthur called the Guv'nor, and I tried not to shout, *get on with it,* and thought about how some people had no time and other people, like the unemployed and the retired, had too much time, and how it should all be shuffled and redealt so everyone had a reasonable amount, except for me, because I liked the pressure.

Meanwhile I got used to his tics. He had a sequence: rub the back of his neck, tilt his head sideways, stretch his jaw in a half-yawn, clear his throat, extend his right leg and shake it. Maybe he had cramp.

I chatted about Eddy and he moved on to Eddy's family. I remembered I had to keep him off families so I said I'd gone out with Peter, and then tried to turn the conversation to the weather. After the statutory grumbles he moved on to the Notting Hill Killer and asked if I had any theories. I had none. I listened to his, realizing that his fantasy was that he'd track him down singlehanded. He must have been retired fifteen years at least. Pity he didn't have something better to think about.

Although as I didn't know yet about his daughter and his wife, perhaps I was making snap judgements. Perhaps what he was doing now was better than what he might have been doing.

Finally he cleared his throat and changed his tone. 'The Guv'nor tells me you're interested in the Christie case,' he said. 'How can I help you?'

I was sorry to disappoint him. I told him that I was a TV researcher and I only wanted to find 10 Rillington Place.

'All right, come on, then. I'll walk you down there.'

As we walked, he talked. He went slowly and paused now and then to catch his breath and shake his right leg. Easier if he hadn't talked, I thought, but probably he was lonely and milking a captive audience. 'I run the Neighbourhood Watch,' he said. 'I still patrol the streets of Notting Hill – and Notting Dale – to keep them safe. I still know what goes on.' He launched into a list of criminals, pointing out where they lived and where crimes had been committed: that corner was the site of last week's GBH; that house was where the local fence lived; that was 'a disorderly house', a quaint old-fashioned term which suggested not so much a brothel, which is what it meant, as a house in which clothes were thrown on the floor and milk wasn't put in a jug.

I adjusted my pace to his, and tried not to

have my teeth set on edge by the hostility in his voice, which didn't seem located to anything I knew, or had asked. I didn't even know whether he was hostile to me or the criminal activities he was describing.

'Not many murderers,' I said to stem the flow.

'Isn't the current bastard enough for you? Four innocent young girls, tortured, raped, mutilated?'

He stopped walking, and went through an aggressive, accelerated version of his tic.

'Of course it's terrible,' I said, but he wasn't listening.

'Three policemen killed in Braybrook Street, over by the Scrubs, remember?'

'When was that?'

'Back in the sixties. Three policemen, just doing their jobs. And before that, Neville Heath, liked tying them up and beating them. You don't want to know what he did to that poor woman's body with a poker, trust me you don't.'

I certainly didn't want to know what Neville Heath had done with a poker nearly fifty years ago, but neither did I trust Arthur. I walked on and he followed me, still talking.

'Over in Chepstow Villas, that was. And a

drug dealer knifed in the Bella, only last week. It's always gone on, believe me, you've got to stay on top of it, keep watching, keep alert, dam the river of evil or else we'll all be drowned in it.'

I nodded, hoping to dam the river of talk. 'Lay off, Arthur, will you? All this is spooking me.'

'Good. That's good. You can be too confident if you're an attractive woman, as I know to my cost. Haven't you a man to look after you?'

'Yes,' I said, to shut him up.

'Does he know you go alone into the houses of perfect strangers?'

'You came recommended, Arthur. Eddy said you were OK.'

We'd nearly reached my flat by now. He turned away from Ladbroke Grove, into a seventies council-built estate of terraced houses. Flat roofs, landscaped public areas with grass and flowerbeds ('No ball games,' 'Do not allow dogs to foul this area,' 'Please respect the flowers'). It being November, there were no flowers, but I nodded to the bedraggled bushes.

'A good estate' he said judiciously, calmer now he was back to business. 'Mostly senior citizens and respectable families. Quite a few privately owned, now, after the council-house sell-off in the eighties.'

We kept walking through it. On our left was the estate, on our right a parking area interspersed with trees, and above us to the right the underground railway, which isn't underground in that section of the Hammersmith and City Line.

'You'll humour an old man, I know,' he said. 'Just in case you're after a real live villain and not telling me, we won't stare, will we, we'll act casual.' Before I could react, he went on, 'Now we're in Rillington Place,' although we hadn't passed any boundary marker that I could see, and it was still a car park. 'And this—' turning right into a narrow street called Bartlett Close, and nodding at the only building in it 'was built over several of the original houses, including number ten.'

It was flat roofed, constructed at the same time as the housing estate but not originally for residential purposes, I guessed. Three floors, and a yard behind with one-storey buildings which looked as if they were used for storage or garages.

'It was light industrial but it was re-classified three years ago,' he said. 'It's flats now.' There were two cars in the back yard.

One was an old Volvo, an estate car which had been loaded and unloaded many times, dented and worn. The other was a hatch-back, black and neat and shiny, a little Peugeot. Arthur walked beside me, surprisingly managing to be casual. He wasn't bad at it. I wondered why he'd stayed a PC so long. To retire as a beat copper – after forty years in – that was something. Although maybe it was more peculiar that he'd survived in the force at all.

'We're OK,' I said. 'Look.' In the small patch of lawn which fringed the building was a FOR SALE board. I walked up to the front door: three bells, presumably one for each floor. Three names: Jacobs, Hobbs, Fairfax. No first names. Arthur was looking at it reminiscently, with a touch of horror. 'He was a very ordinary, respectable man,' he said, 'the kind of man you believed. I thought we had Timothy Evans bang to rights. Then it all went pear-shaped on us.'

I was only half-listening, because I was so pleased. This investigation was going to be easier than I'd thought. Magic. All the chance in the world to see round the flat that was for sale and to enquire about the other tenants.

Tomorrow, I'd send a buyer in. Nick, if I

could find her.

I wrote down the estate agent's name, and number, and followed Arthur, who'd moved away. 'Thank you very much,' I said.

'I'll walk you home,' he said. 'Young girl like you. I don't like to think of you unescorted.'

We were out of the estate now and back onto Lancaster Road. All round us were people, some of them unescorted young girls, walking purposefully and apparently safely through the fog. He was a nutter, I thought, but an Eddy-recommended and therefore harmless nutter, and I submitted to his protection and his criminal information for the ten-minute walk back to my flat.

80

Chapter Seven

I was back at the flat by seven thirty. I closed the front door behind me, flattened myself against the wall so I couldn't be seen from the road and looked out through the small hall window. I watched Arthur pacing up and down protectively for a few minutes then, when he headed away up the Grove, I nipped out to the local shop for basic groceries – milk, bread, butter, water and coffee.

I made myself salami sandwiches and a cup of coffee and pondered the Nick problem, because there was still no message from her.

By now anxiety was pricking me as I ate. I tried her mobile phone again. It was still unavailable. I also rang the office – no luck – and left a get-in-touch message on the answering machine.

Then I remembered Alan Protheroe.

He'd wanted me to see him, that evening. If I saw him it would be quicker than talking on the phone, because I could bully him to the point more effectively, and get a grip on what he wanted me to do. Plus there had been something genuinely urgent about his tone of voice.

I didn't feel tired. What I really wanted to do was put off Alan, put Nick on the back burner until tomorrow, and get stuck into the DESTROY UNOPENED envelope. If I read every word of the letters surely I'd get a handle on the woman, and if I did that we'd have her son bang to rights. I didn't believe he'd be the killer, but if there was even an outside chance that he was, a girl might die while I faffed around with a fussy, cover-my-back producer.

I took Polly's car and went over to Alan's. Such a long-standing relationship must go for something.

Alan lives in a mews house in one of the criss-cross little streets running off Kensington Church Street, super-expensive and super-cramped. He bought it after his divorce. He's nearly sixty now and he should have given up chasing girls, but after his divorce he went for the seriously young and the seriously pretty. He got his fingers badly burnt, and lately his loneliness has been worrying me. I'd found him a joke for years but the joke was wearing thin, either because I'd mellowed or because he was getting sadder. Hard to know which.

I got there at eight, and rang the bell.

No answer.

Odd. He'd said he'd be in all evening; he hadn't rung with a change of plan. He always rings with a change of plan, even if it makes not the slightest difference to the person he's ringing. Pernickety, that's Alan, not to say obsessive.

I rang again, and knocked, then looked up. The bedroom windows were open and a light was on. He must be in, then. 'Alan – hey, Alan–'

I could see through the downstairs window that the living room and kitchen were empty and dimly lit. He might, just conceivably, be upstairs with a girl, if one of his lunches (he believed in lunches) had finally worked.

'Alan!' I called again cautiously. 'This is Alex. I'm going away now.'

His head popped out, above me. 'I'm coming,' he said thickly. 'Don't go away.'

When he let me in I could see how ill he looked. Or, if not ill, sad, I realized as he led me through to the kitchen/dining room. 'Have a beer,' he said, more decisively than

I'd ever heard him say anything. He brushed his wispy hair down with the flat of his hand. 'I'm having a beer and I want you to have one too.'

The house was airless and baking hot. He opened the french windows to his tiny garden and let in some fog, cold air and traffic noise.

'Shall I turn down the thermostat?' I asked.

'What?'

'On the heating.'

'Oh – yes, I suppose.'

I did, then joined him at the small round breakfast table. It was usually bare, but now it was littered: opened post, three photograph albums, two dirty glasses. I moved the glasses to the sink and stacked the post on top of the albums.

He didn't notice. 'I'm worried about my doco,' he said.

'What are you worried about?'

'I'm afraid it's just a bit – dull.'

I was silenced. As a surprise announcement, it was as if Marlon Brando had announced that he had a weight problem. All Alan's documentaries were dull. That was their trademark.

Saying that wouldn't have cheered him up,

84

however. 'Nonsense,' I said as robustly as I could manage. I sounded like a firm but kind primary teacher. Many people sounded like that when they talked to Alan.

It was hard to make a more pertinent comment because I'd had nothing to do with his latest enterprise, which had been dragging on since January. It was a documentary about men, particularly young men, and their unfortunate position vis-à-vis women. Part of the point of the doco was that the whole crew should be male, including the researchers, and that was fine by mc. I'd had enough work on not to want this.

'I don't want it to be dull because it's an important issue. Do you know how many young men commit suicide, Alex? Do you know how many more young men are unemployed than young women? Do you know how much better girls do than boys in the current school examinations, and do you know that's a combination of female teacher prejudice and incompetence, and the redesigning of the exams to favour girls? Do you realize how a simple misunderstanding by a silly girl can escalate to a criminal charge for rape? Do you know how biased the divorce courts are against men, and how little contact divorced fathers are given with their children, who they're paying for? Do you know how many older men are made redundant, and do you know their chance of re-employment?'

'No,' I said.

'I don't care, anyhow,' he said angrily, his shoulders sagging. 'I've come to the end of the road, Alex.'

It was only then that I spotted he was drunk. It was partly the smell of brandy that wafted from him whenever he moved. That and the slurring of his words. Alex Tanner, ace detective. I'd been thrown off the scent because Alan was usually too cautious to drink.

'Which road have you come to the end of?'

'Every kind of road. Have you heard Janey's going to remarry?' He put his hands on the table and looked at them. They were trembling and grubby.

Janey's his ex-wife. Their relationship was evidently still alive for Alan. He looked as if what he needed was a hug, but I was reluctant to give him one in case he misinterpreted my motives. Like a duck, he imprinted on any youngish female who showed him the least attention.

Then he started to moan and rub his

hands, through his hair. He didn't have so much hair that he could afford to do that, so I caught his hands and held them.

'Come on, Alan, it isn't so bad,' I said.

'We had so much in common,' he said. 'I always thought we'd get back together, at the end.'

'At whose end?'

'When I'd – sown my wild oats. And when Janey realized how much I meant to her.'

Now we were well out in the madlands. My impression had been that Janey was mighty relieved to be rid of him and Alan, to my knowledge, hadn't managed to sow even the most domestic of oats.

Also, I had work to do, and this was boiling up into an all-nighter.

For a moment I seriously considered taking him to bed. That would be quickest in the short term. He had tried me a long time ago, when I was eighteen and he was forty-something, but that was while he was still married. I'd looked at him with such surprise and contempt that even he had noticed it, plus he hadn't been seriously keen in the first place.

Now I'd gone up in his rating system because of Barty. Barty was a catch, and I'd caught him. Alan liked what he knew other men liked. I don't think his prick had a personal response. So bed with me would have cheered him up, then I could have exclaimed over how wonderful he was and claimed that I needed to get away to recover from the emotional maelstrom his love-making had induced, and he would have gone to sleep and I'd have been out of there in under an hour, and back to work.

That was the practical solution.

But Barty wouldn't like it, and since he was so far away and my current partner—

'Tell you what, Alan,' I said. 'You shouldn't be alone. Come home with me, I'll make us supper and we can talk.'

I settled him on the sofa, put cushions behind his head, made him an omelette, toast and butter, and a mug of cocoa.

This nursery treatment comforted him. I reckoned he'd fall asleep, so I said, 'Give me an hour to look at these letters, OK? After that we'll talk.'

Then I curled up in the chair opposite him so I could smile reassuringly when he looked up, opened Hilary Lucas's envelope, and emptied the contents neatly on the carpet.

Should I bother about fingerprints? If it

turned out to be serious, I'd better cover my back, though paper doesn't print well. To salve my conscience I picked up the top two, protecting them with a tissue, and wiggled them into see-through plastic folders. Then I added the most recent letter, the one I'd read, and flicked through the remainder.

They were mostly folded: when I straightened them out, the earlier ones were typewritten on quarto paper, the later word-processed on A4. The quality of the printing improved over the years roughly in line with the advance of technology. They were in chronological order, the most recent on top, and all dated, the earliest 1.9.70. As Hilary had said, there was no handwriting.

I numbered them lightly in pencil. One hundred and fifty-three. A lot of letters. A long time. I paper-clipped them together in years. Roughly five a year. Four so far this year. Peculiar, not a scrap of handwriting anywhere. A writer? A typist? Someone who was extremely familiar with keyboards, and someone accurate. No spelling or punctuation mistakes that I could see, running over them, and a high level of vocabulary. Plus the recurrent dates, always in the same format.

A careful-minded, educated woman. Not

an obvious candidate for an unplanned illegitimate child. Maybe she'd had it on purpose.

'Alex?' said Alan drowsily, waking up and looking like a fluffy owl with his face puffy from sleep and his thinning hair poking up in little wisps and erratic tufts. 'Alex, what are you doing? Could I have a drink of water?'

I fetched him the water, and explained what I was doing. No names: the general principles.

'Is it urgent?'

'Could be, very.'

'Then I'll help you,' he said, trying to regain some of the absolute control without which his anxiety levels rose to excruciating heights. 'Excuse me a minute.'

He went upstairs to the bathroom, then reappeared looking combed and washed. 'Got any aspirins?'

'Kitchen. Usual cupboard.'

Back with more water and the aspirins, he sat himself at the desk. 'OK,' I said. 'Get started on these.'

'What am I looking for?'

'Any clue to her identity. Names, places, idiosyncracies.'

'Right.' He started to read, pencil in hand,

90

squared up to the desk and the task. I looked at him with what I was disconcerted to recognize as the beginnings of protective affection. I didn't expect productive work from him, but at least he was trying. We'd talk about his life later.

Chapter Eight

We worked in silence, and in my case increasing bewilderment, for nearly an hour, until I got cramp. 'Want some coffee? I'm making,' I said, getting up and stretching. Then I tried shaking my cramping leg like Arthur Fishburn, but it didn't help. It must have been a guy thing.

'Posture,' said Alan. 'You shouldn't sit hunched over like that for long periods of time. No wonder your back is painful.'

'It isn't my back. It's my leg,' I said.

'Referred pain,' said Alan. 'I'd like some tea, if you have it. Then we'll confer, shall we?'

Confer. He'd be calling a steering meeting next. He was evidently feeling better, or pretending to.

I made the tea and coffee and settled back into my chair again, under his disapproving frown, not pointing out that I was sitting in the chair to work because he'd pinched my desk. 'OK. I'll tell you what I've got—'

'Are you leading the discussion?' he

interrupted querulously.

'Yes,' I said, nearly losing patience, 'I'm the chairperson, Alan, which is what's done for my leg, according to you.'

'Very well.'

'I've got nothing,' I said. 'Nothing concrete. Not a name or a place in any of them. Plenty about her feelings, her memories of their time together, particularly in bed, and some nicknames. I'm fairly sure "Man" is her husband. Her lover's certainly "One" and she's "Two." Their shared child is "Boy." Who d'you reckon "Girl" and "Four" are?'

'Ah,' said Alan. 'May I address the Chair?' He signalled this as a joke by rocking backwards and forwards and making a cawing noise like a minor character from Dickens.

'Get on with it.'

'Four is his wife. I can give you chapter and verse if you like—'

'No, that's fine—'

'And Girl must be the woman's legitimate daughter – older than Boy, because the letters refer to Girl's jealousy and how she overcomes it.'

'Do you have an age for Girl?'

'She sounds about two when Boy is born. Tantrums, etc. So, two years at least older than Boy, who was born twenty-four years ago. Between January and May. In the January letter she's pregnant, and in the next letter, in May, she's talking about the beauty of the child.'

'That's something.' I made a note. 'Anything else?'

'As you know, I've reached 1983. It's a passionate relationship, obviously.'

'On her side, at least.'

'They're still making love, in 1983.'

'They're still making love in 1997,' I said. 'It needn't be passionate on his side, though. They only meet about five times a year. And I think there's something wrong in the last few years, as well. I can't put my finger on it, but her letters seem to lose confidence, as if he might be going off her. Apart from the very last letter, which gets the confident tone back.'

'Let's leave that for a moment. Other than that, the bulk of my letters, like yours, are simply expressions of her feeling, her memories of their times together and her hopes for the future.' Alan cleared his throat. 'I also know where they first acknowledged their love.' Pause. 'In Rome. Which explains the nicknames.'

Significant pause.

'Get a move on, Alan,' I said, trying to sound jocular.

'Do you know the Browning poem, "Two in the Campagna"?'

'No. Explain.'

'It's a love poem from a man's point of view, about a man and a woman in the plain outside Rome called the Campagna. Our woman quotes from it. And that's why she calls her lover One and herself Two. That gives us something, surely.'

'You're positive they were actually in Rome at the time?'

He passed the letter to me and I checked it through. It was clear enough. So if the worst came to the worst I could work on that, though a holiday in 1970 wouldn't be exactly easy to drop casually into conversation.

'This poem – how well known is it?' I said, hoping we could narrow the field to poetry buffs or English teachers. I wouldn't know, my education was mostly crap and though I read a lot, there are still huge gaps.

'Very, I would have thought,' said Alan. 'I knew it.'

'You went to Cambridge.'

'I read history.'

'OK, but still you must have learnt plenty

of this stuff on the way up to Cambridge.'

'I think most reasonably well-educated people of my age or up to fifteen years younger would be familiar with it,' he said.

'Not much help, then.'

'No.'

Alan looked defeated. I remembered I was supposed to be bolstering his ego and cheering him up, and that maybe reading a series of letters from a married woman to her lover weren't exactly the best therapy in the circumstances. I couldn't remember if his wife had had a lover before their break-up, but the chances were she had. People did, even the mumsy Janey.

'Thanks for the info about the poem, anyway. It's been very helpful. Give me your notes. I'll mull over them tomorrow.' He passed them over with the letters and I put them, with mine, back in the envelope. 'Tell you what,' I said. 'Let's watch a video.'

I fished out one of his documentaries from the dusty pile (when would I have time to clean properly?) at the bottom of my main bookcase, and put it on. 'One of your best,' I said as the opening credits rolled.

He didn't even look at his name on the screen. He got up and walked about. 'There's one thing I'd like to clear up, Alex

– you may have thought, earlier in the evening, that I was – a little drunk?'

I nodded.

'I had lunch with Janey, and a drink or two. The alcohol must have reacted with the antihistamines I'm currently taking – and I was upset, of course.'

'Of course,' I said, and ran the video back. 'Look, Alan, I do think the credits on this are particularly effective.'

He sat on the sofa close beside me. After a few seconds I realized he was pressing his thigh against mine. I moved away, gently. He took off his glasses, gave a muted yelp, and leapt on top of me, aiming kisses at my mouth, groping to undo my jeans. 'You know you want it as much as I do,' he grunted into my ear.

I knew I shouldn't laugh, so I didn't. I lay still, saying, 'Al-an' (downward inflection) 'Al-an' (rising inflection) and finally shouting, 'ALAN! STOP IT!'

He didn't stop, and I didn't feel amused any more because he was much stronger than I was and his eyes were fixed and staring. He slapped me, hard, across the face. I gasped, as much from surprise as from pain, though there was enough pain.

I didn't know what to do. I could fight but

I might not win, and I didn't want a broken nose. I could respond, but I didn't want to.

I went limp under him and started to cry. 'Bitch,' he said.

'I'm not a bitch,' I snuffled. 'I gave you supper. You're my friend, Alan. Stop this.'

His fingers were grappling with the fly-buttons of my 517s: I didn't reckon his chances. I stroked his hair and kissed the side of his face soothingly. Gradually, his fingers stopped scrabbling at me. I hugged him. 'Let's watch the video, eh?' I said.

He shifted off me, smoothed his hair back, replaced his glasses, and watched the credits roll. His name would help. It always had.

I drove him home and got back to my flat just before midnight. I was tired but not shattered, and lay down on the sofa with the phone. But first, before making any calls, I thought about Alan.

I'd miscalculated somewhere, writing him off as weak and negligible. Although he was weak, he wasn't negligible. I'd been a whisker from being raped.

Wrong again, I thought. He'd been dangerous briefly, but seriously – precisely because he felt weak and negligible, and couldn't bear it.

Anyhow, for the moment the mess was smoothed over. Neither of us had mentioned it again; we'd both talked resolutely first about the documentary we were watching and, while I drove him back, about the documentary he was working on. Then he'd kissed me on the cheek in his usual unthreatening and noncommittal way. Before he'd closed the door he'd hesitated and I'd thought he was going to offer an explanation – perhaps that the antihistamines he was taking had reacted badly with the cocoa – but he'd said nothing.

I hoped it was the last I'd hear of it. His work was useful, maybe 20 per cent of my research earnings last year. And he was such a long-standing fixture in my life, I'd miss him, foolishness and all.

There was nothing to be gained by thinking of it any more, so I got to work and tried Nick on the mobile. No luck. I left another ring-me message on the office call-minder, then stared at the ceiling and thought. I could ask the Golden Kid, the estate agent who sublet us our office, but not until the morning. At this time of night he'd be out, either clubbing or with any of his innumerable relations.

There was always Laverne, Nick's recent

love-object. She's fifteen, into body-piercing, open-mouthed gum-chewing and escort work. Nick claims Laverne dislikes me more than I dislike her, but I don't think that's possible. I had no reservations about waking Laverne up, because she wouldn't be asleep, though she might well not be in.

She answered after eight rings and her voice was chilly when I identified myself, though no chillier than mine. 'Nah, she isn't here.'

'When did you last see her?'

'What's it to you?'

'She's not around. I need to speak to her.'

'So?'

'So when did you last see her?' Heavy sigh, gum-chewing sounds. 'Did you two fight?'

'I don't have to talk to you.'

'If you don't I'll keep ringing back.'

'I'll leave the phone off.'

'Fine. Pity if you lose work, though. If the agency can't get in touch.'

'Much you care.'

'Plus I'll tell the Social.'

'Tell the Social what?'

'That your mum's taken your baby home to Tower Hamlets. Then they'll take your flat away.'

'Nah, you wouldn't.'

'Try me.'

'They wouldn't.'

'Try them. Just answer the question. Did you fight?'

Heavy sigh, then the economic motive won through. 'Yeah, well. I s'pose. I mean, I didn't but she did. She was pissed off with me.'

'Any particular reason?'

'She stamped and shouted a lot because I had a friend with me, know what I mean?'

'She walked in when you were in bed?'

'Yeah. Sort of. More in the shower.'

'Did she say where she was going?'

'Nah. She just screamed, like, general abuse. Bit out of order, if you ask me.'

'When was this?'

'Last night. Six, seven?'

'Thanks, Laverne.'

'Fuck off,' she said.

After the call I was less anxious about Nick. She'd been upset and angry last night; she must have stamped away somewhere to lick her wounds, specially since she knew that the most she'd get in the way of sympathy she'd get from me was *told you so* and *good riddance*.

I locked the DESTROY UNOPENED envelope in the top drawer; I'd get back to it if I drew a blank at Bartlett Close, Rillington Place as was.

I cleaned the, bathroom before I went to bed. It didn't look as if I'd have much time tomorrow.

Friday 4 November

Chapter Nine

By nine o'clock I'd run three miles, showered, and was in the office with my third cup of coffee, trying to decide if the fog was actually thicker than yesterday or just more irritating because it had gone on too long. Both, probably.

There was still no sign of Nick. If she didn't turn up soon I'd have to sort through her active investigations and deal with anything urgent, but first I had to send someone pretending to be interested in buying a flat in Bartlett Close. If I was lucky, there'd only be one young male tenant in the block. If I was very lucky, he'd be the one selling his flat.

I went through the photograph files, located one of the misper Samantha Eyre, made another mug of instant coffee, picked up my own, and took the lot to see the Golden Kid.

It wasn't far. Out of my door, with its sign carefully hand-painted by Nick, and into the next door with its professional but

107

battered gold lettering: Poneybeat and Unstruther, Estate Agent Est. 1958.

They'd been crooked since 1958, so at least they were consistent. Set up back when Notting Hill was the most notorious area for extortionate landlords who crammed poor, mostly black, tenants into the crumbling decaying terrace houses, Poneybeat and Unstruther had served the landlords. Then they had served the yuppies. Now, they serve themselves and us.

There's no Poneybeat, no Unstruther. There's a Brown, the owner, who is currently serving three years in an open prison for embezzlement, and his assistant, Dermot Molloy, known as the Golden Kid because he likes gold jewellery so much he clanks when he walks.

There was no sign of the Kid in the front office but tendrils of tobacco smoke oozed from the back room, looking like a minor outcrop of the fog. I went straight through. He was squeezing his spots at an ancient mirror, his perpetual Camel in an ashtray by his side.

'Hi, Alex,' he said. 'Be with you a minute. Gissa bit of privacy, right?'

'Get a move on,' I said, retreating to the front office.

'I got a message for you,' he called to me. 'From Nick. She's gone away for a while. Back Sat'day.'

'Where's she gone?' I called.

'To visit an old professor,' she said. 'She wanted to get out of London.'

That made sense. As far as I know the only non-London friend or even acquaintance Nick has is a retired mathematics professor who lives in Oxford.

'When did she tell you this?'

'Last night. Or maybe the night before. Yeah, the night before.'

He came through to join me, his pale redhead's skin now blotched with Clearasil. He's in his early twenties, about six foot and skinny with close-cropped ginger hair. He was wearing his usual suit, dark, very wide at the shoulder, double-breasted and fiercely pinstriped. Under it was a white T-shirt, like the undershirts American servicemen wear in old movies. He had one neck chain, three bracelets, fifteen studs in his ears and two in his nose, all gold. He was also wearing his biker boots.

'Ta for the coffee,' he said, sitting down at one of the four desks the office contained. I was in one of the eight client chairs, which I've never seen occupied. He has no genuine estate agency business – according to Nick, who knows him well, he has only three flats on his books and they're all used for benefit fraud: the taxpayer is paying some twelve non-existent people to live in them. Passing trade very seldom progressed beyond the window with its flyblown sheets of property details, all marked UNDER OFFER. If prospective clients look in they're put off by the Kid's huge Harley-Davidson Electra-glide bike parked in the middle of the office.

The Kid earns some of his money from us: apart from our office rent, Nick uses him for casual work. How he earns the rest, I don't ask, but he never seems to be short.

'Seen Lil this morning?' I asked.

'Nah. Bit early for her, int it? Midday she comes over this way, more like.'

I thought back. He was right, I'd never seen her about before lunchtime. But now I knew where Nick was. I didn't need to see her urgently, anyway. 'How're you fixed today?' I said.

'You got some work for me?'

I nodded.

'Sorry, I've a problem with that. I'm going down south, to visit me brother Sean. He's in a tad of bother, Nick may have told you, and I'm popping down with some readies.'

'Bail?'

'Nah.'

He didn't elaborate, and I didn't ask. The Kid has several brothers. Most of them are in jail some of the time, but never for long.

'I can help out tomorrow,' he offered.

'I'll get back to you,' I said, but I probably wouldn't. I had to get the Rillington Place job done today if at all possible. If I had to, I'd go myself, but I didn't want to because if any follow-up needed to be done I hoped to go in under cover of a residential enquiry.

I showed him the photograph of the Eyre girl. 'Recognize her?'

'Yeah. It's the misper Nick was after. I seen her a few times. She came in once.'

'Why?'

'To look at the bike close up. She liked the Harley.'

I looked at the gleaming blue and silver monster. It was certainly eye-catching. 'Did you talk to her?'

'Bit. She said she'd moved into the area a few weeks ago, was living on the estate down the road.'

'Did she say where on the estate?'

'Nah.'

'Or who with?'

'Nah.'

'When did you last see her?'

'Sat'day. Sat'day morning.'

'Anything else you can remember?'

I took down his description of what Sam Eyre had been wearing – very tight washed-out Levis, a ribbed blue sweater over a great pair, and a leather jacket. 'Fashion leather,' he added scornfully. 'Not leathers, leather.' Then I helped him manoeuvre his bike out of the office, locked up after him, and stood, at a loss, watching his accelerating, swooping progress up the road until even the rumble-roar of the bike's enormous engine was swallowed by the fog.

I felt bereft, which annoyed me. OK, so the Kid couldn't help, so Nick had dropped out of sight, so Barty was in Zaire. So what? I usually like working alone. Only one person to blame, that way.

Doubt was unsettling me. Samantha Eyre was Killer bait. Nick had undertaken to find her, then ducked out. Perhaps that case should be followed up first. But if the unknown letter-writer's son was the Killer, he should be my top priority.

And who could I send to look at the Bartlett Close flat?

A taxi was coming towards me, up the Grove. It slowed down when it approached the cul-de-sac where my flat was, then accelerated and finally pulled up beside me.

My friend Polly tumbled out, talking. 'Oh Alex it's me, it's you, isn't it wonderful, isn't it foggy? Kiss kiss kiss.'

She bent over (she's tall), waved her head ceremonially backwards and forwards beside my ears, swooped back inside the taxi to grab two large leather holdalls, and paid the cabbie, who drove away. 'We're together again! I've got a whole day! Are you busy? Say you're not! What shall we do?'

I looked at her. She's my age, but there the physical similarities stop. She used to be a model. She's very tall, dark, beautiful, expensively dressed. She works as an accountant with a top firm in Hong Kong. Her annual Christmas bonus is more than my entire pension fund. Most of all, she looks like someone who could buy a flat in Bartlett Close with a cheque from her current account. And who might be daffy enough to pay over the odds for a whim.

'You're going to buy a flat,' I said. 'And I'll give you a hand home with your bags.'

Chapter Ten

After she left for the estate agent's, I buzzed around frenetically. I checked through Nick's current work at the office – nothing urgent – sent out some outstanding invoices, put a sign on the door saying NO OFFICE HOURS TODAY, popped over to the library, took a photocopy of the Robert Browning poem, bought some lemons and Perrier water for Polly who's recently been recruited by the caffeine police, cleared my action board, pinned the poem up plus the very short list of facts I had so far about Robbie Lucas's mistress, dusted round Polly's flat to make it look more welcoming, and then got stuck in to washing the woodwork in my living-room.

I wasn't worried about sending her to Bartlett Close, mostly because I didn't believe the flats had any connection with the Killer, but partly because, even if it had, she was absolutely not his type: too tall, too old, wrong colouring. I had given her a brief summary of the background and she'd brushed aside any suggestion of risk, 'With an estate agent? In broad daylight? Get real.'

At eleven thirty, she was back. 'Good news and bad news. The estate agent took me round – none of the tenants were there – and it's either the whole house that's for sale or the flats individually, and two of the flats are under offer, but I said I was interested in the whole house – which isn't a house at all, it's basically workshops and offices converted to flats, but of course you know that...'

'Sit down,' I said. 'Coffee?'

'I don't drink coffee any more, remember I told you. Look look look how it's improved my skin. Mineral water if you have any – fizzy with a slice of lemon.'

'Coming up.'

'And the good news is I've put in an offer for the whole house, so you can go and do my residential enquiry. But the bad news is that the house is owned by a man in his early twenties, who also lives in one of the flats–'

'That's good news, surely?'

'No, because the two tenants are his mates, also men in their early twenties.'

I looked at her. 'Three of them,' I said.

'Yep. Three of them. The owner's Richard

Fairfax, the tenants are Russell Jacobs and James Hobbs. All the flats have two bedrooms and in Hobbs's flat it looked as if a woman was living in the second bedroom, or staying there anyway. Hobbs's flat is also really neat and clean, getting on for obsessive I'd say if he does the cleaning but more or less normal if it's the woman who does, and the other two are what you would expect, Messy. But I didn't see into the garages, which are seriously big – designed for vans, some are used as workshops now. They were all locked and the agent didn't have the keys.' She paused for breath and sipped her Perrier. 'How'm I doing so far?' she said.

'Great. Keep talking.'

'I didn't try to pump the agent much. I stuck to asking practical questions about the property, because I wanted to convince him I was a serious prospect.'

'And did you?'

'Yes. He thinks I'm a cash buyer and he said he welcomed any investigation that would lead to a quick exchange of contracts.'

'Hang on a minute. Have you offered to pay more for the whole house than he'd get for shifting the flats separately?'

'Yes. Not much more, but some. Because if I take the whole thing, then there are development possibilities, because the yard and the garages cover quite a bit of space and you could knock them down and put up three little town houses, and of course re-jig the accommodation in the three flats. I reckon you could get six units out of that.'

'Would it be a good investment?'

'Not really. I don't think so, because there's downmarket housing all round it, so the location isn't much cop, and the yard bit is right under the tube line, so it would be humungously noisy, and probably dirty too – though it *is* on the fringes of a good area come to think.' She paused triumphantly. 'Anyway, I absolutely convinced him I had money burning a hole in my pocket and I said my enquiry agent and surveyor would be right on to it.'

'Well done, Poll,' I said.

'So what are you going to do now?'

'Tip off the police.'

'And do you really think one of those men is the Killer?'

'No. But I have to behave as if I do, just in case. Which means telling the Met.'

'Before you go in and meet the three men?'

'Yes. A.s.a.p. Then I've done the decent thing and the police can work on it – not that I think there's anything to work on – while I identify which of the three is the illegitimate son of my client's late husband.'

'So you'll ring Eddy?'

'Yep.' I reached for the phone, then put it down as I remembered. 'I can't ring Eddy. He's gone to Florida.'

That was when I felt abandoned. Really, abandoned. Bereft. The same feeling I'd had when I watched the red tail lights of the Harley swoop away into the fog.

I'm not at all intuitive – not usually. I don't get feelings – not of dread or hope or anything much. I work from the facts. I feel dread when any sensible person would, and hope when any sensible person would. I don't pulse with New Age sensitivity. Come to that, what had happened to the New Age? First we were going to have it and everything was crystals and peace and love and optimism, then it vanished like all the other media crazes that swirl around for a bit, then drain away unnoticed, while the media tap gushes different rubbish.

Polly was looking at me expectantly. 'So, what will you do?'

'Make a cup of coffee,' I said.

'Hang on a moment,' she said. 'I expect you're going to be busy for the rest of the day?'

There was, a purposeful tone to that, not just her usual friendly exasperation with my obsession with work, so I said, 'Do you want me for something?'

'Just to talk.'

'About anything in particular?'

She hesitated and looked awkward, the way I'd seen her look when she thought she was going to upset someone.

'Something you want to break to me?' I said, to help her and to speed up the process. 'Because if so, tell me straight out.'

'How did you know?'

I shook my head. 'Just don't take up poker, Polly.'

'I'm rather good at poker,' she said, miffed. 'But yes, you're right, I do want to tell you something. I've decided to sell my flat.'

'Why?' I said.

She squirmed. 'Because I...'

'Just say it, whatever it is.'

'Because property prices are picking up so I'll make a bit, and I want somewhere – um, bigger.'

'And smarter?'

120

'Yes, smarter,' she said, relieved. 'Just near here, of course, I don't want to be too far away from you. I've loved sharing the house, so I thought I'd just move up the Hill a bit, but I wanted to tell you before I put it on the market, and—'

She moved over to hug me and, with an effort, I didn't pull away. I'm an unconvincing huggee and I wasn't as upset as I should have been. But I am fond of Polly so I hugged her in return and waited for her to pull away. When she did, I said, 'Thanks for telling me. It's OK, Poll. Really. We'll still be mates.'

'Of course we will.' She hugged me again, then patted me and let me go. 'You've got a lot on, haven't you? With Nick away, and all?'

'True,' I said.

'And you could use an assistant?'

'Well, yes—'

'So I'll help you,' she said, triumphantly. 'I'll do whatever you say. I'm yours till noon tomorrow, with time out for a party this evening.'

She looked so pleased with her offer that I couldn't talk it away.

'Great,' I said. 'Great.'

'So what do you want me to do?'

I couldn't think of anything, yet. Nothing was clear to me. I felt as if London's fog had seeped into my brain.

Polly saw this and tactfully removed herself downstairs to her flat. She said she'd be back in an hour and then we'd go to the Cafe Rouge and have lunch, because we'd have to have lunch no matter what, and talk about it then. I think she thought I was upset about her moving out and needed time to recover myself, and I was happy to let her think that. It was easier.

I wandered into the kitchen to make myself a cup of coffee and found myself drinking a glass of milk. Weird. I don't like milk, much.

I put that oddity aside when I noticed the accumulation of limescale round the taps in my sink. I got scouring powder, a screwdriver and a J-cloth, and started chipping away.

When I next looked at the clock thirty minutes had passed and I still hadn't got rid of every trace of limescale. I was appalled at myself: I wasn't concentrating, I wasn't deciding.

Back at the telephone, I rang Peter, my exboyfriend and Eddy's son. The odds were against him being at home — he's a

122

cameraman who travels a lot – and I intended to leave a message, but he picked up.

We spent a few minutes on the how-are-you bit, then I told him what I wanted: the name of Eddy's hotel in Florida. He gave it to me. 'They won't have arrived yet,' he said. 'They're on the noon plane. You could leave a message, but I shouldn't think he'll be back to you until the early hours tomorrow. Is it urgent?'

'Fairly.'

'Can I help?'

'Nah. It's police stuff.'

'Take care of yourself,' he said. 'If there's anything I can do, just say the word.'

I was touched he'd offered. As I replaced the receiver, I felt encouraged by his protectiveness, and annoyed by my response to it: usually, I resented any male suggestion that poor little Alex needed a big man to take care of her. An adolescent reaction, probably. Maybe it was time to grow out of it and accept any help I could get.

Chapter Eleven

'I think I'm sickening for something,' I said, pushing the menu away. We were in the Cafe Rouge, a local restaurant, part of a chain which advertised itself as having French food which I suspected a French person wouldn't recognize. I liked it though because it served good coffee and cakes at all hours and you could just get a drink, or eat if you wanted to, and they didn't disturb you. I also liked its eclectic clientele: as the area near me gets smarter all the time, most of the watering holes have become the province of particular cliques, with style standards I don't want to meet.

Polly, by contrast, was feeling greedy. 'I'll have pâté first, then Toulouse sausage,' she said.

That made me feel sick. I ordered soup and bread and a lager. But when the lager came I couldn't drink it and had to drink water instead.

'What do you think you're sickening for?'

'Don't know. I just feel peculiar. Woolly-headed and sick.'

'English sick or American sick?'

'English sick, of course. You've been in Hong Kong too long.'

'Well if you're going to be English sick, the loos are downstairs here, so better leave yourself time. I've got some ideas, do you want to hear them?'

'Absolutely.'

'OK. After lunch, I ring the estate agent and get him to fix an appointment for you with the owner on a residential enquiry, yes? As soon as he's available.'

'That makes sense. But I was going to wait until I told the Met, remember? And I can't do that until Eddy rings me back, late tonight. Early tomorrow morning, actually.'

Polly looked disappointed. I'd shot down her first idea. 'Go on,' I said, determined to accept her next suggestion if it wasn't entirely idiotic.

'Well, I thought what I should do is take a look at the woman's letters.'

I shut my teeth on the first response which sprung to mind, that Alan and I had already done that. 'Mmhm,' I said encouragingly.

'Because, face it, I'm your authority on extra-marital affairs.'

That was true enough. Polly's track record

so far was exclusively as the Other Woman. On the only occasion, to my knowledge, that she'd been On the Road to Wifedom in her own right, the man had been gay.

'So I have a sporting chance of spotting things that you won't, because I've Been There.'

'Talking of which, how's Richard?' Richard was her boss, and her latest.

'Same as usual. Fine most of the time. Every now and then guilt breaks through, because he likes his wife. D'you want some more bread?'

'No thanks.'

'I'm starving. It must be excitement... So anyway, I spend the afternoon going through the letters, and you can get organized doing the other things which need your expertise.'

That might be useful and would keep her out of mischief. I gave her the go ahead.

'Now tell me about you,' she said. 'When are you getting married? How's Barty?'

'Barty's fine,' I said. 'As far as I know. He's in Zaire with a crew.'

'Isn't that very dangerous at present? Where in Zaire is he?'

'Not sure. Eastern Zaire I think, with the refugee camps.' Yes, I supposed it was dangerous, but I have faith in Barty. I reckon he can look after himself in most situations and, besides, it's his life investigating and exposing things, and you can't do all of that from Notting Hill, not the kinds of things he exposes: UN incompetence, government corruption.

'And when are you getting married? Come on, you dodged the question. What is it, Alex, are you having second thoughts? He's such a terrific man and you do love him, I know you do, I'm not going to eat another mouthful until you answer.'

She looked at me, sausage-laden fork in mid-air. 'I'm not having second thoughts,' I said in what I knew would be a futile attempt to head her off, because Polly enjoys conversation about feelings. For her, with friends and lovers and anybody she comes into contact with, however briefly, to talk about feelings is to bond.

I don't like the process. Almost always, I end up diminished and angry and entirely unbonded, and I've told Polly that often enough. She just doesn't believe it. I particularly didn't want to discuss me and Barty, because I'm not clear about it myself I don't think I'm in love with him but I'm not sure that matters. Except for Eddy's son

Peter, when I've thought myself in love before it's not lasted long and, when it went, it went completely and I found myself looking at a human being I didn't rate and counting the seconds till I could disentangle myself. It'd never be like that, with Barty. The worst that could happen is that I'd disappoint him, by not loving him enough. He says he loves me and I think he does, though I don't understand why. My low self-esteem? Or his self-delusion? I know he fancies beautiful charming posh tall blondes. That's what his first wife was like. But we do get on. We almost never fight, and when he isn't there I don't exactly miss him but I often think, I must tell Barty that, or want to share a joke.

All that would sound intolerably lukewarm to Polly, and set her off on a further quest to make me admit the emotions she was sure *I* had because *she* would have had them. She was still eating, watching me, waiting for me to go on.

'You are going to ask me to the wedding, aren't you? I so want to be there, Alex. OK, not a bridesmaid – though I'd love to if you wanted me – but I expect knowing you it'll be a registry office job with as few people as possible and a cup of coffee at your flat afterwards, though Barty'll never let you get away with that, thank heavens we can rely on him for decent champagne, and I so want to help you choose clothes because you dress up terrifically well.'

'We're getting married when Barty gets back,' I said, making it sound more definite than it actually was. 'Early December some time. And, of course, as soon as we've fixed the exact date, I'll let you know.'

'Promise promise?'

'Cross my heart and hope to die.'

'Pale green, what do you think? It looks so great with your eyes...'

We finished lunch chatting amicably. When she'd exhausted my wedding outfit we moved on to what kind of person I could bear to buy Polly's flat, and I reassured her that I really didn't mind her selling, though I minded enough for her not to be hurt. And actually I didn't. I sort of knew in a way that when Barty and I were married it wouldn't make sense for us not to live in his whacking great house in Camden Hill, and for me to let my flat. I wouldn't sell it, just in case. But I'd let it and make a tidy profit over what I was still paying on the mortgage and pay off the mortgage quicker, then I'd own it outright.

'Alex? Had we better get to work?' Polly'd paid the bill and was looking at me expectantly.

So we went back to my flat and she took the letters and settled down at the desk near my phone, so she could answer it if necessary, she said. She liked playing Girl Assistant, I thought rather meanly.

I couldn't stay in and watch her work, so I went back to the office and checked the phone for messages. Two requests for a call back from potential new clients. I noted the names and numbers for Nick to deal with. Monday would be soon enough to get back to them. Lastly, a message from Pauline Eyre asking if we'd made any progress. Nothing from Nick.

At least now I'd got the message from the Golden Kid, I knew where she was. I needed her here, though. I tried her mobile number again. Still out of service. Then I got on to Directory Enquiries for the number of her maths professor in Oxford – I had it already, but back in my Polly-occupied flat.

Ring ring ring ring. No answer, no answering machine, no call-minder. That was par for the course, for him. Most likely, he and Nick would be sitting at his squalid kitchen table amid the debris of several weeks no-housekeeping, working on a maths problem and ignoring the telephone. Briefly, I considered going down to Oxford and hauling her back by the scruff of the neck, but that was irritation, not a considered judgement on the best use of my time.

In her absence I'd have to do her work, and actually I was worried about Samantha Eyre, obvious bait for the Killer, who according to the Kid was staying on the estate. The same estate where my other client thought the Killer might live. It was all thoughts and ifs, but the coincidence worried me. The sooner I laid hands on Sam Eyre and got her to phone home, the sooner my responsibility – Nick's actually – would be discharged, and the happier I'd feel.

So I booted up the computer and accessed the file of Nick's casuals. It would be expensive to use them, but it would probably be quick.

The Golden Kid I already knew was out of the picture till tomorrow. Lil was being elusive. I'd use her if she turned up. Then there was Jonno and Solange.

Jonno runs a mobile car valet service and

spends his whole time on the local streets. What he does is log streets for noise and activity, so wherever he works, he susses it, and then when Nick needs information on a particular street for a residential enquiry, she pays him. I've only met him once and he'd made no impression on me at all. I wouldn't be able to pick him out of a line-up of youngish white males.

I tried to remember if Nick'd ever used him for missing persons. I'd got the impression she didn't like him, but that could just be because she doesn't on the whole trust or rate men. Anyway, that didn't matter. I wasn't looking for a holiday companion, just a warm body who could knock on doors, ask questions and give me the answers. Pauline Eyre was paying way over the odds for her investigation and the more bodies I put on it, the better, so I called Jonno's mobile number. He was only three streets away and just finishing a job, so he said he'd be straight in.

While I waited, I called Solange, the last person on the list. She was just up the road and said she'd take a tea break and be right in.

Less than a minute later, she was, and the office seemed suddenly smaller.

I like Solange. She's mid-twenties, mid-height, almost as wide as she's tall, with a fine head covered in corn-rows glistening with oil. All her visible skin glistens, probably with sweat, but she always smells faintly exotic and sweet. She smells how I imagine the West Indies to smell: a combination of soul food sweating through her pores and the particular perfumes she chose to wear, but as I've never been to the West Indies I wouldn't know if it is what they smell of.

Her traffic-warden's uniform is always immaculate, as are her teeth, and as she laughs so much they're all readily available for inspection. Most of her laughter is apparently unprompted, and seems to me to reflect her sense of the absurdity of the British in general and Notting Hill motorists in particular.

'You look stressed, girl,' she said. 'Give me a mug of tea, three sugars, and tell me about it.'

I went into the back hall area just outside the toilet and brewed up on the work surface beside the washbasin. She followed me, and her bulk made it impossible to turn round in the tiny space. 'Where's Nick?' she said.

'Away till tomorrow, and I've got a rush job on. You available?'

'Tonight?'

'Yeah.'

'I'm on till six thirty, then I had plans for the evening. Depends what you want me to do and what you're going to pay me.'

As I gave her the mug and moved back into the office, I knew I had to make a decision about that. I trusted Solange but not Jonno, and whatever deal I made had better go for the both of them.

By this time Jonno had arrived. I gave him the extra mug of tea I'd made, waited while he helped himself to sugar and we settled down. I looked at both of them.

Solange was laughing. Jonno wasn't. He's somewhere in his thirties, tall and stringy with long limbs, long lank greasy brown hair and a long dirty neck. He was wearing once-black jeans, a grey roll-neck sweater and a grey anorak. He looked like grubby spaghetti, and I moved my chair closer to Solange to breathe in her soul-food smell and avoid Jonno's vintage sweat.

'Nick not back yet?' he said.

'Not yet,' I said, then realized. 'How did you know she'd gone away?'

'She said. Wednesday night.'

135

'Where did you see her?'

'Here. Just outside here, in a cab.'

'A black cab?' Nick never wasted her own money on taxis. I should check the petty cash.

'Nah. A minicab.'

'What did she say?'

'What's it worth to you?'

'A tenner.'

'I came to report, see, and collect my money. You owe me for—'

'She'll pay you when she gets back,' I said, sure that whatever fee he claimed from me would be too much.

'That's out of order—'

'Just tell me, Jonno.' I gave him the promised tenner and he shrugged.

'Yeah, well, I said I wanted my money and she said she was going away and she'd pay me Sat'day.'

'That's all she said?'

'Yeah. That's all she said.'

'Was she upset?'

'I was bloody upset. She owed me. Now are you going to get on with this, or what, 'cos I've got a Beemer in Elgin Crescent to muck out by three o'clock.'

'It's a misper,' I said, and gave each of them a picture of Sam Eyre.

136

'Nick's asked me about this one,' said Jonno. 'Haven't seen her.'

Solange nodded. 'Me too.'

'Keep the pictures, I want you to do a door-to-door, as soon as you can. Tomorrow's too late. Three streets each, on the estate up on Lancaster Road. We've information she's living there. I want every single flat or house covered in the streets I give you, but keep well away from Bartlett Close. There's a small block of flats there, but don't touch them, right? Keep well away. Got it?'

'Sure,' said Solange.

'Yeah, get on with it,' said Jonno. 'What're we asking?'

'Has anyone seen this girl, where, and when. I want very detailed notes from the people you speak to, and a separate list of the no-answers so you or I can get back to them. Have either of you done a door-to-door?'

They shook their heads. 'Make it clear you're not from the police, or the Housing Office, or the Social, or the Revenue. We're acting for a worried mum and no way is anyone getting in trouble. If that looks the way to go, tug on their heartstrings. Innocent young girl, Notting Hill Killer, distraught family. Give out our business cards–' I gave them a stack each – 'and encourage them to phone in if they see her. Hint there might be money in it.'

'What if they won't answer questions unless we pay 'em?' said Jonno.

'Say I'm the one who pays, they should ring me, but make a note and I'll get back to them.'

'What's her name?' asked Jonno.

'Her name is Samantha Eyre but she might not be going by that, so don't confuse them up front by telling them. Any questions?'

'Yeah. What're you paying us?'

'Ten quid an hour for the door-to-door. A bonus if you find her.'

'How much?'

'It'll be worth your while,' I said. 'And it's a great hourly rate.'

After they'd gone I opened the door and the window to get rid of Jonno's smell. A faint anxiety was lurking at the back of my mind. I'd set him on the trail of Sam Eyre, and I didn't like him.

But the, fear was unreasonable, I told myself firmly. He was money-grabbing and unappealing to look at and he didn't wash, but that didn't make him dangerous.

And why had Nick taken a cab? If she was going to Oxford, she'd go by train from Paddington. Paddington was well within walking distance, and she walked a lot, eating up miles of pavement with her jittery energy and long athletic stride. She wouldn't have had luggage with her. She didn't even own luggage. And if she was in a hurry she would have taken the tube – Paddington was only three stops away.

I tried her mobile number. Out of service again. This time I was really angry. I'd bought the phone and I paid the rental and bills, mostly to please her, partly because it was handy. So far it had been her toy. Now, when I wanted to use it, she'd switched it off.

I took a deep breath. Angry time was wasted time, and there was plenty to do. It was Friday today. New College would presumably be effectively closed over the weekend, and if I was to track down Hilary Lucas's woman before next Friday, I wouldn't be able to do anything at the college for two days. So I should use this afternoon to get into the place and get some contacts before everyone vanished into the woodwork for the weekend.

Chapter Twelve

Looking at the facade of New College, London it seemed that it had been new sometime in Victorian England, when they went in for mock-medieval complete with turrets and portcullises and a general air of Mad King Ludwig of Bavaria mediated through the vision of a soap manufacturer on hallucinogenic drugs. Not all the turrets were visible through the fog, which was even thicker down here by the river.

I'd come by tube and, as I ascended into the Strand and walked, guided by my A-Z, the hundred yards towards the river to the place where the college was, I tried once more to marshal my explanation of what I was doing to sound a smidgeon more sensible than idiotic. I couldn't. But it didn't matter very much because I've come across quite a lot of academics one way or the other, and although they're presumably very intelligent they're often not very clever, or perhaps not very interested in anything outside their field.

So I went through the portcullised gates – luckily the portcullises seemed rusted shut – and headed towards the main entrance and up some wide shallow steps, and through the entrance door. I discovered I was in the medical school. A passing student directed me to the History Department; several miles, it seemed, along tiled corridors which would do excellently for location filming for any First World War hospital. I fetched up against a door clearly leading to one of the off-shoots of the main building, and then, there I was. History Department Office, said the sign.

Inside was chaos. Several young men and women – students, probably – milling about. Eventually the only adult there shooed them out.

Suddenly I realized how old I felt. When had I gone from being the same age as the students to thinking of them as being just young?

Looking around at them, I realized that it had happened recently. Usually I looked at students and was jealous, because I hadn't been a student. That was what I thought when I looked at students. Now, suddenly, I didn't. Maybe it was because I'd turned thirty. In the sixties they'd thought that, hadn't they, there'd even been a song about it. *I hope I die before I get old.*

'Yes? Can I help you?'

The speaker, the remaining adult, sounded testy, as if she'd been talking for some time and I hadn't answered. That was because I hadn't heard her. I was drifting off more and more: I couldn't keep my concentration. And now I was drifting into thinking I was drifting.

With a huge effort I focused.

She was presumably the department secretary. She was sixtyish and built on unusual lines, as neo-Gothic as New College's design. Her top half was long and slender, her bottom half stumpy and wide, her legs as far as I could see completely straight, as wide at the ankle as they were at the knee, and very short. Her dress made no concessions: her swan-like upper half wore a tight-fitting ribbed sweater, her bottom half a skirt which ended above the knee, her legs thick woollen stockings. Her hair was short, thinning, dyed brown, and her face as weatherbeaten as if she spent her working days on a fishing boat in a North Atlantic gale instead of in this stuffy office.

On one side of the room were pigeon-holes, labelled with names. There was a table with piles of paper, a photocopying machine, several filing cabinets, a desk with telephones and two framed signs on the wall behind the desk. One said 'You don't have to be mad to work here, but it helps.' The other said 'Historians do it with perspective.'

I tried to stop imagining what possible sexual purpose would be served by perspective, introduced myself and explained that I was researching a documentary on heart attack victims and that Mrs Lucas had given me permission to use her late husband.

At that point the woman began to cry. Tears ran down her face, she snuffled, her shoulders shook. After about a minute she stopped, blew her nose, cleared her throat, and said briskly, 'Sorry about that. I'm half Italian, you see. Emotional. Give me a minute.'

She took a phone, dialled, and spoke. it was evident from her side of the conversation that she was talking to Hilary Lucas, confirming my story.

When she replaced the receiver I said, 'And you're half Missourian. Suspicious.'

She gave a half laugh, which was half more than the remark deserved. 'It just didn't sound all that likely,' she said apologetically.

She needn't have apologized to me: I agreed with her, and thought she was sharp enough to be an excellent informant. With any luck I need go no further into the department than the secretary's office. 'What was all that about?' I said, nodding my head at the departing students. 'It was nearly a riot.'

'Bad timetabling,' she said. 'How can I help you?'

'What sort of bad timetabling?'

'One of the lecturers who shall be nameless goes to the pub Friday lunchtime and stays there. Give him a third-year exam class Friday at three and what do you get? Complaints, that's what you get, 'nuff said. What do you want to know? I'm happy to answer your questions if you don't mind me stapling while we talk.' She was taking one sheet from each pile, neatly tapping and squaring them up, then stapling.

'I'll assemble, you staple,' I said.

We worked side by side. 'You were fond of Professor Lucas, then,' I said.

'Very. We went way back. Back to 1965, to be accurate. We were new here together. I was a typist, he was a junior lecturer. He used to share my sandwiches because he couldn't afford to eat out.'

'Was he hard up?'

'Then, he was. Before he married. She has the money, you know.'

'I don't know. I don't know very much at all. She was very reluctant to talk about – anything. It must have been a terrible shock.'

'Oh it was,' she said, crying again, but sniffing so her nose didn't drip on the completed stapled sheets. 'Just like that. He died before he reached the hospital, they said.'

'Where was he when–?'

'Here. In his room. Here. He rang through and I found him. The phone rang and there were just awful noises but I knew it was him and – oh, I can't do this, could you ask me something else please, just till we've finished these notes?'

'Who was his closest colleague in the department?' I said. 'Who would be the best person for me to talk to about how he was feeling, what the job was like, and so on?'

'Me, probably. I'd known him the longest. And he wasn't a gregarious man, didn't make friends easily. His real friend in the university was Philip Gein from the English Department.'

'The one who was killed by muggers?'

'Oh, you know about that. Yes. Philip was his closest friend. He got on well with everybody, did Robbie, but he didn't pal around. He wasn't in all that much, to be honest, did most of his work at home. He liked being at home.'

'So he was happy there?'

She looked at me oddly. 'What's this to do with your documentary?'

Very little, of course. I was hoping for more emotional reaction from her, because she was a possibility. Old enough to be the letter-writer, fond of Robbie... 'An unhappy domestic situation can contribute to stress,' I said. It was common sense, though hardly the latest medical insight.

'Of course it can but you're not going to put that on television, I imagine, telling all England that the marriage didn't work. Not with Hilary's agreement. She's got more sense.'

'And was it an unhappy domestic situation?'

'Not at all,' she said briskly.

'Well then that's why she's prepared to have me ask these questions, I suppose,' I said. 'It must be hard making a childless marriage work. Do you have children?'

147

'I have a son.'

'Oh, how old is he?'

'Grown up and gone,' she said, stapling the last set of notes and pushing half across to me. 'Count,' she said.

I counted, she counted, we agreed the total was two hundred and she stacked the piles neatly on the side of the table.

'The main thrust of the documentary is stress. About lifestyle, really. Had you noticed that he was particularly stressed before he died?'

'The stress around here has gone up every year for the past ten years,' she said. 'Cuts in funding. The pressure to publish. Short-term contracts. More students, because that's the only way to keep funding up. Less-qualified students, who need more teaching. The free-market economy way. It's not just us, of course. Universities all over England. The health service, the schools. Dog eat dog.'

'You don't approve.'

'It's not a question of approve or disapprove. It's just a fact. We couldn't afford the other way, I suppose.'

'And did this particularly affect Professor Lucas?'

She laughed. 'To be fair, it affected Robbie

least of all, probably. They couldn't get rid of him and they didn't want to, he published all the time, he had comparatively few teaching commitments and he'd never been interested in administration or finance so he played no real part in the changes. He spent most of his time at home, as I told you. He kept well out of it.'

'And how about his personality? Was it particularly anxious? Emotional?'

She laughed incredulously. 'Robbie? He had a wonderful temperament. Wonderful. So easygoing. He never blamed me for anything, he always gave me plenty of warning when he wanted something done, unlike some others I could mention,' she said, waving her hand at the piles of notes we'd just been sorting. 'These were in just before lunch, "Can I have them typed and duplicated and sorted by five o'clock. Sorry Elaine I know I should have done them earlier." He's been saying, "Sorry Elaine I know I should have done them earlier" for the last twelve years, naming no names, 'nuff said.'

'The women are better, I suppose,' I said. 'Women usually are. At planning forward and warning you.'

'Some,' she said. 'It depends.'

'If Professor Lucas was eminent, I suppose he supervised quite a few graduate students?'

'Quite a few, although he was very specialized.'

'Did he supervise graduates even in the early days? Way back in 1970, for instance?'

She looked puzzled, as well she might. 'Not so many, of course. Maybe one or two.'

'Because I suppose it can be quite a lasting relationship, that, can't it, if you're interested in the same academic area and then you go on to work in the field, you must keep meeting, I suppose. Maybe I should talk to some of his early graduate students.'

'Possibly,' she said.

'I don't know much about university teachers, but I do know that with some of the other heart-attack victims I've been dealing with, they've been stressed by the increasing demands made by paperwork. Forms and memos and letters and such. Letters, for instance. Was there much increase in Professor Lucas's letters over the years?'

She looked at me, astonished. 'Letters?'

'Yes. You sort the mail, I expect. Did he have more letters than most?' Preferably strongly scented with lipstick kisses and a return address on the back of the envelope, I thought, adjusting my expression to dim but earnest.

'All academics get letters. All academics shuffle paper. That's what they do, most of the time. Did you have anything particular in mind?'

'Not really...' I wished I could just ask her, straight out, for information about what I wanted to know. I thought if anyone in the department knew it, it would be her. Because she wasn't easy to pump, at all, and she didn't trust what I said I was doing, despite what Hilary had told her.

'The memorial service is next week?' I asked, sounding unsure because I didn't necessarily believe what Hilary had said.

'Yes.'

So at least that was true. 'And who's organizing it?'

'Dr Walsh. He's the head of department. He likes public occasions.'

'Perhaps I should speak to him.'

The restrictions Hilary had given me were very irksome. I didn't feel much more progress could be made with Elaine without alerting her to what I was getting at.

'You could certainly try,' said Elaine. 'I'll

give you his telephone number, you can set up an appointment. He's a very busy man.'

'Is he in now?'

'You'd have to make an appointment,' she said again, doing her job as a good departmental secretary, which I was sure she was.

I tried for confidential. 'It's a bit difficult,' I said. 'In something like this, I'd usually rely on the widow to give me most of the background and then check what she said with his friends, because widows only know one side of their husband's lives, of course. But although Mrs Lucas has agreed to let the Professor be part of the programme, she's reluctant to talk about him herself.'

'It was a very close marriage,' Elaine said. 'They pretty much made a life for themselves, and what with no children and Elaine's family money, they could afford to travel. They spent every summer at their place in Italy. And they went away to the sun for Christmas, usually.'

'Whereabouts in Italy?'

'Tuscany.'

'What about research trips?'

'Of course. Mostly to Brussels and Paris and Rome, but there's a lively market in medieval archives so plenty of them are held in Oxford and Cambridge and America.'

'Moving about can be stressful–'

'Not for him. He spaced his trips out and he sometimes took Hilary with him and they combined his research with holidays.'

'And he didn't smoke and he drank alcohol moderately and he had no work worries and no money worries ... it sounds just a bit dull.'

'Dull but lucky,' said Elaine. 'And a very nice man.'

Chapter Thirteen

I left the department a little more informed than when I'd arrived, but distinctly more puzzled. Maybe Robbie Lucas had been the equable paragon Elaine described, or then again maybe Elaine was just a protective secretary, doing her job. She didn't seem a front runner for the mistress, unless she had a daughter she hadn't mentioned.

I stood in the First World War hospital corridor, watching students pass, trying to work out the quickest way out of the building. It couldn't be retracing my steps, because the main entrance wasn't the nearest way out: in getting there I'd walked three sides of a square.

'Excuse me,' I said on an impulse to a purposeful-looking student, 'could you tell me the way to the English Department?'

'Follow me, I'm on my way there,' he said, and swept me along a corridor, up a flight of stone spiral stairs, along another corridor where he pointed at a door, and said tersely, 'Office', and carried on.

I opened the door: the room was apparently empty. In layout and furniture it was not unlike the History Department office, but there the resemblance stopped. Each wall was painted a different colour – dark blue, dark red, dark green and terracotta – and hung from floor to ceiling with posters of poems. On every possible surface were plants, bursting with health and vitality and in some instances making determined efforts to grow up the posters.

'Can I help you?'

The voice came from a corner of the room behind a filing cabinet, some plants and several ferns. Then a face emerged, framed by fronds and tendrils: a youngish female face, my age I guessed, round and cheerful, surrounded by a halo of frizzy blonde hair and wearing thick, distorting glasses.

I explained who I was and what I was after, and that I'd just come from the History Department.

'Let me finish spraying the plants, and I'll be with you,' said the girl. 'I'm Maisie and I'll tell you what I know.'

'Henry James,' I said. 'Were you called after the book?'

'No way,' she said, 'it's a stupid enough name anyway but no Eng. Lit. tit can resist referring to it so I get my retaliation in first. Right,' she said triumphantly giving a last decisive spray and emerging completely.

She was just a little taller than me and her whole body was as slender as Elaine's sylph-like top half had been. She was wearing black woollen tights, highheeled clumpy shoes, a short narrow leather skirt, a red skimpy sweater, and an amused alert expression which I guessed was permanent. 'D'you want a cup of coffee? I'm just making.'

'Great,' I said. 'Black, no sugar.'

'Just as well. Some slob's pinched the milk.'

'Are you the department secretary?'

'That's me. Bit different from History, eh?' She waved her hand around the office.

'Just a bit. Maybe you can explain something to me – why do historians do it with perspective?'

'To make their dicks look bigger?' she suggested.

'And how do Eng. Lit. tits do it?'

'Like rabbits. Here's your coffee, have a chair and tell me what you need to know.'

'Anything at all about Professor Lucas and what might have caused or precipitated a heart attack.'

She leant against the edge of the desk, sipped her coffee and watched me. 'You needed Philip Gein – you know who I mean?' I nodded. 'They were mates.'

'That's why I came here. Elaine wouldn't tell me anything even if there was anything to tell: protecting her department. She made Robbie Lucas sound like a candidate for Man of the Year award. Great boss, great husband.'

'He was, I think,' said Maisie. 'A really nice guy, apart from an obsession with irrigation and drainage.'

'Why don't you tell me what Philip Gein would have said if he were here to say it? You could probably guess.'

She laughed. 'Nobody could guess what Philip would say. Never. Unpredictable, he was. Typical of him, really, to die the way he did.'

'Which was?'

'He just walked out of here one afternoon, said "See you tomorrow", and the next we heard, he was dead. Mugged on the way to the Strand.' She was serious now, and sad.

Something struck me. 'When was this?'

'August,' she said.

'He was mugged on an afternoon in August? And killed?' That was really odd.

London muggers seldom kill people. When I'd first heard it I'd assumed it was late at night, in the dark, some kids who were drunk or high. Even that would have been unusual. 'Did the police ever catch them?'

'No. They had no idea. He was found stabbed on the street, that's all they knew, and his wallet had gone so they classed it as a mugging. It's been dull round here since he went. I still can't believe it, actually. I expect him to walk in ... But you don't need to hear this. What else can I tell you?'

'I was wondering, really, if Professor Lucas had other friends in this department. Philip Gein sounds as if he made friends easily, while Lucas didn't, according to Elaine. So I thought maybe there were other people in this department who were close to Gein who sort of got to know Lucas.'

'I see what you mean ... you could try Barbara Gottlieb. She was probably closest to Philip.'

'Close close?' I said.

She shook her head. 'Not Barbara, though Philip wasn't averse to as much close close as he could get, which was plenty. She's in her office, I think. D'you want to go along and give her a try?'

Barbara Gottlieb's office was absolutely businesslike. No plants, no posters. Bookcases entirely full of books and files and papers, a desk with a computer and more papers, and one chair. No chair for her and clear floor space otherwise, to leave her room to manoeuvre her wheel chair, which she did skilfully, with strong arms. The lower part of her body, under a rug, seemed almost wasted to nothing. She was in her forties, probably, though the dark-brown hair which fell straight to her shoulders was untouched by grey and the thick skin on her handsome face was virtually unlined.

She could be the right age for the mistress. I needed to find out if she was married, so I went for it. 'Are you Herman Gottlieb's wife, by any chance? I worked with him on a documentary once.'

'No,' she said. 'I'm not married.' She appeared uninterested in Herman Gottlieb, which was just as well. I don't like inventing when I don't have to. I explained myself, again, and my cover story sounded no more sensible on the third run-through. As I talked, she waved me to the chair, and watched me with her large clear grey eyes expressionless. When I'd finished, she nodded.

160

'Hilary Lucas has agreed to this?' she said.

'Yes. Elaine in the History Department checked with her.'

She nodded again. 'You'll forgive me if I have a word with Elaine.'

'Of course.'

While she telephoned, I looked around the room, at the high arrow-slit windows and the bookcases going all the way up to the Gothic ceiling, and wondered how she ever reached the books on the upper shelves, and why a German had come to London to teach English literature, because although she was absolutely fluent she had a decidedly German accent.

When she put the phone down, she looked puzzled.

'All right?' I said blandly.

'Not really,' she said. 'I don't quite understand. Hilary's a very private person, very self-contained, and she was absolutely devastated by Robbie's death. We all were, of course, it was so unexpected, but for the widow in a good marriage – '

'Especially a childless marriage,' I said.

'Indeed. For the widow in a good marriage a death like Robbie's must be as if the world had stopped. That's one reason why we left it so long before the memorial service.'

161

'When was Professor Gein's memorial service?'

'In September,' she said briefly, as if the memory was painful, then returned to her point. 'I could understand if Hilary was co-operating in scientific research which might help other potential heart-attack victims, but yours is to be a popular programme, isn't it?'

'We have properly qualified advisers,' I said, hoping she wouldn't ask me to name them, knowing she would.

'And those would be'

'I'm afraid I'm not dealing with that aspect of the research,' I said weakly.

'No,' she said.

'I'm dealing with lifestyle. Such as, were there particular stresses in his work, in his domestic life? Was he a good mixer with plenty of friends, or a more solitary person? That kind of thing.'

'That kind of thing,' she repeated. 'So, ask me your questions, if Hilary wants it.'

'Were you a close friend of his?'

'Not so much. I was a friend of Philip's and I saw something of Robbie because of Philip.'

'What was Robbie's life like? Can you describe it to me?'

162

'It was very pleasant, I think. He was devoted to his wife, and proud of her. She is, as you probably know, very successful. He was successful too, in his own field, which interested him. She has plenty of money of her own, and she also earns a great deal, and his salary was good. They had a beautiful London flat and a villa in Tuscany. They enjoyed good food, which Hilary cooked, and good wine, which Robbie chose. They were minor collectors of modern art. They went to the opera, they listened to music, they had a small circle of friends whose company they enjoyed. Hilary's sisters have children, and they took an interest in them. Robbie's brother also has children, several children, and they took an interest in them too. A quiet but pleasant life, I think. Good people. Kind. Generous. Intellectual.'

'The small circle of friends,' I said. 'Who else should I talk to? Professor Gein's widow, perhaps?'

'Philip did not leave a widow. His wife died three years ago. She had myasthenia gravis.'

I scraped around my information bank. 'The wasting disease?'

'Yes. She was in a wheelchair, like me. And I have been paraplegic so long, I knew about disability. Sometimes, as his wife sickened, I could tell him what to expect, how to help her, what to do for the best.'

I said nothing because nothing seemed tactful. 'So who else do you think I should talk to, about Professor Lucas?'

She looked at me, expressionless. 'It depends what you want to talk about. He saw a great deal of Hilary's family.'

'That's an angle I must pursue, then. But on the work side,' I said remembering Hilary's suggestion that the mistress was probably an academic, 'someone else in his field? I imagine he went to conferences and read papers about his subject?'

'Sometimes, of course, but he did not make friends easily. He was very self-contained. I don't remember him mentioning anyone in particular.'

'A society, then? Is there an irrigation and drainage society?'

'Not as such. There are Historical Geography Societies, of course, but again, I can't remember him mentioning anyone in particular. You could ask.'

We seemed to have reached an impasse. I wanted to ask her, straight out, who his mistress was. She might even have told me. Her reaction would have told me something, at least. But that was exactly what Hilary didn't want, and I still had nearly a week.

'Thank you,' I said.

'I cannot have been of much help.'

'It doesn't sound as if he's much of a candidate for stress, no, but that in itself could be interesting.'

'If you say so. And you know where I am. If there is anything else I can help you with–' she began, and stopped.

I let the silence go on, hoping she'd fill it. She didn't.

Chapter Fourteen

When I got back to the flat I found Polly sitting on the floor surrounded by letters and full of herself. 'I've solved your problem!' she said.

For a moment, I was disappointed, the kind of disappointment that comes when someone else fills in the last clue in your crossword puzzle. Then I adjusted my face to grateful, which I actually was, and said 'Great! Who is she?'

'Who is who? Oh, your woman. I'm not talking about that, though I have some suggestions about where to look. I meant, your problem about telling the police. All done.'

A surge of rage gripped me. What the devil did she think she was doing? And who had she told? And what kind of a mess had she got me into with Hilary Lucas? And what did the heck did *Nick* think she was doing, skiving off and leaving me making do with Polly?

'Don't be cross,' she said. 'Listen, I didn't

167

mean to interfere, but it seemed such a wonderful opportunity, oh do stop looking so cross, listen – Arthur Fishburn, the old ex-policeman chappie, Eddy's friend, dropped in to see you and I gave him a cup of tea and we got to chatting – I just think a chat was what he wanted, because he didn't seem to have a message for you or anything. And then I thought, he's Eddy's friend, he's got contacts and his old friends of course, and he knew all about how the serial killer hunt is organized and who he should tell, and who would act on it, and he said he could do it without naming names, so I told him, but not with the names, and he said he'd speak to someone this afternoon, and then let us know when it was done, and I gave him your card so he has your number here and in the office.'

She stopped, and looked at me half-defiantly, half as if doubts were creeping in.

Not half as many doubts as I was having, but there was no point letting her see that. What was done was done, and she wasn't to know that Eddy had given me health warnings on Arthur, nor that I had my own reservations about him. Now he knew I was a private investigator, and I'd deliberately kept all that well away from him. 'Oh,

Arthur,' I said heartily. 'Of course. Good thinking.'

She wasn't entirely convinced, but she wanted to be. 'Because I thought, if you didn't need to wait to talk to Eddy, then you could go over to the house and get stuck in this evening, so I rang the estate agent and made an appointment for you, for eight o'clock. That's the first time one of them will be in, apparently. It isn't the owner – it's the one who has a girl in his flat. James Hobbs.'

'Thanks, Polly,' I said rather limply.

She obviously felt I wasn't enthusiastic enough, and she was right, because she'd meant well and she hadn't done too badly, always supposing that Arthur Fishburn could or would do anything sensible. 'D'you want to give Fishburn a ring and call him off?' she said. 'Or cancel the appointment with Hobbs?'

'Absolutely not,' I said. 'I'm making coffee and I'll get you some water, and then you can tell me what you've sussed from the letters.'

'OK,' said Polly, who had moved to the desk and was marshalling the letters in piles in front of her, 'what with talking to Arthur and really concentrating on each letter, I haven't gone through all of them. I read the last letter, the one about Rillington Place, but apart from that I stuck to chronological order and I'm up to 1986. This is what I've got so far. First thing is, they know each other very well and see each other a lot. Apart from their private meetings, that is.'

'Evidence?' I said.

'She never uses the letters for practical details. Nothing at all to say next week at the usual place or don't forget to book the table.'

'Which you would otherwise expect to find?'

'Of course. It's not easy making arrangements with a married man, believe me, unless you work with him or see him regularly for some other reason. Plus it isn't the other usual thing, where you make detailed arrangements for the next date at each meeting, because the gaps between meetings are too long. They make love about five times a year, with a minimum of two months between. Two months in advance is a long time to make firm dates. Plus they don't talk privately on the telephone, because some of the letters are just saying very simple things like, I'm missing you very much or I wanted to tell you I love you ... things which she could perfectly well have said on the phone, if they could safely have used it.'

'Maybe she preferred writing it.'

'OK, even if she did, that last letter – the one about wanting him to talk to their son – she'd surely have said that on the phone if she could have, and discussed it with him. But apart from the arrangements question, the other reason I have for saying that they see each other quite often as well as meeting to bonk, is that she doesn't describe or explain important events in her own life or his, she just refers to them, and quite often they're things that have happened since their last bonking session, and the really obvious example is when their son is born. They don't meet privately from January that year until July, but she writes to him in May, taking it for granted not only that he knows about the child but that he's seen it, probably several times.'

'OK,' I said. 'Supposing you're right—'

'I am, and do you see what that means? It means we're not looking for a work colleague. It's got to be a friend of the family. Or a member of the family, sister, sister-in-law, maybe.'

'A work colleague could bring in her baby

for general admiration and the ritual pre-
sentation of cuddly toys.'

'But a work colleague wouldn't expect him
to be so familiar with all the current details
of her home life. They don't meet often for
their bonking sessions, she's not going to
waste them describing the difficulties she's
having with her newly installed french
windows.'

'French windows?'

'Yes, back in 1980 that's what she's
referring to, as if he knows all about it. Plus
the original falling-in-love bit happened in
Rome, yeah? During the holiday time. In
August. Where I'll bet anything they were all
holidaying together. Her husband was there
anyway, because she says she found it hard
to face him, that night. And also, I think the
nicknames are so she doesn't have to use the
names.'

'Because she's worried about someone
reading the letters and identifying her?'

'I don't think so. More because she feels
guilty, and it's easier if she doesn't have to
name his wife or her husband, who I think
she loves, the husband I mean but possibly
the wife too. Close friends or family, trust
me.'

'Hilary's got sisters. And Robbie's

172

brother's married.'

'Not a bad place to start. Other things to look for, the son went to boarding school – Alan noticed that, actually his notes aren't bad–'

'I haven't had time to read them–'

'Don't worry, I'll tell you his as well as mine, but there aren't that many anyway, not real facts. She doesn't half go on about her feelings. And she quotes a lot.'

'Is that surprising?'

Polly grimaced. 'It is and it isn't. What kind of professor was Robbie?'

'Historical Geography. Medieval drainage and irrigation.'

'Then I suppose *she's* something literary. Writer, teacher–'

'Why do you say that?'

'Because she's a smart cookie, I think. Skilful. I get the impression she's keeping him ticking over, keeping him interested, and the feeling/literary bit would tie in if he was that way inclined, but if he's into sewers, I suppose that must be her...'

'I don't think it's the sewer kind of drainage.'

'Whatever. It's not culture, is it, and the letters are culture which I'd assumed they shared.'

'OK,' I said. 'Hang on a minute.' I fetched my list from the action board. 'This is what I've got so far. The woman is now at least in her late forties.'

'Yes.'

'The son is twenty-four, with a birthday in the first half of the year.' Polly nodded me on. 'He has an older sister, at least two years older,'

She hesitated. 'There's something odd about the sister.'

'Such as?'

'I wonder if she's handicapped. There aren't many mentions of her – nothing about her at school, but quite a lot about the son at school.'

'She might assume her lover'd be more interested in his own son than in her daughter.'

'Could be... It's hard to pin down, but there's something ... a sort of indulgence, when she writes about her.' Polly started riffling through the pile of letters, then stopped. 'I'll find it later. Just put, query handicapped, and go on.'

'The woman was in Rome in August 1970.' Nod. 'She lives with her husband.' Nod. 'The letters seem to change in the last few years, but you haven't got that far, so you wouldn't know. And that's all I had.'

Add the son who went to boarding school when he was thirteen, and the friend/family bit for the woman, and her maybe being a writer or a teacher of English. Listen, Alex, I've got to go and get ready soon, I'm going out tonight, I told you, but I've photocopied the letters and can I take a set, cos I haven't finished them and I'll probably have more ideas on the ones I've read, there are things floating round in the back of my mind I haven't pinned down yet, and also can I show them around a bit this evening, I can't give your client's name away however much I drink, because I don't know it?'

'Sure,' I said. 'Who're you going to be with?'

'The girls. In their time, Other Women every one.'

The girls were models from the agency Polly had worked for. More than ten years ago they'd agreed to a reunion dinner every year; so far they'd kept the tradition going, although the original group was depleted by one suicide and one overdose, and only one was still a model.

'I'll see you tomorrow morning before I go anyway, my plane isn't till the afternoon, so I'm off now, kiss kiss, look after yourself at

Rillington Place, I hope the Arthur Fishburn thing is all right, I'm sorry for interfering, but I did mean it for the best...'

Chapter Fifteen

Without her, the flat settled back into quiet with a sigh of relief, or perhaps that was me.

It was six o'clock: I had two hours before going over to keep my appointment with James Hobbs. Two hours sorting-out time.

I turned up the thermostat, opened the windows to get rid of the Polly-perfume, expensive and musky, which I didn't usually mind but now was making me queasy, settled down on the sofa with the telephone, and called my old school friend Michelle. She lives with her two kids in the council tower block where I grew up when I wasn't in care.

She's always in – she's been agoraphobic since she was raped at thirteen – and she spends a lot of time on the phone, so I wasn't surprised to get the engaged tone.

I tried Nick's mobile. Still out of service. I tried her Oxford professor. Still no reply. I called in to my office phone and picked up the three messages.

The first was an offer of work, the second

Pauline Eyre again, could I get back to her please, the third Arthur Fishburn. He sounded his full age, older than he'd looked, and he wasn't comfortable with answering machines.

'Oh – er – this is a message for Alex Tanner, sent at ... wait a mo ... five thirty on Friday, that's five thirty p.m., seventeen thirty I mean. This is a message to say that as requested by Miss Straker, I think that was the name, I've informed the SIO, that is the Senior Investigating Officer from the Met, that is the Metropolitan Police, and also at the SIO's request the receiver at the Major Incident Room in Notting Hill Police Station of the suspicions expressed concerning a tenant of the flats in Bartlett Close formerly Rillington Place in connection with the on-going investigation into the murders of young women perpetrated in or about Notting Hill, that being all the information available to me. Oh, this is Arthur, Arthur Fishburn, formerly police constable Arthur Fishburn, retired. I think that's it ... Oh, if I can be of any further help–'

The machine had cut him off.

I wondered if anyone in the Met would listen to anything Arthur said. I wouldn't, in their place, particularly since he couldn't give a source. But the first part of my work for Hilary Lucas was done.

I re-dialled Michelle. This time she answered, swamped by a background of gunshots and screams. 'Alex, hi, will you turn that down Warren, I won't tell you again – TURN IT DOWN!' The gunshots died away and a door slammed. 'OK, I can hear you now – he's off to sulk.'

'How're the kids?'

'They're kids, what can I say? Going through a stage, know what I mean? How're you? Going to come over and see me? Bring Thai. I've got into Thai. More subtle than Indian and spicier than Chinese. I'm even tried cooking it but the shopping's hard to get, round here, or so Mick says but I'm not sure I believe him, lazy bugger.' Mick was her latest man and he'd not only lasted for a whole year but he also had a job, as far as I knew the only man in the tower block who did, though most of the women were employed. 'I've been thinking about you all this week,' she went on. 'Warren's made a guy. Do you remember our guys?'

When she said it, I remembered. For years she and I had been a team. Primary school, comprehensive school, we'd sat together, spent breaks together, covered each other's backs. Often I'd eaten tea at her place, either because my mother'd been out of it – she was schizophrenic then, now she's got Alzheimer's – or when I escaped from the current foster parents. I could still taste her mother's fry-ups. They were never good exactly, but they were comforting and familiar and she'd been generous to me. Looking back, I realized just how generous.

Shell and I had made a good profit on the guys. We'd had a five-year run, eight to thirteen. After the rape she'd quit. I'd gone on alone, because I could look younger than my age and I liked the money, and I hadn't minded doing things alone. I couldn't swear to it that I'd given her a share, even though she was too scared to go out and I'd done all the work. I hoped I had.

'Of course I remember,' I said. 'We made over eighty quid one year.'

'It was a good laugh, wasn't it?'

'A great laugh. Good times.'

Pause. I don't know what she was thinking, but I thought about the disaster of her life, and the purely joyous bubbly sound of her long-ago giggle.

'I'll come and see you soon, but things are hectic at the minute...' I waited, briefly, for her to ask me what I wanted, then realized with an embarrassed shock that she was probably the only person I knew who I regularly rang up when I didn't want something. 'I need advice,' I said.

'From me? Gerrover! Since when have you listened to me, Smarty?'

'I'm listening now.'

'OK,' she said seriously. 'I'm listening too. Get it out, c'mon.'

'Yesterday and today, I can't concentrate. I feel sick. I'm sensitive to smells. I'm drinking milk, and I hate milk.'

'Peeing a lot?'

'Not that I've noticed.'

'Nipples?'

'Two.'

'Ha bloody ha. Sounds as if you're in the club, love.'

'That's what I thought.'

'Go down the chemist, get yourself a test, give it a try tomorrow morning. You trying for this, were you?'

'Absolutely not. I'm on the pill. And we use condoms.'

'Determined little sod, then. Takes after his mum. But you better read the instructions on the test, the pill may do something to it... You all right, Alex?'

181

'I'm fine,' I said.

'I'm really pleased,' she said.

'Why?'

'Because you'll come back to me.'

'What do you mean?'

'You'll find out. When're you going to tell your mum? How is she? Still in hospital?'

'How do you expect her to be? She hasn't made sense for years. She doesn't even recognize me. Of course she's still in hospital,' I said irritably.

'You've still got to tell her if you test positive,' said Michelle coaxingly. 'It stands to reason. You've got to tell your mum.'

I didn't argue. When she says 'it stands to reason', she means the exact opposite: that reason is nowhere, but that deep feeling or conventional belief is involved and that nothing will move her. She'd said, 'it stands to reason' that she'd be safer if she never went out. I've often tried to persuade her to get help for her agoraphobia. I still try, off and on.

We talked for another ten minutes but I'd switched off.

I'd known I was pregnant just before Polly left. It hadn't been a thought process, the putting together of clues – such obvious clues. It had been a fraction of a second's shift from total ignorance to total certainty. Talking to Michelle had just been a way of acknowledging it, the beginning of a long road of female confidences and obstetrical gossip, the kind of thing I'd spent my life avoiding because wombs are boring. I just hoped my own womb would be a page turner.

Abortion wasn't an option. It was Barty's child, he wanted children, we were due to be married anyway, and I wanted children.

Some of the time, I wanted children. Some of the time I didn't. But now I edited out the thoughts about not wanting children, same as, when the child came, I'd edit my words.

I'd stop taking the pill, I'd carry a supply of dry biscuits for the sickness (Michelle's advice), I'd tell Barty when I had independent confirmation.

Meanwhile, if I could, I wouldn't think about it, who unless I was very unlucky wasn't an it but was a him. Or her. I had work to do, and with any luck my brain would stay on-line enough to do it. But right now, I suddenly realized I needed to sleep. An hour's nap, that's what I wanted. That's what my womb wanted, I supposed, because unpregnant Alex never took naps.

Chapter Sixteen

It was well dark by seven thirty, and as I walked through the streets to Bartlett Close I remembered, with a slight frisson between my shoulder blades, Arthur Fishburn's insistence that it was dangerous to walk alone in the Notting Hill streets. It wasn't. I knew it wasn't. And it was typical of the over-protective, wanting to make himself important, Arthur to say that. But all the same I didn't feel easy, possibly because I was now walking for two, and I crossed over the road once because there were some particularly threatening footsteps behind me. But once you start worrying about that kind of thing you become a prisoner in your own house, waiting for someone to go out with you. It was inconceivable. In England's climate there are large stretches of the year where if you only went out in bright daylight you'd hardly be able to go out at all, and I wasn't going to give way to that.

I took a roundabout way through the rest of the estate to check on Jonno and Solange.

I saw them both; both involved with door-step conversations. Neither of them saw me, and that was fine. I'd get their reports tomorrow morning.

Bartlett Close was quiet. On the estate there had been people and lights. In Bartlett Close, with only one building, there was silence, and thin gleams of light escaping from around the rims of the curtain of the top flat. The rest of the block was in darkness.

I went up the steps, pressed the buzzer marked Hobbs, and identified myself to the intercom crackle. There was no verbal response, but the door swung open in front of me. In the streetlights I could see a hallway crammed with bicycles, and the timed switch for the hall light, which I pressed and pressed without result.

'Doesn't work,' called a flat voice from the top of the stairs which I could only dimly see at the back of the hallway. 'Must get around to fixing it. There's a torch on the table to your right.'

I saw the torch, put it on and headed up the stairs. The beam of light gave a spooky air to a perfectly normal hall, I thought, impatient with myself. I felt a dread which was absolutely unwarranted by anything that was happening. And it couldn't be Rillington Place. I wasn't sensitive to atmosphere, and I didn't believe in ghosts: not the malevolent ghost of the necrophiliac Christie, nor the pathetic ghost of the half-witted Evans, nor the even more pathetic ghosts of the murdered women and the toddler child.

At the top of the stairs was light from the opened door, and the young man who'd spoken to me. When I reached the top he was still standing on the small landing, blocking the doorway, and we were standing closer than I liked. 'Can we go in?' I asked.

'Sure,' he said, leading me into the living room. He was a very ordinary-looking young man, about five foot ten, with an unremarkable face, collar-length dark-brown hair untidily brushed back from a high forehead, and pale-blue eyes behind a pair of glasses which had once had elegant metal designer frames but were now held together at the bridge and the sides by what looked like insulating tape. He was dressed for comfort and warmth: shapeless brown corduroy trousers, check flannel shirt, thick, once cream, now beige, Arran sweater. The building was chilly: I wished I had a sweater too, even though I don't normally feel the cold.

187

'Hi,' he said. 'You're Alex Tanner? I'm James Hobbs, except I'm known as Jack, but that's old stuff unless you're into cricket. He was a batsman. Call me Jack, if you like, everyone does. Take your coat?'

'No thanks.' I huddled into my leather jacket and looked around the room.

It was oblong, quite big, quite tidy, and had been converted from light industrial to residential with the mean features of a low-budget building: low ceilings, poky windows, a central light fitting with three high-powered bulbs and no shade. The walls were still unplastered breeze-block, painted magnolia, the paint partly worn through where someone had scrubbed off the inevitable grubby marks round the light switches. Magnolia gloss woodwork, sparkling clean, even on the doors. Posters Blu-Tacked to the wall, about 50 per cent well-known and modernish works of art, 50 per cent female actresses and singers. The art was all powerful, nothing pretty: *Guernica, The Scream,* plenty of abstracts. Cheap DIY bookcases crammed mostly with paperback thrillers; two sofas, not matching, with covers so old that the original floral pattern had faded and worn to yellowy beige. A desk with a computer. A wall rack with a music system, big speakers, hundreds of CDs. Not a speck of dust anywhere, that I could see, but apart from that the room was unremarkable, like its tenant.

'So what do you think?' said Hobbs.

'Very nice,' I said.

'Is it?' he said, looking round as if for the first time. 'It does me because I don't really notice where I live – it's the workshop that goes with it I need, really. D'you want a drink? Or d'you want to work? Measure the noise level, or something?' His unexpressive, unsmiling face was as flat as his voice. Not hostile, not welcoming. If I hadn't felt so spooked I'd have liked him, I thought. I like direct, practical people.

'A drink would be good,' I said.

'Lager do you?'

'Great.'

He vanished back into the hall, presumably on the way to the kitchen. I sat on one of the sofas. Ouch. No springs. I went much further down than I expected and cracked my chin on my knee.

'Here.' He was standing right in front of me, and I hadn't heard him come back. I jumped, as much as it was possible to jump when I was effectively enveloped by the exhausted sofa. He didn't seem to notice, just kept standing there offering me the glass. His hands were big, strong-looking, discoloured, not as if they hadn't been washed enough but as if they were ingrained with some dark substances that he worked with, day in, day out. I also caught a whiff of an acrid, unfamiliar smell. Paint or something – maybe he was an artist.

I took the glass and tried to drink from it, then noticed that the liquid was juddering, nearly spilling over. My hand must be trembling, I thought, lowering the glass gingerly.

'Train,' he said. 'Give it a minute.'

Then I noticed the noise. It wasn't so much loud as all-pervasive, an elemental experience shaking the sofa and the room and the building. 'Is that the Hammersmith and City line?' I said.

'Yep. About every seven minutes. It does knock off between midnight and six, though, and you get used to it. Crap building, in my view. The flats should have been soundproofed. Still could be, of course.' He sat down on the sofa opposite, sipped his drink and looked at me, expressionless.

I felt rattled. I wanted to be out of there,

and the more direct I was, the quicker it would be. 'Sorry to be so nervous,' I said. 'I reckon it's age. I've been most peculiar since I turned thirty, but you wouldn't know about that of course.'

He smiled.

'How old are you?' I said.

'Twenty-four.'

'There you are. You've a long way to go, but it depends on your temperament. What's your star sign?'

'Aries,' he said.

Aries. March-April. Twenty-four. He could be Boy. 'Good temperaments, Aries.'

'I thought Aries was sensitive and jumpy,' he said. 'Not that I'm a great believer in astrology.'

'No, men tend not to be. Women, now I bet if you had a sister, she'd read her stars in the paper every day.'

He smiled again.

'Do you have a sister? I've always wanted a sibling, but I'm an only child.'

He shook his head. 'No sister. I'm an only child too.'

I relaxed. He wasn't it. I banished the tendrils of anxiety that had been distorting my normal perceptions, took a notebook from my bag, sat as upright as I could, and said briskly, 'I won't keep you long. I just wanted to introduce myself, so that if you see me snooping about taking photographs or using a noise meter, you'll know what I'm doing.'

'I'm only a tenant you know,' he said. 'It's Richard Fairfax you need to meet, really.' He grinned. 'And you can talk to him about sisters, if you like. He's got one.'

'Richard Fairfax?' I made a note. 'Does he live here, too?'

'Yes, the ground-floor flat. He's out tonight. So's Russell. Russell Jacobs, he's the flat in the middle. They're out together.'

There was an odd note in his voice. Jealousy? Relief?

'Are you and Russell Richard's friends? Is that why you've got the flats?

'There won't be any trouble getting us out, if that's what you're worried about. We haven't got leases, or anything.'

'Very good friends, then,' I said

'Yes. Old friends, anyway. I was at school with Rich.'

'Where was that?'

'St Botolph's.'

I looked a question.

'Minor public school,' he said. 'In Surrey.'

'Were you a boarder?'

192

'We both were.'

'Is he older than you? Looked after you, did he?'

Clumsy as it was, he didn't balk at this. 'Rick is two months older than me. Not enough to make a difference,' he said. 'We were just friends.'

'And was Russell at St Botolph's as well?'

'Not Russell. He met Rich at Aberdeen.'

'University?'

'Yes.'

'I never went to university – often wondered if I'd missed anything.'

'Depends what you're interested in. I went to art school instead.'

He showed no sign of finding my questions odd; he just sat, blinking at me, unsmiling, not hostile, not anything except perhaps awkward. Awkward because he lacked social skills, or awkward because he found women difficult, or awkward because he was hiding something? Impossible to tell, but I'd make the most of my chance to pry.

I looked at my notes. So far Richard Fairfax, the owner, remained a possibility for Boy. 'Your mate Richard owns the freehold, does he? Of the flats and the work shops?'

'Yes.'

'Lucky man.'

'He's got plenty of property. Mostly industrial and commercial.'

'Must be worth a bit. Wealthy family?'

This was too much, possibly because it was about money, the great English taboo. 'You'll have to ask *him* about that,' he said.

'Sure. I'll try and see him tomorrow. He won't be working on Saturday will he?'

'He won't be at work, no, but I don't know what other plans he's made.'

'I'll arrange it through the estate agent,' I said.

Now I needed to get into the Christie murders, which Boy had apparently been so morbidly interested in. I sipped at the lager without swallowing much – I'd really gone off alcohol – and said, 'Rillington Place used to be somewhere round here, didn't it?'

He hesitated, maybe calculating whether he'd mess up his friend's sale of the property but deciding that if I'd already guessed, the site would be easy enough to establish independently.

'Yes. These flats are in what used to be Rillington Place.'

'So, where would number 10 have been, then?'

'Follow me,' he said, and moved quickly

and silently towards the door. I put my drink down, stuffed the notebook back in my bag and followed him, almost running to catch up.

He went down into the hall, opened a door in the far end, and went outside.

The yard was bounded on one side by the flats and on the other by the workshops/garages. Behind and above the garages was the railway line, beginning to vibrate with the rumble of an approaching train.

'Wait for the train,' he said loudly, seconds before we were swamped by the sound. The carriages were blurred by the fog and I could just make out, through the fuzzy light of the windows, the backs of heads and the curious, distorted face of a child pressed to the glass.

Chapter Seventeen

It was cold: I shivered, huddled into my leather jacket and waited for the great wash of sound to recede. As soon as it did, James started to speak.

'We're standing in what was Christie's front room. Where he buried his wife, finally, and where he hid his first victim, Ruth Fuerst, for a night when his wife came back unexpectedly. Next day he dug her up and buried her in the garden, over there, where the workshops are now.'

'Ruth Fuerst?' I said, not because I wanted to know more but because I wanted to know if he could tell me more.

'Austrian girl, lived in Oxford Gardens, twenty-one when she died. Started as a nurse but was probably a part-time prostitute when Christie met her. He says he strangled her while they were having intercourse, but actually he probably killed her first, then afterwards he wrapped her in her leopardskin coat and hid her under the floorboards in the front room, with the rest of her clothes–'

I was chilled, by the cold, or the bleak cruelty of the event, or the lack of sympathy in his voice. 'So this was the front room,' I said, 'and that was the garden. It must have been a very small house.'

He nodded. 'They were. The Christies had the ground floor – front room, back room, kitchen, outside lavatory and wash-house. All the tenants shared the lavatory and wash-house, which was mostly used for emptying chamberpots. The first floor also had front room, back room, kitchen; the top floor only had bedsitting room, kitchen.'

I could imagine it. Typical of the houses in the meaner streets of North Kensington. I'd been round several of them ten years ago when I was looking to buy, so proud, now I'd got a regular salaried job, that I could. What I remembered most clearly was the smell: old vegetable water, dry rot, mildew and urine. It seemed to seep from the dank flimsy brick walls. The area must have been full of them in the forties and fifties, when landladies still put notices up in the front window: NO DOGS NO BLACKS NO IRISH NO CHILDREN. Now most of them had been gentrified. Job-driven media types had gutted them, made an open living space on the ground floor with a little conservatory tacked on the back full of plants maintained by a garden service, torn up the sodden floorboards and replaced them with polished wood.

But back with Christie – 'Where did the Evanses live?'

'Top floor. One room and kitchen.'

'So to get to the lavatory they'd have gone through Christie's ground-floor flat?'

'That's right.'

I swallowed, thrust my hands deeper into my jacket pockets, waited for the next train to go by. When I could speak and be heard again, I said, 'Where did the Evanses live before they came here?'

'With Timothy Evans's mother, stepfather and sisters, in St Mark's Road.'

St Mark's Road, just a spit away. So near safety. If, of course, the family was safe. 'Loving family?'

'Very loving, apparently, but there wasn't enough room for them to stay there with a baby on the way.'

I'm not one for generalized guilt: I think it's a kind of vanity to make yourself miserable, when you have something, by thinking about other people who have much less, unless you're going to take practical steps

199

on their behalf. So, although I had a vivid picture of my baby's possible accommodation – his or her father's six-bedroom, three-bathroom house in Campden Hill for starters – I refused to entertain it. But I did imagine what it must have been like for Mrs Evans.

'How old was she? Evans's wife?'

'Beryl. Beryl was about nineteen when they moved in.'

Nineteen. In one room and a kitchen, with a baby, and an outside lavatory two floors down.

I pulled myself together. I was supposed to be finding out about this man's attitude to the murders. Get on with it, then. 'Some of the others were buried in the garden, weren't they?'

'Just one. Muriel Eady, the second victim. And this bit here–' he moved a short distance towards the workshops – 'was the washroom, where he put Mrs Evans and the child Geraldine.'

'How old was Geraldine?'

'Thirteen months, born October 1948, died November 1949.'

Thirteen months. I clutched my belly protectively, and then forced my hands away when I realized what I was doing. Whatever

I called my child if she was a girl, it wouldn't be Geraldine. I began to feel sick and groped for a biscuit to nibble.

'You all right?' He stepped closer, and the pungent smell of his hands hit me powerfully.

I moved away. 'How big was the garden?' I asked, looking at the area he was describing and forcing myself to concentrate on that.

'It was a bit smaller than the workshop on the end; the one I use. About fifteen feet by twelve. Plenty of room for two graves, come to think of it. Sure you're all right?'

'Yeah, I'm fine. Go on. How did the second one–'

'Muriel Eady,' he prompted, when I groped for the name.

'How did she die?'

'She was a bit different from Ruth Fuerst. Older – early thirties – and respectable, with a steady boyfriend. Worked with Christie in the radio factory at Acton. He was in despatch, she was in assembly. She had chronic catarrh and Christie said he'd cure it. He invited her over, fixed up a contraption so she could inhale Friar's Balsam–' he saw my confusion – 'that stuff you put in a bowl of hot water and then breathe in the steam, with a towel over your head. Never had it? Plague of my childhood, my mother was dead keen on it – anyhow, he also gave her a whopping great dose of gas as well, then moved her to the bed, strangled and raped her.'

'What was Christie like?' I said.

'Pathetic, really. Self-important, bullied by his mother and his sisters, called "Reggie-No-Dick" at school, petty thief, gassed and invalided out, of the First War.'

'So he was quite old?'

'Middle forties when he started killing people. Sad wanker in a mac, basically, could only get it up with a corpse.'

Another train roared past. I waited, then said, 'There were other victims, weren't there?'

'Three, walled up in the alcove at the back of the kitchen. Kathleen Maloney, Rita Nelson and Hectorina Maclennan. He killed those after his wife – you look terrible,' he said bluntly. 'Are you squeamish?'

'Not usually... Why did he kill the baby?'

'To cover his tracks and implicate Evans, once he'd killed Mrs Evans. It wasn't a sexual thing. Come inside, I'll make you a cup of tea.'

He sounded concerned enough, but I felt sick and didn't want to throw up in front of him, so I thanked him and bolted.

Halfway home, feeling much better, I could have kicked myself. I hadn't even seen inside his workshop, and I couldn't make up my mind about Hobbs. He didn't have a sister so he couldn't be the Boy of the letters, could he? And also Boy's mother had said that he thought the women had got what they deserved, that he'd taken some kind of pleasure in it. I hadn't got that impression from Hobbs. He certainly didn't admire Christie – 'sad wanker in a mac' was hardly the description of a role model. On the other hand, he'd known all about the case: he'd given me every name and date I'd asked for, and I'd got the impression that he could have gone on talking for hours and not run out of facts.

Just knowing facts could hardly be held against him – it was the nature of the facts he knew, that he'd bothered to acquire. Surely that argued a morbid preoccupation? On the other hand he'd been concerned about me, and not so involved in his description that he hadn't noticed my reaction.

I was concentrating on my thoughts and so, what with the fog as well, I was nearly going up the steps to my front door before I noticed there was someone standing there, ringing my doorbell.

I recoiled, instinctively expecting it to be Arthur Fishburn. But it wasn't. It was Janey Protheroe.

Chapter Eighteen

What did Alan's ex-wife want with me? I greeted her and took her in. In the full light upstairs I saw she looked older – hardly surprising, since I hadn't seen her for years – and also worn and frazzled. She'd cut her thinnish greying hair short, and it looked limp and straggly. She also had one of those fine white skins that, when they line, collapse into parachute silk. Hers had collapsed. Mind you, she was well on in her fifties.

I sat her down and gave her tea, mostly hoping it would stop her apologizing. It was very aggressive apologizing, though – she was clearly angry, but didn't know how to express it. A fermenting cocktail of emotions. Not at all the Janey I'd known and hadn't liked much – she was boring and smug. But she'd been useful: everyone who worked with Alan relied on her to manage him and soothe his fears. Married Alan had been a lot easier to deal with than divorced Alan, with his perpetual pursuit of dis-

appearing girls and his untempered ob-
sessiveness.

But now the usually calm Janey was
boiling up inside. She even looked on the
unkempt side of casual – she was wearing
battered old green synthetic trousers and a
not-white-enough shirt under an anorak
which one of her sons had probably grown
out of some years earlier. She didn't look at
all like a woman about to enter into a happy
second marriage. And turning up, un-
heralded – I know plenty of people who
would think nothing of appearing for
getting on for ten at night without an
appointment, but Janey wasn't one of them.

She'd retained her polite conversation,
however. 'Out with it, Janey,' I said eventually, when it seemed as if she'd still be
talking about the awful fog when Britain
joined the EMU.

'This isn't going to be easy,' she said.

'Just tell me,' I said, 'or I'll have to ask you
to leave.'

She looked at me. The sharpness of my
tone had cut right through her self-pos-
session. 'It's about Alan,' she said. 'I don't
think you're good for Alan.'

I took this amiss. All I'd done for Alan was
listen to his bletherings, feed him and nearly

get raped for my pains. 'What do you think I've done?' I said.

'Your affair with him.'

'I'm not having an affair with him. I wouldn't dream of it,' I said firmly, almost too firmly to be polite, because she had married the man, after all.

'Is that true?'

'Absolutely. I work for him, and I hope he thinks of me as a friend–' he'd bloody better, I thought crossly, since I'm one of the few under-fifty females in London who'll waste ten minutes on him – 'but that's as far as it goes.'

She sighed. 'I thought so,' she said to herself. She didn't seem relieved: if anything, more worried, but also more purposeful. 'He told me about it, you see. And I thought he was probably – embroidering the truth, a little, but I had to be sure.'

'Why?' I said bluntly. She'd divorced him years ago.

She looked at me with gentle superiority, a look I remembered from back when I'd been a gawky twenty and she'd been a confident solidly married forty. 'Because he's the father of my children,' she said.

'I don't follow,' I said, unhelpfully. 'Explain.'

207

She sighed. 'Alex, I thought we were friends.'

I knew why she thought that. She'd first known me when I was eighteen, scrambling my way into a life of my own after a child-hood of foster parents. I was skilled at seeming grateful for being patronized. Janey had thought me a poor little thing who flowered under her instant affection and interest. She'd welcomed me into her immaculate house in a solidly middle-class-with-pretensions village outside Princes Risborough, and gossiped with me in her welcoming pretty expensive kitchen. She'd been proud of the house, of her children, and thought that she had much to offer me – an older woman's guidance, a posher woman's experience, because after all my own single-parent council-flat mother was mentally ill. I'd wanted to offer her a punch in the teeth. I'd been chippy then.

But I needn't be so chippy now, so I smiled. 'Sure.'

'So I can trust you?'

'To do what?'

'Not to tell Alan that I came to see you.'

I considered. 'Yes, unless he asks me directly.'

'Because I'm really concerned, and I don't

see much of him now, and you're the only woman I know who sees him all the time. Has he ever – hit you?'

'No,' I lied, because Alan was more my friend than she'd ever been. 'Has he hit you?'

'Yes. Twice, recently. Both times he'd been drinking. But it isn't like him, at all. I think he's desperate. I don't want him to do anything silly, because...'

'Because of the children?'

'And because of me. Because of our time together. Because I love him, I suppose. And violence, even minor violence – he didn't really hurt me – made me wonder, might he do something silly? Because it is so unlike him.'

'Suicide?'

'Suicide, of course, and... I just don't know. It's absolutely absurd, I know it is... And I lied to him,' she said defiantly. 'I don't believe in lying, I always taught the children never to lie. But I did lie to him, I said I was getting married again. And I'm not. Absolutely not. I have a friend, but there isn't any chemistry between us, whereas with Alan'

'Why did you lie?'

'I thought it might push him on a bit,

because I'd like us to get back together again.'

There was chemistry between them. Chemistry, with Alan? He should snap her up, I thought. She must be completely rattled. She'd been married to the man for years, she must know that the way to him was flattery, full-frontal flattery, no matter how extravagant.

'Why didn't you just say you loved him and needed him and wanted him back?'

'You wouldn't understand. I wanted him to make the first move. I know it was stupid. Do you think he's unstable, at the moment?'

'Yes, a bit. Stressed,' I said. 'He needs you. Just speak to him frankly. Men usually like that,' I concluded maliciously. *She'd* never hesitated to tell *me* what men liked – according to her, regular meals and tidy houses near Princes Risborough.

Her eyes wandered round my living room, and she brightened perceptibly, probably thinking how she would refurbish it. 'You're probably right,' she said, in the tone of one who wasn't paying the least attention. That was the other thing about Janey, I remembered. She had the concentration span of a newt.

After she left, getting on for eleven, I'd intended to work. I lay down on the sofa and closed my eyes for a moment.

The insistent buzz of the telephone woke me up, and I knew as I grabbed it that it had been ringing for a while.

'About time,' said Eddy, irascibly. 'You weren't asleep, surely? You left a message asking for an urgent call-back.'

I checked my watch. Just after midnight. No wonder he was surprised. I'm usually a night owl.

'How's Florida?' I said, playing for time enough to remember why I'd wanted him to call.

'Florida is long, thin and low-lying, as always, and I'm tired, jet-lagged and pissed off, so get to the point, young Alex.'

Now I remembered. I'd left a call-back message at his holiday hotel before Polly had interfered by recruiting Fishburn as my go-between with the Met, involving him far beyond Eddy's explicit instructions. Lucky for me that Eddy was three thousand miles away.

A full explanation, it had to be. I gave it.

When I finished, there was an ominous silence. Then Eddy spoke, in even more ominous, gentle tones. 'Did I or did I not

211

ask you if you were working on a doco?'

'You did.'

'And did you or did you not tell me you were?'

'I did.'

'Don't you ever lie to me again, you little squit.'

'Sorry, Eddy.'

'Sorry doesn't begin to cover it. Sorry isn't in the same country, continent, planet or solar system, my girl, believe me.'

'Galactically sorry, Eddy.'

'Shut it, you little bleeder, I'm thinking. And while I think, let me tell you about Arthur. Back in the early sixties, Arthur was a DCI.'

'A Detective Chief Inspector?'

'Happy family man, lovely wife, lovely teenage daughter, great future. Then his wife and daughter were raped. Messy rape. We caught the toe-rag and he went down for five years. The night after sentencing, Arthur's wife killed her daughter and herself.'

'Ouch,' I said in futile sympathy.

'Then he went peculiar. Not peculiar enough to be booted out, not after what he'd been through, but peculiar enough to be safer as a beat constable, all things considered.' With the tribal loyalties of the Met, I thought, no peculiar would have been peculiar enough to boot him out, and I was relieved not to be told what things they'd had to consider. 'I warned you,' Eddy went on. 'I asked you and I warned you and you lied to me. And if you even begin to think you can tangle with the Killer – not that I believe this has anything to do with the Killer, mind you – then you're even fuller of smart-arse feminist shit than I already know you are.'

'Sorry, Eddy.'

'And stop saying that or I'll have a heart attack. I'm not pleased, Alex. Don't push it... Right, this is what you do. I'll call the lads in the incident room and tell them what you've told me, in case Arthur hasn't, and get them to look out for Arthur. You keep away from him. Keep your nose out altogether, you hear me?'

'I'm going to see the other men at Rillington Place tomorrow. I've got to keep on it, for my client.'

'You want to finger the stupid slapper who let a married man shaft her stupid for thirty years and wrote crap about it, go ahead. But don't mess in anything else, got it? Hear me?'

'I hear you.'

After he rang off I brushed my teeth and lay down on the sofa again with a glass of water, reassured by Eddy's bollocking. He'd been right, anyway: he'd taken over with the Met, and he was in Florida and likely to remain so for two weeks.

Next I knew, the room was full of giraffes, squealing. I dragged myself awake to shake off the dream and looked at the time display on the VCR. Two thirty. I was definitely awake, but the room was still full. Of squealing models, milling around the sofa with their long legs and long necks and tiny heads.

'Polly!' I snapped at the lead giraffe. 'What the hell!'

'She's always like this when she first wakes,' said Polly. 'Coffee, girls!'

Suddenly they'd all vanished into the kitchen, where they'd be hard put to mill, or even move. Only Polly remained, looking slightly drunk, extremely pleased with herself and extraordinarily beautiful in a tiny tight black dress which just grazed her nipples and reached a few inches down her thighs. 'Isn't it handy I've got a key? Because you didn't answer when we

214

knocked, not though we knocked for ages, and you'll really want to know this, we've spent all evening on it practically because it was like a competition, adultery consultants, that's what we called ourselves, D&E specialists–'

'D&E?'

'Dick and Ego, and it was such fun, although a bit disappointing–'

'What was disappointing?'

'The winner, although not really I suppose because it's what you'd expect–'

'Polly, why do you all look so tall?'

'Shoes,' said Polly, taking hers off and waving them in demonstration. 'Clumpy high heels, hope they'll be out again soon, my ankles are taking a pasting, put three or four inches on so the shortest of us is well over six foot. Oh good here they are...'

I now saw there were only three other models in the herd. One, blonde, held a mug of coffee, another, black, a carton of milk, the third, a redhead, a bowl of sugar. Each one of them was beautiful and wearing about as little as Polly. 'Pity I'm not a man,' I said. 'Plenty of milk, please.'

When they'd stopped squealing and sat down I was introduced to them. I forgot their names immediately, and hoped that

215

wasn't a side effect of pregnancy but attributable to being jolted awake. Names didn't turn out to matter because they all spoke at once. 'We worked on the letters – it was such fun! Polly wanted to help – we've all Been There – haven't we just – and we were looking for tips, because thirty years and a husband – bloody good going – but *we* didn't get it...'

They looked at me expectantly. I was disgruntled. If they'd woken me up to tell me they hadn't got it...

'Because my mother did!' said the redhead triumphantly. 'She's Been There in a major long-standing way, and she read them too, and *she* worked out what happened.'

'What happened when?'

Polly nudged me in the ribs, over-emphatically.

'You told me you'd noticed a change in the letters a few years ago. You said they'd changed but you didn't know why. We can tell you.'

'So tell me.'

'The lover's wife died.'

Of course. Of course. Under their choral explanations, I saw it for myself. When the lover's wife died, the lover was free. But the mistress wasn't. And the boat was thoroughly rocked. He could find another woman as a permanency. A younger woman or just a fresh woman. No wonder the tone of the letters had changed, become less confident, more tentative.

The models were still talking. I met Polly's eyes. 'But that means—'

'That means they weren't written to your client's husband. Because she's still alive, of course.'

'But my mum knows who they *were,* written to,' said the redhead.

If her mum knew that, I thought, as well as being a prime brood giraffe she was also psychic. 'How come? What do you mean?'

'She doesn't know his name, of course, but she knows who he'll *be.* A colleague at work, a good friend. And, most likely, he'll be dead.'

'*Recently* dead ... because the envelope will have been inside *another* envelope with your client's husband's name on it ... in the event of the lover's death, don't you see, and then it goes to his best mate, to destroy unopened ... so that there isn't a scandal... What's the matter, Alex?'

Philip Gein. That was what Barbara knew. Philip Gein the English professor, whose mistress might very well lard her letters with

217

literary references. Who was always trying his luck – whose wife had died four years ago – and who had been killed by un-identified muggers in broad daylight just off the Strand, right after he'd been asked to remonstrate with his illegitimate son who just might be the Notting Hill Killer...

'Oh, shit,' I said.

'Aren't you pleased? We thought you'd be pleased.'

'I'm dead grateful. Really. You've all done brilliantly ... oh, shit.'

Saturday 5 November

Chapter Nineteen

I woke at seven thirty with the conviction that something was hanging over me that I didn't want to remember, plus a cosmic crick in my neck because I was still on the sofa.

Cosmic took me to Eddy, and the Fishburn cockup. I groaned and stumbled upstairs to the bathroom, where the faintest, slightest, hint of nausea reminded me I was probably pregnant. Then I remembered Jack Hobbs, my irrational dread of Rillington Place, my reluctance to go back there, and the likelihood that I'd be going back that morning.

Down in the kitchen, making coffee, I remembered the small-hours invasion of the Giraffe People and the possibility that Philip Gein had been murdered by the son of the letter-writer, the man I was tracking down.

None of it looked better in the morning.

Except possibly the pregnancy, which hadn't looked all that bad to start with.

I took the mug of milky real coffee and stood by the living-room french windows, staring out into the darkness. It was still foggy.

And there was still, I realized, something else that I didn't want to remember, something I hadn't clocked properly the first time round ... something to do with Alan Protheroe...

Thump, thump on the door. Polly's voice. 'Alex, can I come in? Alex are you awake? I bet you are. Alex–'

I opened the door, groping for my thought. 'Belt up, Polly – I'm trying to think. What's the doorknob effect?'

Polly went straight to the kitchen where she filled a pint beer glass with mineral water and came to join me in the living room. 'I haven't got a hangover, Alex. Do you know why?'

'Because your head's so feeble you get pissed on two glasses of wine?'

'Wrong! Because I don't drink coffee! It's really handy, you should try it!'

'It would be handy if I drank much alcohol, but I don't because I'm drinking coffee. Listen, Poll, really, what's the doorknob effect?' I went back to the door and held the knob, trying to recapture the flash of memory I'd half had.

'It's the shrink thing, actually everyone

knows it but shrinks have a name for it, when people say the really important thing they wanted to say to you when they're just leaving. Hand on the doorknob, you know. Aren't you pleased with what we found out last night? Wasn't it clever of us?'

'Very clever, well done,' I said, picturing Janey Protheroe just leaving, turning at the door, saying – what had she said?

She'd given a nervous laugh – 'You'll think this is really silly. I know it is. But it was just – in all the papers, they do go on and on, I blame the media – all, that stuff about the Notting Hill Killer. It makes you think, doesn't it? People must know the Killer, mustn't they, and they'll all think it couldn't possibly be him, but some of them will be wrong, because it will be. The man they know will be the Killer.'

Then she'd shut the door behind her, leaving me with the absurd inference: Alan Protheroe, serial killer. And I'd dismissed it immediately, hardly even processed it through my brain. But it had taken root there and grown while I slept. Alan! He couldn't possibly. But two days ago I'd have sworn he couldn't possibly rape me. But then again, I'd have been right, because he hadn't.

What I needed, I realized, were facts. When the killings had taken place. Chances were Alan would have been working out of London and he could be ruled out straight away.

No, I wouldn't bother, it was ridiculous.

I remembered Eddy. Talking about police work. 'When I have a suspect, I don't waste time poncing around with what he could or should or might have done. I find out what he did do.'

I realized Polly was still talking. '...so I am actually putting the flat on the market, Alex, and I wondered, do you want first refusal? It wouldn't be a bad investment, considering how the prices have gone, and the letting value is high, and I know how you like owning things, and maybe you wouldn't want some stranger buying in, just think about it, for a week say.'

'Name your price,' I said.

She named it: a very fair price. Well above what I could afford, though, was my first thought. But no, hang on, if I was letting it would more than cover the mortgage – a good investment. Actually she was being generous, even if she would save estate agents' fees. 'Thanks, Polly, I'll be back to you within the week.'

'That's good, then ... I won't be moving, far away, honestly...' She hugged me. I hugged her back. No Polly in the house – a baby – everything was changing fast. I felt a lurch in my stomach which was nothing to do with pregnancy, as I had a vision of myself as a mollusc clinging to a rock with the sea coming in and swamping me, and me clinging on pretending nothing at all was happening. What water? I don't see any water...

We were still hugging. Unusually, I found it reassuring.

Finally, she let go and wiped her eyes. Her emotion steadied me. She'd always been the emotional one; some things were unchanging. 'I've got to pack. Is there anything I can do to help before I go?'

I gave her the task of making an appointment for me to meet Richard Fairfax – that morning, preferably. Maybe Philip Gein was the man the letters had been written to, but I still had to prove it, and the easiest way to do that was to identify the Boy of the letters. Fairfax was my best bet for that: he had the right birthday, he had a sister, he'd been to boarding school. I was almost sure it was him. That didn't mean he was the Killer, of course, but if Gein had been murdered, it might mean that Fairfax was the murderer. or, it might mean nothing of the sort. Sometimes a mugging is only a mugging.

I showered for a long time, hoping the water would sluice away the tension in my whole body and the nagging feeling that I was being swamped by events. There was too much in my head, too much on my plate.

I needed Nick. According to the Golden Kid, she'd said she'd be back today. Early, I hoped.

Meanwhile it was still only eight and I felt restless, unable to concentrate. So I went for a run.

I did my warm-up exercises in the street. Stretching, deep breathing. The deep breathing was a mistake: chilly acrid fog seared my lungs. I set off very gently, at a jog, so slow that walkers easily kept up with me – I wasn't sure how possibly pregnant women were fixed vis-à-vis running – but as the blood started pumping I felt better, and decided to listen to my body. It had told me it wanted milk and more sleep: now it told me to run, so I did.

My route took me past Bartlett Close, but I didn't look in at the flats; I went straight past under the railway bridge seeing only the pavement in front of me and hearing only the sound of my own breathing. I deliberately emptied my head. When I reached the Scrubs I set off anti-clockwise to run the perimeter, one-minute sprints alternating with three-minute lopes.

Over an hour later when I reached my flat again all I could think about was stopping. My legs were rubber, hauling me up the stairs, and I collapsed on the sofa, moaning. Physical exhaustion felt good.

Now I could face the day. Now I looked forward to all the things I had to do. I pushed away a nagging anxiety, that pregnancy was already making me more moody than I was used to. I was usually contemptuous of women who had mood-swings and said 'Now I feel like it now I don't feel like it', and had tended to think they should pull themselves together and get on with it. Who cared what they felt? But now I was behaving like that myself, so how far could I trust my own judgement?

By nine thirty I was in the office, coffee-mug in my hand and ready to go. The one fixed point in the morning was the noon appointment Polly had made with Richard Fairfax for me. I checked for telephone messages, but there was nothing that couldn't be left for Nick to deal with, apart from another what's-happening-about-Sam call from Pauline Eyre, which I'd return just as soon as I'd talked to Solange and Jonno.

I might as well check the e-mails, while I was at it: I didn't use e-mail nearly as much as Nick, but there might be something from Barty.

I logged on, quite quickly. America hadn't woken up yet, of course. The usual ten or so messages for Nick. I didn't look at them. One for me. I clicked it open. It wasn't from Barty, nor anyone I recognized. It was sent from the local Internet Cafe, in the Portobello Road. I knew that much, because when Nick had bullied me into learning how to use e-mail, a few months back, she'd gone to the Internet Cafe, sent me messages and made me answer them, so I recognized their e-mail address. But this message was unsigned, and it made no sense.

Have collected the following accounts: Lagrange, Atiyah, Leibniz, Ireson, Abel. Do not pursue these clients: debts paid in full. Actively pursue Bourbaki. Consult Seymour.

Had Nick hired a debt-collection agency? We hardly had any outstanding accounts. Nick prided herself on making non-payers' lives a misery. And I didn't think we'd ever had clients with those names, but I tried them on the computer anyway.

Nothing.

A joke, perhaps? If so, I didn't get it. I kept the message in case it was actually for Nick and would make sense to her, then I closed down the computer and took a pen and paper.

I needed an updated action list. I needed an action list I'd act on, too. Focused, effective, immediate action. Catch all the gnats buzzing about in my head, fix them on paper in a numbered list, go through them one by one. Then put a nice thick black line through them.

I worked on it for several minutes, scribbling and rearranging, then finally making a fair copy, on paper, in my own writing. No messing about on the computer. Nick always teased me about that, but it wasn't the same thing. When my hand wrote, my brain thought. Face it, I was thirty. Only a few years younger, another generation, and I'd probably be using the computer to make coffee.

Nick: Ring mobile, Oxford. Talk to Golden Kid, Jonno. Grace Macarthy
Sam Eyre: Solange, Jonno. Ring Pauline Eyre
Hilary Lucas: Richard Fairfax. Noon. Ring Barbara Gottlieb? Philip Gein
Alan Protheroe: Check Killer dates, details in library – ring
Me: P test tomorrow (buy kit)? Tell Barty if he rings. Stock up on dry biscs, check running
Polly's flat: Rental income? Monthly interest, mortgage

I read them through. As is the usual case with lists, some of the items would take much longer than others; I started with the quickest: Nick's mobile. Still out of service. I dialled the Oxford number of Nick's professor. No answer. I already knew the Golden Kid wasn't in his office – I'd looked in as I passed. So I rang and left a call-back message on his machine. Maybe Nick'd told him more details than he'd given me, like what time I could expect her back today. Or, more likely, maybe not. Her continued absence was making me itchy enough to worry away counter-productively at what little information I had, like a dog with a sore paw.

As a very long shot, I then rang Grace Macarthy, a well-known feminist professor and annoyingly good friend of Barty's who'd taken an interest in Nick and who Nick had been in unrequited love with before she fell for Laverne. Grace's whimsical answering machine message told me she was in Adelaide. Good. I hadn't wanted to speak to her anyway. Typical of her to have such a show-off message, surely an invitation to burglars, although knowing Grace it was just as likely to be misleading. She might be tucked away in her study in West Hampstead listening to voices on the machine and picking up when she wanted. Just in case, I left a message.

Jonno next, on two counts, Nick and Sam. Mobile, answer, he'd come straight in. Seeing as I owed him. Solange on Sam, ditto, though she didn't mention money. Then something struck me and I rang Solange back. 'Seen Lil about this morning?'

'Loony Lil? She's in Westbourne Park Road. I can hear her from here, still on about the fog.'

'Ask her to come and see me right away, would you?'

231

'Sure.'

I crossed things off the list. Then I tried New College, London, on the off-chance that Barbara Gottlieb would be there, or that they'd give me her home number. She wasn't, and they wouldn't. And I had no idea where she lived, so I couldn't get it from directory enquiries, but it'd be worth checking through the London phone books in the library. I was sure Gottlieb knew much of what there was to know about Gein, and she had offered to help, after all.

By which time Solange and Jonno had arrived. Solange went into the back to make tea for herself and Jonno and coffee for me while I argued with Jonno about the money he said Nick owed him. He was wearing the same clothes he'd had on the day before and, it appeared from the smell, without removing them to sleep or wash.

When the drinks came, I lost patience. 'Nick'll pay you what she owes when she comes back, OK? Enough, already.'

'Charming,' said Jonno.

'Tell me what you found out last night and tell me the hours you worked, and I'll pay you for them.'

'Stupid cow,' said Jonno.

Solange looked at him with contempt. For

once, she wasn't smiling. 'You got no manners and I got no time to waste on you.' She turned her back on him and talked to me. 'Your girl livin' in Bartlett Close, I reckon. That why you told us to stay away from there? Plenty of people seen her comin' in and out. She workin' in the pizza shop up Notting Hill.'

My stomach flipped. *Sam* the girl in Hobbs's flat?

'What's up?' said Solange, watching my face.

Come to think of it, I didn't know. There was no real reason to believe that Sam was less safe in Bartlett Close than anywhere else. 'Nothing,' I said. 'Let's have your notes.' She passed them over: very detailed, in painstaking, loopy writing. 'Great. Three hours' work plus a bonus.' I counted the banknotes into her hand.

'I earned the bonus too,' said Jonno aggressively. 'I got the same information, I get the same bonus.' He shoved his notes at me: greasy pieces of scrap paper, tiny scribbly writing, and a claim for five hours' work.

'Five hours?' I raised my eyebrows.

Solange laughed. 'Two and a half,' she said. 'I watched him come and I watched him go and two and a half's max.'

'Three hours and a bonus, Jonno.'

He took the money before saying, 'Stuff your bleeding work, then,' and slamming the door behind him as he left.

'Is he always like this?' I asked.

'Nah, you just had the very best of Jonno – he's usually a rude boy. My break time's over, I'm back on the street, thanks for the tea, keep me in mind if you've anything else. Lil should be along right about now, she said she'd something else to do first.'

Chapter Twenty

I had enough hard information about Sam Eyre now, to ring Pauline and put her in the picture. But it was her husband who answered, snapping. 'Dr Eyre. Who is this?'

'Could I speak to Pauline Eyre, please?'

'Not until you have identified yourself. I don't countenance anonymous calls annoying my wife.'

'Oh, does she get many?' I asked blandly.

'I don't see what business that is of yours, whoever you are.'

'You introduced the subject, Dr Eyre.'

Pause. Then he said, 'Am I speaking to Alex Tanner?'

'Yes,' I said. 'Good morning.'

'Why did you not introduce yourself?'

Unreasonable people make me unreasonable. Of course, normally, I would have said who I was. But his tone and his whole attitude suggested that he was censoring his wife's calls not for her benefit but for his. I wasn't surprised his daughter had run away.

235

'My dealings are with Pauline,' I said. 'Is she there?'

'No, she is not. Any information you have for her, you may give to me. Samantha is my daughter.'

'When is Pauline likely to be back?' Never, if she had any sense.

'I repeat, give me the information. I will pass it on. If you have found Samantha, I am relieved to hear it. She should come home immediately. She has duties in this house, duties which she has neglected. Duties to me.'

Perhaps he was hiding concern behind aggression, but all I could feel was the aggression, his will against mine. He wanted to dominate me: I wanted to end the call.

'Please tell Pauline I rang,' I said, and put down the receiver.

That didn't end the tension, though. I could feel it in my neck muscles and threatening to burn like acid in my stomach. I'd wanted to talk to Pauline because the coincidence, if it was a coincidence, of Sam being at Bartlett Close was worrying me. Now all I could think of was the Eyres and their home life.

What must it be like to live with him, I wondered. In my office I'd assumed that he was behaving particularly badly because he was upset about his daughter, angry with his wife's independent action in hiring a detective, and feeling vulnerable off his home ground. But, if anything, he'd been worse just now. Maybe I shouldn't give Sam's address even to Pauline, who I hoped would ring me back. If her husband gave her the message.

Then I heard Lil.

'The raw morning is rawest, and the dense fog is densest, and the muddy streets are muddiest, near that leaden-headed old obstruction, appropriate ornament for the threshold of a leaden-headed old corporation – The Royal Borough of Kensington and Chelsea. And hard by Kensington High Street, in the Town Hall, at the very heart of the fog, sits the Lord Mayor in his High Court of Pomposity.' She finished, with an exultant shouting flourish, just outside the door of the office. Then she knocked.

'Come in." I called.

She came in tugging Benbow behind her. He had his muzzle wedged firmly in a KFC box and was making slurping noises. 'Morning, Lil,' I said. 'D'you want some tea?'

'Strong, some milk, three sugars,' she said, and sat down heavily. She's somewhere in

237

her late seventies and small, probably shrunk from medium height. She's slender and fine-boned, though you could hardly tell that in winter through her layers of clothes, today green woollen tights, lace-up brown walking shoes, green calf-length wool skirt, beige fine wool sweater and cardigan, green Barbour jacket, two red scarves, a dark red felt hat and red mittens. She and her clothes are always clean, a welcome change from Jonno, although her constant prowling of the streets and habit of quoting, or sometimes reading, passages of the classics out loud to an indifferent if not actively resentful public give her the superficial appearance of a bag lady.

I gave her the tea and we both watched Benbow crunch the last KFC bone, chase his tail three times and collapse as heavily on the floor as his owner had in the chair. 'He's a young dog, you know,' she said.

'Only two. I tell you this because most people assume that an old woman has an old dog. But he's young and he needs walking and the family that kindly took him in don't have the time.' Plus you like his company, I thought. 'And I need his company,' she went on, and grinned all over her long, bony, weathered face. 'What can I do for you? Where's Nick?'

'I'm not sure,' I said. 'The Golden Kid gave me a message from her, saying she'd gone to stay with a friend and she'd be back today.'

She tilted her head to one side, considering not just the information but my method of delivering it. 'The Golden Kid? Do you mean Dermot, next door?'

'Yes.'

'A verbal message?'

'Yes.'

'And you don't consider him trustworthy? In matters like this, I mean. He's clearly untrustworthy in a professional capacity or in relation to the Department of Social Security, but since I neither wish to buy a house nor have I any especially warm feelings for the DSS, I consider him rather a good egg. What motive would he have for misleading you?'

'I don't know. It's not like Nick just to bunk off. And her mobile phone isn't on, so I can't get in touch. When did you last see her?'

She thought. 'Wednesday morning,' she said finally. 'It was raining. She let me shelter for a while.'

'How did she seem?'

239

'Silent. Restful.'

When Nick first worked for me, she was an elective mute. She still talks very little, socially. I consider this a major advantage but I was surprised that Lil did.

'If I were you, I'd wait till tomorrow to worry,' she said, 'if she doesn't turn up. She's usually reliable. What can I help you with?'

'Not much,' I said. 'I just wanted to check with you about Nick, see if you had any extra information. The only work I need doing at the moment is research.'

'Research? Where?'

'In the library.'

'Before my retirement, I was a librarian,' she said, rubbing her swollen, arthritic knuckles.

'What about Benbow?'

'I can take him home. To his home, that is. A comfortable basket in a warm kitchen. He's had plenty of exercise this morning.'

She looked eager, but would she be efficient? I'd never actually used her, though I knew Nick did, but what exactly for? I was beginning to realize quite how much of Nick's day-to-day running of my business was a closed book to me, and I didn't like it. But meanwhile I needed someone in the

240

library. 'What's your hourly rate?' I asked.

Left alone in the office, I tried to make sense of what I knew. Sure as anything, Sam was the girl living in Jack Hobbs's flat. And Nick'd been working on the Sam case. Could something have happened to Nick? But what, and why? It wasn't as if Bartlett Close was a black hole. I'd been in there and nothing had happened to me. No, I was just fussing. Nick'd turn up.

I crossed Sam off on the action list, which was now looking pretty good, by which time Lil was back, still with Benbow at her heels. 'Thought I'd do this little chore before I took him home,' she said, puffing and excited, enjoying her own efficiency. She thrust a photocopied sheet at me. 'I've marked the likely one,' she said, 'but I brought the others in case. If I'm wrong, drop in to the library and tell me on your way to your appointment at Bartlett Close.'

The one she'd marked was a B. Gottlieb only two streets away from NCL.

When I looked up to thank Lil, she'd gone.

I tried the number she'd given me, and it was right. The Germanic voice on the call-minder message was definitely Gottlieb's. Pity she wasn't in, but that was too much to hope for. So I left a message.

Then it was time to go to meet Fairfax.

I locked up the office very securely and set off on the short walk, picking my way through the various guys that littered the roads. It was 5 November, the last day to make a killing for the kids with their guys, and it being Saturday there were more visitors about, heading for the Portobello Market. Today it was Australians. Perhaps there was a package tour in town, or perhaps it was the Australian school holidays or something.

Anyway the Jamaican boy on the corner near the pub was doing a particularly good trade. He had a large sign saying DIRECTIONS TO PORTOBELLO. Tourists stopped to ask for directions, which they didn't need because there were perfectly good street signs, and then they had to give him contributions for the guy, much of which, I suspected, went to his elder brother, the muscle-bound drug dealer.

I gave him nothing. He had a rubbish guy, dressed entirely in the Manchester United football strip.

Chapter Twenty-One

When I reached the turn-off to Bartlett Close I hesitated. The reluctance I'd felt earlier came back in full force now. Irrational it may be, but it was real. I stood on the corner and peered into the fog, which seemed thicker here. I could just make out the building: lights glowed dimly on every floor. A train rattled by.

I waited for comparative quiet, took a deep breath and walked to the front door.

Richard Fairfax must have been waiting for me. He answered the bell straight away, smiling.

He was a perfectly inoffensive man. Blond, with regular smallish features, medium height. He had none of Jack Hobbs's social awkwardness – he scooped me in, chattering. 'A detective, what fun. I've always been captivated by the idea of detectives – love them on TV – come in, it isn't very tidy but after all...'

It wasn't tidy. It was a young man's flat, disorderly. CD cases left empty, CDs and mugs and beer cans scattered on the floor round the player, clothes littered about the living room, but underneath the surface mess it was clean. Sam's efforts?

The room was the ground-floor duplicate of Hobbs', but it looked very different: coherent, as if it had been decorated and furnished at the same time, possibly even by a designer. That would make sense, of course, because Fairfax was the one with the money. A designer with minimalist leanings. Cream and black. Cream curtains and cream-painted plastered walls, wood floor with rugs – old-looking, valuable rugs – and black and steel furniture, with a black leather sofa that would probably fart if you sat on it, the kind of simple desk that would cost far more than an ornate one, with a top-of-the-range PC and printer and a laptop beside it. The cream walls were varying shades of cream; something pricey had been done in the way of dragging or stippling or whatever it was called when interior decorators got their hands on a large bankroll and a tin of paint.

'Well – great to meet you, but how exactly can I help?' he said when he'd offered me coffee, which I'd refused, unusually for me and possibly rudely. But I still didn't like the feel of the place and I didn't want to stay there longer than I had to, despite Fairfax's apparent amiability.

And why shouldn't he be amiable? Even if he was Boy, even if Boy was the Butcher of the Bella, even if he'd killed Philip Gein to cover his back, why shouldn't he be amiable? He didn't know I was after him. He shouldn't suspect it.

But as we sat down – me on the leather sofa, which farted, and he on a rather beautiful chrome and leather chair which he'd cleared by picking up a pile of clothes and throwing them on top of an existing heap in the corner – I got the impression that he felt superior; that he was even, in a polite way, laughing at me.

'Tell me what you want to know, what sort of thing you do,' he said, 'and I'll answer your questions if I can.'

I explained about noise and neighbours and the details that I usually checked out with property enquiries. 'Surely most of that you do talking to other people, not the vendors themselves?' he said.

That was true, of course. I didn't want to dwell on it, for obvious reasons, so I said something about how useful it was if the vendors were prepared to help, and how

245

useful it had been talking to Jack last night, and how the noise from the trains was very intrusive, wasn't it, and how did he cope?

A train went past as I spoke. We waited for the noise to pass. I was trying to work out what was odd about his clothes. He was wearing cavalry twill trousers, a beige check flannel shirt, an old but well-cut tweed jacket and probably hand-made brown leather lace-up shoes. Perfectly ordinary, really. The kind of thing Barty wore when he was going to the country–

That was the oddity. Barty was in his mid-forties, and very posh, and when he went to the country he often stayed with the kind of people who owned Range Rovers not because they were pretentious but because they needed them, to drive off-road on their estates. For Barty it was a sort of uniform. But for Richard Fairfax, an ex-minor public schoolboy who sounded lower-upper-middle-class and who lived within kebab-sniffing distance of Ladbroke Grove, it was a costume, a dress-up. Unless... 'Are you going away this weekend?' I asked.

He shook his head. 'I like London,' he said. 'Plenty going on, don't you find?'

'What do you do?' I asked, deliberately open-ended, hardly expecting him to reply

'I'm a serial killer' but not about to look a gift horse in the molars if he did.

No such luck. 'I'm a civil servant,' he said. 'As civil as I can manage.' He smiled at me. Very regular teeth, like his features. Civil servant could be anything, from a high-flyer in the Treasury to a clerk in the Driver and Vehicle Licensing Authority. It was more likely to be the latter than the former, otherwise he'd have specified. 'But I don't have to live on my salary, fortunately. I had a doting great-aunt who left me her property portfolio, useful stuff, bits here and bits there. Nice to have the money of course but it's also time-consuming. Accountants, managers, brokers, you know how it is.'

I made no effort to look like someone who knew how it was.

'About the noise of trains,' he said, his smile dimming.

He was losing patience. I wasn't being impressed enough. I smiled. His smile recovered wattage. 'About the noise,' he repeated. 'I got the impression from the agent that the purchaser, Polly Straker, is it? was considering an investment. Building, in fact. If the new building was soundproofed, it wouldn't matter, would it?'

'There's that, of course,' I said. 'Perhaps I

could see the workshops, this morning.'

'It's not convenient at the moment,' he said. 'Sorry. Of course your surveyor will be able to. He's coming next week, I think?'

'Monday or Tuesday,' I said, knowing the survey would never happen. A train was passing and I looked around under cover of the noise, hoping I'd missed something I could use as a lead-in to identifying him as Boy. Family photographs, ideally, with a mother and a sister so I could find out if she was called Girl or if she had a learning disability or had died a few years back. But there were no family photographs. Just clothes. Different clothes, I realized. Some as deliberately country-gentleman as the ones he was wearing: others quite different, more Italian Eurotrash smart.

'Hi,' said a voice. Another young man was in the room: I hadn't heard him come in.

'Hi, Russell. Meet Alex Tanner, the detective. Alex, Russell Jacobs, the other tenant.'

Jacobs was the tallest of the three, over six foot, and the thinnest: gangly with prominent wrists and a massive Adam's apple bobbing distractingly up and down a long neck topped off by a too-small head. He had cropped dark hair, small dark currant eyes set deep under a bony forehead and a shadowed jaw. He was in jeans, a thick dark sweater, and trainers. He grinned at me, revealing widely-spaced teeth, said, 'Russell Jacobs, the other tenant,' and flopped down on the sofa beside me. Involuntarily, I moved away, feeling crowded and outnumbered, especially since he and Fairfax were exchanging a conspiratorial glance. Or maybe just an intimate glance. Were they gay?

'You're the smallest detective I've ever met,' said Jacobs in a flat Essex whine.

Annoyance came to my rescue, banishing neurotic pregnant-woman fear. I wasn't going to take that from anyone, no matter if he looked like Frankenstein's monster. 'How many detectives have you met, then?'

'You're the first.'

'Then I'm also the largest detective you've met,' I snapped, taking out a notebook and flipping it open in a businesslike, verging on aggressive, way.

'Largest detective I've met,' he said.

I looked at him sharply. Was he sending me up? But Fairfax didn't react, and that was the second time Jacobs had echoed me. A mild form of echolalia, perhaps; a nervous habit.

Suddenly, poignantly, I was reminded of Nick. On the one occasion I'd agreed to play Scrabble with her she'd come down on me hard for making the word 'echolalia' when I could have made a much higher score by adding one high-value letter to an already existing word. I just liked words: she hardly saw the words, only the patterns and the scores. Which was why she was a mathematician, I supposed. Plus she'd been annoyed by not knowing 'echolalia', and she'd taken her annoyance out by denying such a condition existed ... I was drifting off again.

'Vacant possession won't be a problem, will it?' I said directly to Fairfax. 'My client's a bit concerned about that.'

'Why should she be?' said Fairfax. 'Won't her solicitor be dealing with those issues?'

'In due course, if we proceed that far. But protected tenants can be a major problem, as you'll appreciate. Let's see: there are three, isn't that right? Russell here–' I indicated him, and he grinned placatingly – 'Jack and – isn't there a girl upstairs?'

'A girl upstairs,' said Jacobs. 'Yeah, but she doesn't have a lease. She just rents a room from Jack. An informal arrangement.'

'And she is?' I waited, pencil poised.

'Samantha Eyre,' said Fairfax.

I wrote that down without a sign of recognition. 'Is she in at present? Maybe I could talk to her.'

'She's out at work,' said Jacobs.

'Right. Another time. Now tell me, this was Rillington Place, wasn't it?'

'You went through all that with Jack,' said Fairfax. He'd been interested enough to debrief Jack in some detail about our meeting, then. Could just be natural curiosity. Could be because he was genuinely interested in the sale to Polly. Could be because he was suspicious of me. He seemed to be watching me warily now, but I didn't trust my own judgement, the place spooked me so much.

'Do you get any sightseers? Murder buffs, ghouls?' I said.

'Not that I know of,' said Fairfax.

'Never seen any,' said Jacobs.

'And you don't feel the place is haunted?'

'Haunted? Hardly,' said Fairfax.

'It never crossed my mind,' said Jacobs.

'That was years ago, right?' said Fairfax. 'Christie was years ago. Before the war.'

'Before the war,' said Jacobs. 'Years ago. And I don't believe in ghosts.'

Chapter Twenty-Two

I didn't come away from Bartlett Close with much. I'd definitely located Sam Eyre, that was a plus, but as far as identifying the Boy of the letters I was no further than I'd been the night before. Richard Fairfax was still the best, indeed only, candidate: boarding-school educated with a sister. But the atmosphere hadn't been conducive to the kind of chat that might have revealed anything about Fairfax's sister, or his mother, or whether he knew Philip Gein, or if his mother had been on holiday in Rome in August 1970.

Neither Fairfax nor Jacobs had seemed interested in Christie's multiple murders. But they'd both been tense, I thought. Or maybe I was imagining it. My antennae kept overreacting: Fishburn spooked me, Jonno spooked me, Bartlett Close spooked me; Nick's absence was spooking me, and even poor Alan Protheroe had given me a few chills down the spine.

It must be hormones, I decided, and

dropped into the local chemist where I bought the cheapest pregnancy test they had.

As I turned the corner of Ladbroke Grove to my office, I was sure that Nick would be there. Irrationally sure: I just had one of those pictures, much more vivid than reality, of the light being on and the door unlocked and me hearing the flat click-click of the computer keyboard as Nick caught up with the outstanding work and her sulky face when I bawled her out for skiving.

From the corner I could see it was dark. From ten yards, I could see someone standing outside. From three yards I could see it was Lil, silent, without Benbow.

I let her in, turned on the light to chase away the gloom, and put the kettle on.

When we settled down, her with tea and me with coffee, she still hadn't said anything. None of the earlier eagerness and bounce. She passed me some photocopied sheets. I glanced at them. A long feature article on the Killer, two weeks old, from the magazine section of a quality Sunday.

'Most of it's in there, I think,' she said. 'He's a good journalist, that one, accurate and well in with the police. It's reasonably up to date, and obviously there haven't been any more murders since. I don't know how much more you want. And these are my notes.'

'This'll probably be enough,' I said glancing through them. 'Why don't you tell me the highlights?'

'I'm surprised you haven't kept up with this yourself,' she said. 'Most people seem enthralled by serial killers.' Her voice was flat.

'But you're not?'

'No. I find it sad and frightening that one human being should do that to another, and that others should want to know about it.' She looked at me almost defiantly. 'I know I'm old-fashioned. That's because I'm old.'

'I'm sorry I asked you to research this, then,' I said.

'I like research,' she said. 'I'm good at it. But this – it reminds me of how much the world has changed for the worse.'

'Lil, how old were you in 1947?'

'None of your business,' she said spiritedly.

'OK, but remember the late 1940s?'

'Naturally.'

'When the world was so much better?'

'Yes,' she said. 'It was. We didn't have so many possessions, of course, but–'

255

'But Reginald Christie was living just round the corner in Rillington Place and quietly killing women and stashing them in his garden because he was sexually inadequate? And when it came out, in the fifties, the paper boys were shouting "Christie Murder", and I bet the newspapers' sales shot up?'

'Well,' she said. Then she smiled. 'You're right. I agree with you about that specific point, but I still feel—'

'Not now, Lil, OK?'

'Later, perhaps? That was almost a discussion, you see. Nobody ever discusses things with me any more.'

'I'm not surprised, since you just stand in the streets yelling out Dickens.'

'In the place where I live, I mean. The staff are too tired and the inmates are too senile.'

'Sorry about that,' I said dismissively. 'Now, are you going to brief me on the Notting Hill Killer, or do you want to go and find a counsellor to complain to?'

'You're decidedly bossy,' she said neutrally.

'I'm also your boss,' I said equally neutrally.

We looked at each other. Then she unwound her scarves and took off her hat,

256

revealing wiry, curly grey hair. 'Tell me what you want to know.'

There wasn't much I hadn't actually known already, I thought as I closed the door behind her, after I'd sent her up to check that Sam was actually working at the pizza place on Notting Hill.

I sat back down at the desk and looked at the notes she'd given me. According to the article, they were short on forensic evidence. No sperm, no saliva, no blood. A careful murderer, or perhaps a deliberate campaign of misinformation by the police.

Apart from that, now at least I had the dates of the murders so I could check and eliminate Alan Protheroe as a possibility. If I could be bothered: suspecting him was absurd.

There were details I'd forgotten. In each case the girl had disappeared while out shopping on a Saturday, although not always from the Notting Hill area. I'd been wrong about that. The first was from Notting Hill proper, the second – from the north end of Ladbroke Grove near where it met the Harrow Road – only Notting Hill if you were an estate agent or a journalist stretching a point. The last two were from different districts of London, one from Hampstead and one from Islington.

The Saturday suggested the killer was someone who worked a Monday-Friday job or, since all four girls worked Monday to Friday jobs, someone who knew it would be easier to pick them up then.

I made myself another mug of coffee and nibbled on a dry biscuit, not because I felt sick but in case I did. I ought to eat some proper food, with vitamins. In a minute I'd do the pregnancy test, and listen to my messages, and ring Barbara Gottlieb and probably Mrs Eyre, but right now I was beginning, despite myself, to be interested in the Killer. Not the man himself, but the puzzle. What, apart from their physical appearance, did the victims have in common?

Victim one, from a house in Lansdowne Crescent, just up the Grove in the smart direction, was eighteen and had died in January. Her father was a merchant banker, her mother a graphic designer. She had an older sister. She was on a gap year, waiting to go up to university, and earning some money working locally as a receptionist in a cable television company. Her parents knew better than to co-operate with the media, but an unnamed friend described her as 'jolly, with lots of friends, no special man'. She'd gone out shopping – not for any particular item, just browsing – and been due to meet her sister for lunch at one in an Italian restaurant near Harrods, but had never appeared. So presumably she'd been picked up in the morning.

Victim two, twenty, March, the north Ladbroke Grove one, was much less upmarket. She lived in a council flat on a big estate with her single-parent mother, a checkout operator at the local Sainsbury's, and three younger half-siblings. Her mother had sold her story to a tabloid so there was plenty of information about the girl, most of it sentimental rubbish, which boiled down to a harmless, aimless young woman who liked clothes and make-up and clubbing and her boyfriend. She worked as a Post Office counter clerk. She'd slept in that Saturday until noon and then gone out to the Portobello Market. At seven o'clock that evening she didn't turn up to meet her boyfriend at the local pub to go clubbing, but the boyfriend thought he'd been stood up and her mother thought she was with the boyfriend and she wasn't actually missed until her body turned up on Tuesday.

By now perhaps the killer, assuming he

was local, thought it was safer to move further out for victims. Victim three, eighteen, May, a dental hygienist, was the only child of elderly and careful parents. She'd disappeared between twelve and one: she'd popped out to the local electrical shop two streets away from their house in West Hampstead, to get some spotlight bulbs for her bedroom. Her father had gone out to look for her when she was late back for twelve thirty lunch. Her father was a dentist, her mother a housewife, and the girl sounded as respectable as you'd expect from her background. No boyfriend. Presumably Daddy Dentist would have threatened prowling youths with root canal work.

Victim four, nineteen, July, had disappeared even further afield: in Islington. She'd come south from Liverpool, worked on the switchboard at a local computer components manufacturer and lived in a flat-share. She'd last been seen by one of her flatmates at ten o'clock when she set off to do the last-minute shopping for her cut-price package holiday to Tenerife. She was due to depart in the early hours of Sunday morning. Her flatmates had supposed she was in Tenerife until her body was found, on Wednesday. According to them she was 'fun-loving,' which being translated and considering she'd been murdered, probably meant 'a right scrubber'.

What connected them? I couldn't see it – not surprisingly. It was ludicrous to hope that I would see at a glance what the police had failed to see in months.

All that struck me were the differences. The girls came from utterly dissimilar backgrounds, assorted classes, educational levels, temperaments, sexual experience, religions – January was Church of England, March Roman Catholic, May Jewish, July nothing. Three of them still lived at home, but at their ages, with their income levels and the cost of housing in London, that was normal.

So the killer chose them for their looks, and nothing else. The four faces, in photocopied black and white, were equally pretty, equally ordinary. In the colour which would have shown their blonde hair and blue eyes they'd have looked not just like sisters but like quadruplets. And Sam Eyre's photo added in made quintuplets.

He picked them on looks. Blonde, pretty, young and small. But where had he seen them? Victim three, May, was perhaps the oddest from that point of view. The other three were all heading for busy shopping areas, which the killer could be patrolling, but May only intended to walk through two quiet streets in a backwater. Was it sheer luck that he'd seen her? Or had he known where she lived and waited for her? Spotted her in a more public place and followed her home, and then bided his time?

And once he'd located them, how did he persuade them to go with him? And where did he keep them, for the three or four days before the body was dumped? For most of that time they'd have been alive, according to the article. Alive, and being tortured, so presumably noisy.

In a very isolated area, perhaps – in which case, not Notting Hill. Or a soundproofed room. Which might be anywhere.

Then he dumped them in Wormwood Scrubs. Which didn't necessarily mean that he lived near Wormwood Scrubs, of course.

So the Butcher of the Bella might have nothing whatever to do with the area.

I put the article in my desk drawer, closed it, and took a deep breath.

Pregnancy test time.

Chapter Twenty-Three

The test had been easy enough. Dip the little white plastic stick into the urine sample, and wait two minutes to see if two lines appeared in the display area. I deliberately spent the waiting time making coffee. When I looked again, there they were. Two distinct lines.

It wasn't a shock, at all. I'd known it. But it was an irreversible event, a door closing and a door opening, into areas I'd never really thought I'd enter. Not actually. I thought I'd talk about it and plan it but it would never be the right time.

How do you make God laugh? Tell him your plans.

I wrapped the test kit in newspaper and put it inside a plastic bag. I knotted the plastic bag and put it inside another plastic bag and knotted that, and put the package into a black bin liner and went outside and stuffed the whole thing in the litter bin a few yards up the Grove, outside the chippy.

Then I went back in to my office. I'd tell

Barty on Monday. Or rather I'd set about telling Barty on Monday – I had a telephone contact number of an aid organization somewhere in Africa, not, I didn't think, in Zaire itself. I'd get him to call me back. Which might take days. And until that was done, I couldn't tell anyone else.

Which meant, I thought perking up, that my clear duty was to get on with business as usual. Which meant I was putting it off. Which meant I was running away. Which meant that I was being unfair to Barty. I made myself pick up the phone and make the call.

It was a good line and the person who answered – she sounded Scandinavian – knew who Barty was, but her manner was strange. 'You wish him to telephone you? of course, yes, if – but it might not be so easy, you understand? We are not sure...'

'Whenever he has a minute. Not urgent,' I said.

'But– And you are, please?' I told her. I said 'fiancée' for the first time, to hear how it sounded. It sounded silly. Pregnant part-ner it would be from now until delivery.

'But conditions are difficult, you under-stand. Do you understand?' She sounded even odder now, with the local-conditions

264

arrogance you often get from people who work in uncivilized areas and assume that anyone not familiar with them thinks it's just like being in London.

I assured her I understood to shut her up, and rang off.

Then I listened to my telephone messages. only one. 'Er ... Arthur Fishburn here for Alex Tanner. Please could you get back to me as soon as possible, that's utmost urgency, please, as soon as you receive this message. I'm leaving this message at noon on Saturday, repeat noon on Saturday, please telephone me as soon as you receive this message. I'll wait for your call.' He added his telephone number. Then there was a pause, when all I could hear was his heavy breathing. I imagined him going through the convolutions of his tic. Then, almost shouted – 'For your own safety! Please!' Another rasping pause. 'Er ... this is Arthur Fishburn, ex-detective constable, Metropolitan Police', then a crash as he replaced the phone.

He'd sounded sincere. A bit self-dramatizing, that was his style. But sincere, and possibly even frightened.

I dialled his number. The phone rang and rang. I left it ringing until it was obvious that no one would answer, then I let it ring some more.

He'd left the message two hours ago. Maybe he'd got tired of sitting about waiting for my call and gone out. That was most likely. If he thought it was really urgent he might come to the office. He was probably on his way to me now.

I rang Nick's mobile number. Still out of service. I tried her friend the ex-maths professor's number, in Oxford, and waited out the ringing even longer than I'd done for Fishburn. No answer. Barbara Gottlieb next. Answering machine, with lots of pips to show she hadn't picked up her messages yet. Fishburn again, in case he'd been in the loo the first time I rang. Still no answer.

So I put on my jacket, locked up the office and headed north to his place.

I turned left off the Grove and into Fishburn's narrow, empty street. Nobody was out and about, and I didn't blame them. Half past two on a November afternoon, there should have been some natural light. But above the fog the sun seemed very far away and indifferent. There was a glow from the street lamps and a little dispirited artificial light leaking from an occasional window, but the fog was blanketing that too and seeping, acrid, down my throat.

I stopped outside Fishburn's house. There was a light in his front room, and the curtains were open today, and the little gate leading to his front path was swinging wide.

I went up the path and rang the bell. No answer.

I stepped onto his handkerchief lawn to look in the front window. The light came from a low-wattage bulb in a heavily red-lampshaded standard lamp in the far corner, so the whole room was red-tinted and the front area, near the window, not very bright at all. It was just bright enough for me to see that the walls were covered by pin-boards. On the pin-boards were clippings from newspapers and magazines, none of them legible at first glance.

Certainly, Fishburn wasn't in there.

I stepped back from the window and looked up and down the street, to see if a watchful neighbour was studying me. No sign of any movement, no twitching curtains that I could see. Dead quiet, suddenly broken by the half-familiar roar of a revving engine from the end of the street. Then, soon, quiet again.

I rang the bell again to establish my good

intentions, just in case. Still no answer. I peered into the window again, squinting at the nearest wall. At first the newsprint just blurred, then it swam into focus and I could make out the headlines at least. They were all about the Notting Hill Killer. Every one I could read. And when I knew what I was reading, I could make out more of them on the back wall, I recognized the magazine article Lil had brought me.

The shock was so great that I backtracked and was away down the road towards the comparative crowds of Ladbroke Grove before I knew what I was doing.

It was classic serial killer stuff to keep clippings, to gloat over your handiwork.

Then I slowed down. Fishburn was too old to be the Killer, surely. I already knew he was obsessive and I'd guessed that he was fantasizing about catching the Killer.

I stopped. He'd said he wanted to speak to, me urgently. He wasn't answering his phone. Maybe something had happened to him. He was an old man. Maybe he'd had a heart attack from excitement, and was even now lying in his bleak kitchen, dead. Or not dead yet, but very ill, possibly dying, in which case I could help him. I should help him.

I turned and ran back, in through the gate.

I tried the front door, pushing it hard. It held solid at top and bottom – probably bolted. Round the back. Down the narrow concreted path by the side of the house, into the tiny concreted yard. The yard was bordered by a fence. There were no tubs of flowers, no shrubs, not even boxes or garden tools. There was absolutely nothing.

The back door was half open. There was no light in the kitchen. I stepped cautiously towards the door, listening. No sound. Faintly I could hear a dog barking, and the steady hum of traffic on the Grove, but nothing from inside the kitchen or the house.

There was no point in waiting. The longer I hesitated, the more reluctant I got. I forced myself through the door in a jumping-into-a-cold-swimming-bath rush and was inside, by the table, before I realized my trainers were squelching and sticking. Looking down through the dimness my once-white Air Nikes were two spattered islets in a lake of blood. I opened my mouth to scream and shut it again as the deep pre-scream breath sucked the sweet, stomach-turning smell into my nose and throat.

I looked for the source of the blood, at first distinguishing nothing in the shadowed kitchen. Then, wedged between the table and the door, I saw a hump of clothes, someone's kneeling back...

Fishburn.

I shifted from squelchy foot to squelchy foot. I didn't want to look closer, and he couldn't still be alive, but if he was, I'd kill him by being squeamish.

I moved towards the kneeling hump. As I got nearer, I saw the angle of the head, wedged sideways against the wall, hardly attached to the body, only held in place by the wedging – his throat had been cut, right back to the bone. No blood was pumping from where his neck had been.

So he was dead. Thank God, I thought, feeling guilty even as I thought it, thank God he's dead, so I can get out of here.

I went back, in the same footprints as far as I could manage it, to the door. Then I untied the laces on my trainers and stepped out of them, leaving them on the back step. That procedure took much longer than I wanted, much longer than I could have imagined because my fingers were shaking and slippery with sweat.

Then I walked back to the road, the fog-damp concrete making my socks sticky in a dreadful mimicry of blood.

Chapter Twenty-Four

I was nearly home before I could stop walking. My feet were walking but I was running in my head, and my mouth was silent but I was screaming in my head.

I had no answers or explanations for what had happened. But I knew, at least, that the police had to be told, so I stopped at a phone box and dialled 999, and in a raspy voice as close to baritone as I could manage, I reported Arthur's death, gave them the address, told them not to waste time on my trainers, and rang off when they asked my name. I was going to keep out of it until I'd spoken to Hilary Lucas. She'd wanted confidentiality and although after this she couldn't have it, I wanted to warn her first. Plus I wanted time to think and freedom of movement. Once the police knew I'd discovered the body, chances were I'd spend the rest of the afternoon, if not the entire evening, sitting round in a police station.

I went back home. As soon as I got inside

the hall door I removed my sopping, disgusting socks, and as soon as I was inside the flat I put them in the rubbish. Then I noticed that the bottom few inches of my jeans were soaked with blood, so I stripped them off and put them in the washing machine, on cold rinse, and fetched a pair of clean jeans from upstairs.

I turned on the central heating and the hot water, ground beans, made myself a decent cup of coffee, wrapped myself in a duvet and sat on the sofa with the telephone. I needed to work things out. Badly. And I didn't know where to start.

I called Hilary Lucas.

Answering machine. I left an urgent callback message. If she didn't get back to me quickly I'd tell the police the whole story anyway, with everything I knew. Which actually amounted to very little.

Fishburn's death might be related to his dealings with me. If so, it'd be connected with the Killer and Bartlett Close, because those *were* his dealings with me. Plus his urgent message to me suggested that I was involved. On the other hand, he probably wasn't Mr Popularity in his own neighbourhood, waging as he did a single-handed war against the local criminals.

But he had clearly been pursuing the Killer on his own account long before he met me. I shuddered at the memory of the Killer Shrine Room, which was somehow more scary even than the Kitchen of Blood. Those clippings were the work of months, not days. He might have stumbled on an unrelated lead.

Philip Gein had been stabbed to death and Fishburn's was a stabbing death too. It involved a knife anyway. I resolutely blocked the mental picture of what the knife had done. Similar m.o. I'd been pretty sure that Gein had died because he'd accused his illegitimate son of being the Killer, and it looked as if that was Richard Fairfax.

It was all guesswork.

Fishburn had left the message for me at noon, so he was still alive then. I'd found him at two forty-fiveish. How long had he been dead? I should know, roughly, from the blood, surely. How congealed had it been? I forced myself to remember. Squelch, squelch. I imagined picking up my feet. The blood had been sticky, almost solid. And the spatters at the bottom of my jeans had been globs rather than splashes. So, he wasn't all that freshly dead. It would help, of course, if I knew anything accurate

273

about congealing blood.

Between noon and twoish was my best guess. And I'd been with Fairfax for a lot of that. On the other hand the whole procedure needn't have taken long. Less than five minutes in a car from Bartlett Close to Fishburn's house, a quick murder, less than five minutes back.

He'd have been covered with blood, though—

The doorbell rang.

I went to the kitchen and squinted down through the window, but whoever had rung was standing too close to the front door to be seen.

I opened the window, shouted, 'Hang on a see,' scrambled into clean socks and a pair of DMs and grabbed my bag and keys. In my present state of mind there were very few people I'd have been happy to let in, and no strangers.

I opened the front door to a stranger, but an instantly classifiable one. An average height, square-built, cheap-suited beige-macked man in his late thirties who showed me his warrant card but who might as well have had CID tattooed across his forehead.

'Alex Tanner? Sergeant Cairncross. I'm

274

working on a murder investigation and I've heard from Superintendent Barstow that you may have some information. Can I have a word?'

It wasn't a question. He was moving forward as he spoke. 'Sure,' I said, slipping past him onto the steps and closing the door behind me. 'We'll go to my office. Just along here, come with me.'

Looking rather disappointed, he followed me. 'Not convenient for me to come in, is that it?'

That was precisely it, I thought, bearing in mind my jeans, still slurping around in a pink-tinted rinse, and the fact that the Killer might be a policeman with a perfectly valid warrant card. 'I'm expecting someone to meet me at the office,' I said. 'Wouldn't want to keep them waiting.'

He made a noise expressive of impatience, distrust and an intention to intimidate. Quite a lot to pack into one grunt. 'I'm a busy man,' he said.

'Sorry.' I said, 'but the office isn't far and you can have a cuppa in the warm. You look cold.'

He looked, more than anything, tired and unhealthy. His brown eyes, set deep behind a prominent forehead, were shadowed, and his greyish skin stretched tightly over a not unpleasant face. He had the kind of straight, fine mouse-brown hair that recedes early and always flops: it hadn't been cut recently enough and it straggled down inside the collar of his shirt. He didn't seem hostile but he did seem preoccupied and he didn't seem actively interested in what I might tell him. This was nothing to do with Fishburn's murder, for sure. This was the reluctant follow-up to the information I'd asked Eddy to pass on.

Maybe when I told him what I knew about Arthur it would cheer him up. It must be very demoralizing to work on a prolonged, important investigation which made you look more of a wally as every unsuccessful day went by, as every successive body was heaped up in reproach.

'Tea's just coming, unless you prefer coffee,' I said unlocking the office door, putting the light on and waving him to the client chair. 'Take your mac off, sit down, make yourself at home.'

He ignored what I'd said and began a tour of the room, inspecting Nick's naïve attempts at office decoration. 'Much work for you in Cambodia?' he asked.

'It's been dropping off recently. Thailand's

looking good, though.' This time, his grunt expressed mild impatience and even milder amusement.

'The guv'nor says you're all right,' he said. 'And the guv'nor's a good copper. So I take his word for it.'

'But?'

'But what he told me you'd said about the Killer sounded like a load of bollocks, excuse my French. I don't take kindly to members of the public taking up a little light detecting and starting work on a serial murderer to get their faces in the tabloids.'

'It's not like that,' I said. 'I have some information. I don't know how big a load of bollocks it might be. That's for you to decide. You're better equipped for that than I am.'

He gave his mildly-amused grunt.

'Now, Sergeant, do you want a drink, or not?'

He put his head on one side and considered. Could he afford the time? 'Yeah,' he said finally. 'Tea. Milk, two sugars. I'm not on duty. This is by way of a favour to Eddy. You're off the record. And call me Andy.' Then he smiled. He looked quite different when he smiled; years younger, for a start. He was probably my age or less.

I went into the little hallway at the back and put the kettle on, feeling relieved. I'd tell him everything I knew, including that I'd discovered Fishburn's body, and then I'd be back on the record quicker than he could grunt. OK, so the rest of the afternoon and the whole evening might go down the tubes, but the police worked slowly and I was grateful I didn't have their job. I didn't want to see the mutilations on the dead bodies of the girls. I didn't want to interview the nutters who might have done it. I didn't want to trawl through mountains of tedious information looking for the speck that might be useful. The least I could do was be a co-operative member of the public.

'Two sugars?' I called.

'Yeah. Actually, make it three.'

The sugar bowl was nearly empty. We kept stores in the battered cupboard under the sink. I opened the cupboard and nearly dropped the mug I was holding.

Inside the cupboard, its red charging light glowing like a warning of danger, was Nick's mobile phone. The phone she never, ever left. The phone that was damaged if it was left charging for more than twelve hours, as she'd repeatedly told me. 'You must read the instructions, Alex. It's ridiculous to spend money on equipment and not read the instructions.'

She'd never have left it on charge. She'd never have left it at all. Not voluntarily.

So where the hell was Nick?

Chapter Twenty-Five

It took everything I had not to show Cairncross I was poleaxed. I hadn't time to think, I had to make an immediate judgement call. Of course if I told him everything, even about the disappearance of Nick, the Met were much better placed than I was to intervene; with all the information I'd give them they could pile into Bartlett Close.

Eventually.

They'd want to dot the i's and cross the t's and do everything by the book first, because the Killer was the last person they'd want to wriggle away free on a technicality.

And I didn't even know if Nick was in Bartlett Close or if she'd fallen foul of the young men of Bartlett Close. That was where Sam Eyre lived, sure, and she'd been on the Eyre case. That was where I'd pointed Fishburn to. But was it where Nick had gone?

By the time I brought Cairncross his syrupy tea I'd decided. Above all, what I

281

couldn't afford to waste was time. I needed him out of my office. I needed freedom of movement. If Nick was with the Killer – wrong size and shape and colour as she was –she might, just might, still be alive. She'd gone on Wednesday evening. The shortest time he had kept a victim was three days, Saturday to Tuesday night. The three days weren't quite up yet.

So I told my edited story to Cairncross as quickly and dully as I could. I told him about Hilary Lucas, the betrayed widow. I told him about the letters from the mistress and gave him the last letter which mentioned Boy and Bartlett Close. I left out everything else.

I felt treacherous because as he relaxed, listening to me, he turned into a human being – 'Call me Andy'. He was sharp enough. He spoke warmly of Eddy, said Eddy had spoken well of me, even made quite good jokes which I had to force myself to laugh at. Under other circumstances we'd have got on, but concealing my involvement in the recent discovery of a murder victim was hardly conducive to a bonding process.

Eddy had chosen him well. He took the information seriously, made notes, asked intelligent questions, gave me a card and urged me to ring his mobile if I remembered anything else. He'd be back to me, he said, and meanwhile I was to keep my nose out and myself safe.

Yes, I said, I'd keep away from Bartlett Close. Then he asked me about my work and looked as if he was settling in for a coffee-sipping, getting-to-know-you chat. Any other time I'd have joined in. Apart from liking him, good contacts in the police are always useful, and I was going to be seriously stuck when Eddy retired.

But now, I wanted him out, so I pretended breathless interest in the details of the mutilations the Killer inflicted on his victims. He looked surprised, as if he hadn't pegged me for a ghoul, then disappointed and weary, as if the human capacity for bad behaviour was a weight on his shoulders. He couldn't get shot of me fast enough.

I shut the door behind him, looked at the card he'd given me with his mobile phone number on it, and guiltily promised myself I'd tell him all about finding Fishburn as soon as I could.

Just moments before, I'd been struggling to disguise the fact that every inch of my body was itching with the imperative need to get rid of him and do something to find

Nick. Now I could do something I was appalled by the realization that I didn't know what to do.

Yes I did. I needed to look in the workshops at Bartlett Close. Fairfax had kept me away from them earlier that day. They'd be a good place to keep a prisoner: they were isolated, and the noise of the trains would blanket any screaming.

Lil opened the door, and I jumped.

'Not now, Lil,' I snapped.

'What's up?' she said calmly, sitting down and unwinding her scarves. 'I've come to report about Samantha Eyre. You asked me to check, remember? I went up to Perfect Pizza and she is indeed working there. I saw her. She'd just come off duty and was eating with two young men.'

'What did they look like?'

She described Fairfax and Jacobs.

'What time was this?'

'Half past one,' she said.

'Are you sure?'

She waved a notebook at me. 'I was observing,' she said. 'I like pizzas. I stayed to have lunch. I had an American Hot, with added pepperoni, and a cup of cappucino.' She took a receipt from her pocket and, passed it to me.

'Were they still there when you left?' I said.

'Yes. All three of them were still there when I left, just after half past two.' She tapped her notebook.

That made timings for Fishburn's murder tight, if Fairfax had done it. He could have nipped up to Arthur's after I left and still been in Notting Hill in time for lunch – but how had he known Arthur was a threat to him? How had he been a threat? And would Fairfax have been able to sit and eat normally?

'How did the blond one seem?' I said.

'In good spirits. Rather full of himself. I didn't take to him at all. Everything he said was I, I, I.' She looked at me brightly. 'Tell me what's the matter,' she said. 'Why are you so jittery?'

I kept pacing round the room. For a moment, I considered telling her everything. At least I'd hear myself talk and maybe it would make more sense to me. But that would take time, and also I was reluctant to involve anyone else in the danger. I'd involved Arthur, and now he was dead.

'When did you say Nick would be back?'

'This afternoon, I think,' I said as steadily as I could manage. Was she reading my thoughts? 'Why do you ask?'

285

'I was hoping for a game of Scrabble. We play regularly on Saturday evenings. She's very good.'

'I've really got to go out,' I said. 'Urgently.'

She went on as if I hadn't spoken. 'Dermot is next door.'

'The Golden Kid?'

'Yes. Perhaps you could press him further about Nick. Just a thought, because you said you were concerned about his reliability. Shall I get him?'

My first instinct was to say no, but then it occurred to me: if I was going to poke around the workshops at Bartlett Close, I could take the Kid, not so much for protection as for company. I didn't think he'd have any moral objections to breaking and entering and he might well have skills I could use.

'Get him,' I said.

The Kid sauntered in with Lil chivvying him like a sheepdog. 'What's all this about Nick, then?'

'She isn't back yet,' I said. 'And she's left her phone on charge.'

'You found the phone,' he said. 'Good. I was going to mention it to you but it slipped my mind.'

'Mention what?'

'She left it by the sink, so I put it away in the cupboard when I locked up, in case the rat knocked it over.'

'The rat?'

'Yeah. I've got one too, unless it's the same rat commuting. Didn't Nick tell you?'

'No.'

'She was handling it. The pest control people are due in on Monday–'

'Dermot,' I interrupted, 'Why did you lock up?'

He looked puzzled, fiddled with one of his earrings and looked at himself more closely in the dim mirror Nick had placed in the darkest corner of the room. 'It gives an illusion of space', she'd said loftily when I'd pointed out that the mirror was murky and tarnished enough without giving it no light rays to work with.

'She asked me to.'

'Do you often lock up?'

'Only when she asks me to. I've got a key, of course, and I check the messages for her sometimes.'

'The messages?'

'Yeah. E mail. And telephone. If she's out in the field and I'm here, it's no big deal, right?'

'So when you saw her on Wednesday evening, where exactly was it, and what exactly did she say? And will you stop squeezing your spots?'

'Lighten up, OK?' he said reproachfully.

'I'll make us all a nice cup of tea,' offered Lil, and went into the back hall.

I took a deep breath. 'Sorry, Kid, but I'm tense.'

'Yeah, I see that,' he said.

'Tell me exactly what happened when you last saw Nick.'

He gave a martyred sigh. 'It was maybe six thirty, sevenish. I was next door working on the bike. Nick barged in, pissed off about something but she didn't say what. She said to tell you she was going out of town to see an old professor, be back Sat'day, she had a minicab waiting, would I lock up and keep checking for messages? So I said yeah, and she went, and I locked up maybe ten minutes later. I've told you all this, OK?'

'Did you see the minicab?'

'Nah.'

'Do you know why she was taking one?'

'Get real. How would I know that? In a hurry, maybe? Why don't you ask 'em?'

'Ask who?'

'Them on the corner. The cab company,

288

the Spaniards.'

'They're Portuguese,' I said.

'Whatever.'

Lil came back with mugs of tea. 'I'll go over and ask, shall I?' she said.

'Please,' I said, and off she went.

I was beginning to find the Kid's easygoing responses reassuring rather than irritating, though I was still strung tighter than piano wire. Maybe Lil would get some useful information from the cab company, though, and I had to wait for that.

Meanwhile I collected what I thought I'd need. A torch. The mobile phone – might as well use it. Wirecutters and a chisel, which Nick kept in the bottom drawer of the desk, though I'd been careful never to ask why.

Lil was back. 'Not very helpful, I'm afraid,' she said. 'Nick hired the cab to go to Paddington via the estate down the road. She got the cab to wait outside the estate, then came back and paid it off. He remembered because it was such a cheap fare. He wouldn't have accepted it if he'd known, and she wouldn't pay extra for the trouble. She didn't even tip.'

That was Nick, all right. 'Which estate?' I said, though I was sure I knew.

'Over by St Mark's Road.'

That confirmed it.

I'd just opened my mouth to ask the Kid to come with me to Bartlett Close when he looked out of the window, said, 'Shit! a warden! Back in a minute,' and set off at a run down the street.

I took Lil's tea and sipped it. I hate tea and this was particularly vile, the kind of metallic orange paintstripper brew I imagined her dispensing in air-raid shelters in the war.

Then I heard the noise. A familiar noise. The noise I'd heard outside Fishburn's house before I discovered the body. A noise I couldn't believe I hadn't identified at the time, because it was so familiar now I heard it in context. The deep, rumbling, primitive roar of the Kid's Harley-Davidson.

Chapter Twenty-Six

I gulped Lil's tea. The Kid, the Killer. Or the Kid, just Fishburn's killer.

It was ludicrous. How could it work?

But actually, of course, it could. Say the men at Bartlett Close were nothing to do with it. Then we were left with Nick, in pursuit of Sam, who might well have been earmarked by the Killer as his next victim. Say Nick had put two and two together and spotted the Killer. If it was the Kid he'd be well placed to get rid of Nick. He could have picked up the message to me from Fishburn and known Fishburn had some information.

It could be cobbled together, but I didn't believe it. On the other hand did I not believe it firmly enough to take the Kid with me as back-up? Hardly. Bartlett Close was spooky enough without having to watch your back-up.

I needed someone else, so I grabbed the phone and rang Peter, Eddy's son. He'd offered to help, he doesn't live too far away and he's reassuringly burly. Also his sexuality is basic and straightforward, and he likes women.

None of which turned out to be relevant, because only his machine answered. 'Peter? Peter, are you there? Pick up if you're there. It's Alex, I need to speak to you. Do us a favour, pick up.' No response, only the metallic beeping of the machine, then silence.

I replaced the receiver without leaving a message. Lil was watching me, her hands wrapped firmly round her mug of tea. 'Let me help,' she suggested.

'Not now, Lil,' I said.

There was a blessed quiet as the Kid's engine cut out. He must have ridden the bike into his office. Then he came back in, sat down and drank his tea. He looked just the same as he always did; gangly, spotty, ludicrously perforated and gold studded, harmless. But then the Killer would. If he stalked the streets muttering threats and waving a bloodstained knife the Met would have caught him long ago.

'Got a job for me, then?' he asked.

'Not today,' I said. 'Maybe Monday.'

'Be seein' ya, then. You going to the fireworks?'

'I am,' said Lil. 'I like fireworks.'

'What?' I said, then remembered. Every year the council gives a bonfire party and firework display in Wormwood Scrubs, hoping to discourage individual displays which so often result in accidents. I'm not mad on fireworks and I dislike parties so I never go, but it's a big local event. Due to start any time now. 'Surely the fireworks will be invisible in the fog?'

'I expect they'll produce an eerie glow,' said Lil. 'They can't possibly cancel now, it's too late, and I'm going anyway. I hate to miss a party.'

'Me too,' said the Kid.

'Off you go, then,' I said.

One good thing about the fog, I thought as I stood outside the flats at Bartlett Close, was that it'd give me good cover. It didn't look as if anyone was at home: there was one light in the main building, but it was a hall light. Presumably one of them had got round to repairing it since I'd stumbled past the bike on the way to visit Jack Hobbs.

Only last night, that had been. It seemed further away.

I could hardly put off moving much longer. I could walk straight past the flats into the yard behind, and then to the workshops. It didn't look as if there were any cars in the yard, but I couldn't be sure. Back there, it was out of the street lamps' reach, and dark as well as foggy.

I checked the mobile phone to see if I'd get a signal. Yes, quite strong. Then I checked, twice, that I'd switched it off. Bit of a giveaway if it rang mid-burglary.

The roar of a passing train kick-started me. Now, I thought, walking quickly and purposefully straight past the flats and through the yard to the workshop at the far end.

Which was unlocked.

I pulled one of the heavy doors just open enough to slip inside and then pulled it to behind me. Darkness. Smell of oil, and damp. Torch on. Everyday objects, spot-lighted in turn: garden tools, tins of paint and anonymous bottles on shelves, cardboard boxes against the walls, a space in the middle where a car was sometimes parked, judging by the patches of oil on the bare concrete floor.

I went over and looked inside the cardboard boxes. Ordinary junk.

No Nick. No sign of Nick.

Out into the yard again, closing the door

behind me. The windows of the flats were still black and blank, apart from a glow from the hall light filtering through Hobbs's living-room windows on the top floor. I couldn't have seen the road from where I was standing even without the fog.

So far, so good.

The next door was chained and padlocked. I stuck my chisel through the chain and twisted. It gave way. Nobody could have heard the noise of it breaking, if there had been a noise – a train was passing.

I went in and closed the door. This time my torch was less tentative. A large old Volvo estate took up most of the space. Two walls were lined with racks holding plenty of plastic storage boxes with electric cables and microphones and plugs. There were some booms and windbaffles and some battered metal Sammy boxes, used for film sound and camera equipment. I looked inside the largest box first: it was easily large enough for a body, even a big body like Nick's, but it was empty. So were all the rest of them, and so was the car.

Somebody was a sound recordist. It had to be Russell Jacobs. Perhaps his echolalia was a human version of his working life. I wasn't happy with the car being there; it evoked his hulking presence and I shivered. He's out, I told myself firmly. It was very common not to use a car in London. Besides, he had been with Sam Eyre and Fairfax when last seen. I hoped they'd since met Hobbs and were all together in Fairfax's car, taking a nice drive, preferably to Aberdeen or Exeter, or through the Channel Tunnel and on to Vladivostok.

Back in the yard, I looped the chain round the handle a few times so the doors looked secure.

Still no sign of anybody. Maybe I should be searching more thoroughly, looking for more signs of Nick's past presence as well as her body? Fat chance, burgling with a torch.

I tried the doors on the last workshop, Hobbs's studio, and they swung open at my touch. As I shut them behind me I did wonder – surely art studios needed light? There hadn't been any windows in the other two workshops – would there be any here? And even if there were windows at the back, they wouldn't have access to much except a view of the underside of the Hammersmith and City line.

Then the smell hit me. A much more powerful, all-encompassing version of the pungent smell I'd noticed on Hobbs's hands. I fumbled with the torch. The beam sprang out at random and shone high up on the side wall. On – I couldn't believe it. The torch slipped through the cold sweat of my fingers until I got a firmer grip and could direct it to the object again.

It was a dog. Standing on a shelf, ten feet off the ground. A spaniel, like Lil's Benbow, but unlike Lil's Benbow, absolutely still and silent.

A real dog, but it couldn't be a real dog. Not immobile, not that distance off the ground. At last I worked it out. A stuffed dog.

A model, for his art? Or, if he was a sculptor, part of his art? I swept the torch round the space.

It was his art. He was a taxidermist. The workshop was full of groups of animals.

The smallest I could see were tiny mice, the largest a Great Dane. All the groups were doing human things in human settings: eating Christmas lunch, with crackers and decorations and plates heaped high with model food; watching television on a model sofa with beer and Coke cans and half-eaten pizza. A slender animal I couldn't name – a ferret maybe – bathing a ferret baby in a ferret-sized bath. Plenty of hamsters and gerbils and guinea pigs and a few white rats sunning themselves in absurd trappings on a crowded holiday beach. A proud squirrel father recording the birth of his child on a tiny camera in a miniature squirrel labour ward.

I took a deep breath and moved to the back, running the torch from side to side, checking each group separately and looking under the tables that supported them. The place was so cluttered I had to search systematically. Running the full length of the back wall was a working counter with a sink set in it. Hanging on the wall behind were tools, many of them sharp-looking knives. There were also shelves, with bottles and boxes, and a tall fridge.

Beside the sink was soap, and that was where the smell came from. Camphor. That was it, camphor. Used in the preparation of the skins, presumably. Now I'd identified the source of the smell, I rather liked it.

Come to that, I didn't mind the animal groups, either. They were rather charming, taking their human activities so seriously, and rather clever too. It was a social comment, I supposed. Death warmed up, death prettied up. Behind human celebrations and family life, the emptiness of mortality. But a celebration of life too, because unless you disapproved of taxidermy in principle, you couldn't look at the groups without identifying with their evident pleasure and pride in the moment or without admiring the skill and charm of the artist who'd had the idea, and the skill of the craftsman who'd restored these dead creatures to a sort of immortality, clothed in shiny healthy coats, adorned with delicate little whiskers. Nor could you look at them without feeling sad at the ultimate futility of people's personal and domestic enjoyments and rituals.

Equivocal, that's what it was. And that suits my own world view, although equivocal is a poncey word for it.

Enough art appreciation. I had to open the fridge. I did, and shut it again. It was a small-animal mortuary. No Nick.

That was it, then. I'd drawn a blank. I wandered back through the human-animals, wishing I could look at them in proper light. Maybe he was accumulating them for an exhibition. If so, I'd go, because I wanted to see all the detail. Maybe I'd even buy a group, except Hobbs'd probably charge a fortune. I could ask Barty to give me one.

I turned, nearly at the door, for a last look. Then someone spoke, behind me.

Chapter Twenty-Seven

I jumped away from the voice, bumping into a table, rocking the Christmas dinner. I hadn't taken in whose voice it was, or what it said. Every bit of me tensed in an effort not to scream, because if you screamed you were vulnerable.

Then the lights came on, bright overhead spots, momentarily blinding.

'It's only me,' said Jack Hobbs. 'You need the lights to see, don't you?'

His voice was as flat as ever, the statement practical. He didn't seem surprised or angry to find me there. He was wearing the same pair of ancient corduroy trousers as he had the night before, unless he kept several pairs with identical blotchy stains, and the same Arran sweater.

My heartbeat steadied and I switched off the torch. He was between me and the doors but the doors were wide open and there was nothing threatening in his manner. I stopped feeling scared and felt mildly embarrassed instead.

'Sorry,' I said. 'I wanted to see the workshops and nipped in, since the door was open.'

'Richard told me the surveyor was looking at them on Monday,' he said.

'I was curious.'

'You're a detective,' he said. 'I suppose that's your job, prying.'

Prying rankled. 'Detecting, I'd call it,' I said.

'Detecting. What exactly are you detecting, here?'

'Actually I was admiring,' I said. 'Admiring your work.'

'By torchlight?' He didn't seem angry, but neither did he seem flattered. 'What are you really after, Alex?'

'I told you. I'm doing a property enquiry.'

'If you say so,' he said, trying to meet my eye. 'I rather wanted to talk to you about that, actually.'

What was he getting at? Did he suspect I was after a particular quarry? I hoped not. And why should he? 'It must be very difficult, taxidermy,' I offered.

'Not difficult exactly. Not the preservation bit. That just takes method and patience.'

'But you make them look natural and human and expressive as well,' I said.

'Glad you think so,' he said more warmly. 'That's what I aim to do.'

'Anyhow, I'll get out of your way,' I said moving towards the yard.

Instead of stepping back, he closed the doors behind him. 'I need to keep the fog out,' he said in explanation. 'Damp's not good for them. Don't go yet. Tell me what you think about the group I'm working on now. The baby bath scene, over here.'

The mother and baby ferrets were towards the back of the workshop, and I was deeply reluctant to move further from the doors. I wasn't afraid, exactly, but I'd be happier outside, I knew. As a distraction, I pointed up to the spaniel, alone on its shelf.

'Are you going to put that in a group?' I asked.

He stopped walking, quite close to me now.

'That's the first animal I ever did,' he said. 'My apprentice piece. Years ago now. I hadn't got the concept then. I keep her for sentimental reasons.'

'Her?'

'She was the family pet. I really loved her. We all did.'

'Doesn't it upset you, looking at her like this?'

303

'Oh no. It isn't Girl, up there. Just her skin.'

It hit me so hard I felt as if my heart had leapt right out of my body to perch beside Girl.

Girl, the dog. No wonder the references in the letters made her sound handicapped. Because she wasn't a girl at all. She was a spaniel. Hardly surprising they hadn't sent her to boarding school.

And here I was with Boy, who wasn't Fairfax but Hobbs. Hobbs, whose own mother feared he might be the Killer. Hobbs the patricide. Hobbs who showed his affection for the family pet by scraping the flesh from her coat and sucking the brains from her skull. Hobbs, who was standing between me and safety while the latest train thundered overhead and rattled the stuffed creatures on their plinths.

'What's the matter?' he said.

'Nothing,' I said. Stupidly, because if I looked half as dreadful as I felt, I must look terminal or worse. 'Or maybe a little faint. Some air...'

I made to pass him, going for the yard. He put out a strong arm and stopped me. 'Hey – lie down, that's the best thing for fainting, lie here on the floor and I'll open the doors.

Really, it's a circulation thing, get your feet up and blood to your head, you can't faint lying down.'

I tried to pull away but he held on, and he was much stronger than I was.

So I abandoned subtlety and kicked him in the balls.

It was an effective kick, thanks to a combination of fear and Doc Martens boot. He collapsed immediately into a groaning heap, and I took off for the street.

I stopped running just outside the flats, and tried to look casual as I turned into the estate.

Two shapes were approaching. As they got nearer I could see it was Fairfax and Jacobs. I looked behind me – no sign of Hobbs.

'Hi,' I said, and kept walking.

'Alex, do you have a minute?' said Fairfax, with a confident smile.

'Not now, I'm afraid,' I said, not pausing.

'But I have a job for you. I want to hire you,' he said, sounding miffed.

'I must get back. Sorry,' I said over my shoulder. 'I'll give you a ring.'

'But this is urgent,' he said to my retreating back.

'This is urgent,' echoed Jacobs.

'I'll ring right away. Promise,' I called.

By now I couldn't make out his expression, but I guessed it was petulant – tough.

Off the estate, back in the more populated Lancaster Road, I nearly stumbled over a lifelike guy propped against a wall with its lower body on the pavement. 'Watch it,' said the guy's owner, who was, surprisingly, not a child but an adult, shoving an upturned motorcycle helmet at me coercively. The Golden Kid, in fact. 'Gissa quid for the guy, go on.'

I stopped. 'What the hell?'

'Quite all right,' said the guy.

It was Lil.

'What are you doing?'

'Obbo,' said the Kid. 'Lil thought you needed some looking after, and you can't have just a guy, can you, stands to reason, there's got to be someone taking the readies.'

It would have been ungrateful to point out a) that they were a ludicrously unconvincing duo, or b) that I could have been murdered in Bartlett Close while they were attracting attention in Lancaster Road.

'Good scheme, don't you think?' said Lil proudly. 'I learnt my tradecraft from John Le Carré.'

'If I were him and I heard you say that, I'd sue.'

'Now now Alex, you're just jealous you didn't think of it yourself,' said Lil, attempting to get up. The Kid put his hands under her armpits and scooped her up as if she was weightless.

She dusted herself off, settled her hat more firmly on her head, and said 'I'm glad to see you. We were just about to come to your rescue.'

'Yeah,' said the Kid, shaking his helmet, 'and we made upwards of twelve quid. Not bad.'

Chapter Twenty-Eight

We were all back in the office. Despite my broad hints, they'd refused to be shaken off.

'Tea for everyone?' said Lil.

'Ta. You make a great cuppa,' said the Kid.

'Coffee, please,' I said, and sat down wearily behind the desk.

'We'll need more milk,' said Lil. 'Dermot, could you?'

He stood by the desk, waiting. I unlocked the petty cash and gave him some. He seemed to have embezzled the Guy Fawkes contributions in the short walk from Lancaster Road.

When he'd gone, I said to Lil, 'Can we get rid of him?'

'Why should we?'

'Because until I've found Nick I don't know which men I can trust.'

'You think she's been kidnapped?'

'Yes.'

'Why?'

'Because even though she left her mobile phone behind she still hasn't been in touch yet. Because she isn't back. Because I feel it in my bones.'

'Why are you wary of men, particularly?'

'Because I think she's been kidnapped by the Notting Hill Killer.'

'Do we know the Killer's a man? There's no physical evidence left on the bodies.'

'They've been raped.'

'The rapist could have been a woman using an appliance,' she said. 'In any case, Dermot can't be the Killer. That's absurd. He's a perfectly decent young man from a very close family. And he likes large dark women.'

'How do you know?'

'He's made approaches to Solange.'

I didn't want to waste time arguing with Lil. I wanted to think in peace, and plan my next move. I could feel the sands of Nick's life trickling away while Lil and the Kid drank their tea and told me how clever they'd been.

'I'm going home for about half an hour. There's something I need to do. Snap the Yale on the door if you go before I get back,' I said, and refused to meet her outraged and reproachful eye.

The flat was warm and wonderfully empty.

I took off my boots and picked up the phone for messages, just in case I was completely wrong and there was a call from Nick.

Only one message. 'Hi Alex it's Polly, about four thirty, the plane's been delayed and delayed and I'm coming home, see you soon, maybe we could go out tonight or I could help you work, whatever you want, I've been missing you in Hong Kong you know, we should spend some quality time and—'

Her time was up on the call-minder so I didn't hear any more, though she was probably still burbling into a phone at Heathrow.

Four thirty, she'd said. She should be here soon.

Better Polly than Lil, anyway. Better still, though, would have been Nick. I was beginning to realize how much I missed her taciturn pragmatism. But when she was back I'd have plenty to say about the lax security in the office. I'd no idea the Kid was wandering in and out at will, listening to messages, using the computer. He could spend hours on the Internet at my expense. Plus Lil obviously had the run of the office some of the time.

When Nick was back I'd give her a

bollocking, for sure. Except it wasn't for sure she'd be back, not at all.

I lay on the sofa, under the duvet, stared at the ceiling and tried to make sense of what I knew.

It was like peering through fog. Close up were the figures I could see, that I knew about. Fishburn, in pursuit of the Killer and pointed by me at Bartlett Close, dead. Sam Eyre, who Nick was tracing, still alive and well and living at Bartlett Close. Alive and well even though she was made-to-measure for the Killer.

Made-to-measure. The phrase stuck in my head. Why? I niggled at it, but nothing came.

Leave it, it'd emerge in its own time. What else did I know for sure? Further back, blurred by wisps of fog, was Hobbs. He was certainly Boy. His mother thought he might be the Killer, and a mother's opinion on something like this should go a long way. And Gein had conveniently died when the finger was pointed at Hobbs. And he did know all about the long-ago murders at Rillington Place. And he produced most unusual works of art.

But I liked the works of art. On balance, I was surprised to find, I liked Hobbs. I'd attacked him because I was frightened: by the stuffed spaniel, by Bartlett Close itself, because he wouldn't let me go. He could just have been trying to help a fainting woman, and he was right, of course, you couldn't faint lying down.

Behind Hobbs, there were the really shadowy figures. Fairfax and Jacobs, neither of whom I liked, Fairfax because he seemed vain and shallow and arrogant, Jacobs because he was a coarse yes-man to Fairfax. And then there was Jonno, who seemed grabby and dirty and misogynistic, and the Kid whose bike might have been in Fishburn's road – how many big Harleys were there in Notting Hill? Very few, surely. And even Alan Protheroe who was desperate with impotence and who'd been working since January on a documentary on the plight of men wronged by rapacious women.

And behind all of them, faceless, the Killer, who pounced from nowhere and went back to nowhere and who might have Nick, and who, as Lil had pointed out, might be a woman anyway.

I sat up. Andy Cairncross. I'd have to tell him, or failing him, any policeman. I'd have to tell the police, because I had no answers and no place to go, no place to look for Nick. She wasn't in the flats at Bartlett Close; she wasn't in the workshops. I had no idea where else she might be.

Time to call Cairncross.

I reached out for the phone. As I did, the doorbell rang. I jumped. Then I looked out of the window. Damn. Lil. But she'd seen me and I had to let her in.

She settled on the sofa, looking at me with a kind of peering intensity. 'I know you wanted a bit of peace, but I thought you ought to see this.' She offered me a sheet of paper.

'What is it?' I said.

'An e-mail. It arrived a few minutes ago. I printed it out for you.'

I looked at the origin first. Inge Ericsson, EAPWU, Nairobi. EAPWU? Nairobi? Oh, the Scandinavian I'd spoken to about Barty, probably.

Lil was still peering at me as I read the message.

You should not worry too much, but I do not think you understand the situation here. Eastern Zaire is at war. It is mostly jungle. Maybe a million refugees and more Zaire IDPs are wandering through it, trying to escape the RPF, Kabila, Interahamwe, mercenaries, the Zaire, Ugandan and maybe Burundi armies. It is chaos. There are two holed roads, no better than wide farm tracks, and one rusty railroad for a region the size of France. The only comms are in the big towns. They weren't reliable in peace, and now men with guns are destroying everything they can't steal, they work worse. Nobody knows what is going on. So do not worry too much when I say there is no way of telling Barty anything because there has been no contact with him and his crew for three days – people are always disappearing into the jungle and coming out two weeks later completely OK. We do know that he left Goma Wednesday, trying to reach some refugee camps NW to talk to the guys who organized the Rwanda genocide in '94 before Kabila kicks their ass. This area is now very confused. Barty has GPS, so he knows where he is, but if his satcom isn't working he can't tell us. CNN say there are reports of white journalists caught in fighting near Ubundu, but it's too far for Barty. Anyway, there are reports of everything. The chances are soon Barty will come out of the jungle and reach you by satellite, but we just don't know. So be ready for a long wait and do not think the worst. Things are bad there, but probably not as bad as the TV makes out.

I read it, then I read it again. I must be tired, I thought. Or else my mind was refusing to grasp it.

I read it for a third time and the mists in my brain cleared. Inge was trying to be tactful. She'd been trying to be tactful on the phone, and I'd not listened and thought she was being patronizing. Barty was in a war zone and hadn't been heard from for three days. She kept telling me not to worry, which probably meant *she* was worried, and she knew a sight more about it than I did.

He might have been dead for three days.

Chapter Twenty-Nine

Lil asked who Barty was and I told her. She was brisk and reassuring. 'Zaire is a mess but he must have known that when he went,' she said.

'He did. That's why he went.'

'He's competent and sensible?'

'Very.'

'And experienced in theatres of war?'

'Minor ones, very.'

'Then don't let's worry about him until we have something concrete to worry about. Must get back to the office – things to do. I'll let myself out.'

I hardly noticed she'd gone, what with concentrating on not worrying about Barty. I fetched a glass of water from the kitchen and patted my stomach absently as I drank it. Time enough to think about life as a lone parent when – if – I knew that's what it had to be. Meanwhile, get on with work, which meant finding Nick, which meant ringing Cairncross.

First, I'd wash. Displacement activity,

probably, but I went upstairs to the bathroom and did it anyway.

I only just heard the telephone over running-water noises and leapt downstairs two at a time, mouth still sticky from toothpaste.

'Alex? Lilian Seymour here.'

'Lilian Seymour?'

'Loony Lil,' she clarified crossly. 'We've just received a telephone call from a Richard Fairfax. He seemed to be expecting you to ring him about a job he wants you to do.'

Fairfax was following up? Surely, by now, he'd have talked to Jack Hobbs. They were mates. Would he want to hire a detective who'd kicked his friend in the balls? Unless Hobbs hadn't told him, because Hobbs was guilty – but of what?

Useless to speculate.

'Thanks, Lil,' I said. 'We'll leave it, I think.'

'I took details of the job,' she went on remorselessly. 'Apparently he owns a derelict industrial property on the fringe of the Scrubs. It's frequently vandalized. He wants you to identify the vandals: he thinks it's a gang of youths. I quoted the usual rate and he accepted it. He's particularly anxious that you start straight away.'

'Straight away? Like, now? Five thirty on a

Saturday evening?'

'Yes. And I said you would.'

Pure rage swept through me.

'That's bullshit, Lil,' I said. 'No way. I've got plenty on at the minute, and frankly, it's not up to you to decide.'

'I've committed us,' said Lil, calmly. 'I know that's what Nick would want. She feels very strongly about never turning away work that we can easily do. We're still building a proactive business profile.'

If she'd been in the same room I'd have given her a proactive punch in the nose. 'I'm not going to do it, Lil,' I said, through grinding teeth. 'Ring him back and tell him we'll deal with it next week.'

'No need,' she said. 'I'm free. I'll do it.'

'You'll miss the firework party,' I said, trying to let her down gently. It was a mistake. Offer a sop to an alligator, you get your hand bitten off.

'Thank you for your consideration,' she said, 'but much as I enjoy parties, I enjoy work more. The usual rate, please.'

'Lil – wait in the office, OK? I'll be with you in a minute. Where's the Kid?'

'He's gone to the party. I understood you wanted me to get rid of him.'

'Just wait for me. Don't do anything.

Don't answer the phone, don't–' I broke off, realizing I might put ideas into her head. 'Just stay exactly where you are and make some tea.'

I put my boots on again and went into the kitchen to turn the heating off.

Then I changed my mind and left it on – an extravagance, but I didn't know what time the police'd be finished with me, and I knew I wanted to come home to warmth and a bath. I was still in the kitchen when I heard knocking at the door of my flat.

I let Polly in. 'It took me over an hour from Heathrow, this fog is ridiculous, London has bad feng shui, it must be that, feng shui is very important, my flat in Hong Kong is wonderful to live in because the architect was guided by a feng shui consultant. Where are you going? Can I have some water? What's the matter, you look furious, aren't you glad I'm here? Put me in the picture, do.'

The last thing I wanted was to go through for her what I'd just been through for myself, about Nick's disappearance and the possible candidates for the Killer. But neither did I want to confide in her about Barty and my pregnancy.

Practically, she could be useful. She was

quick, she was bright, she was an outsider, she was an extra body, I could trust her absolutely. And I needed help. Much as I never like to admit it, I needed help.

So I fetched her the water and put her in the picture.

When I finished, she said nothing for a while. Then she said, 'It's all supposition.'

'Fishburn's body isn't supposition. Nick's disappearance isn't supposition.'

'Nick could just turn up.'

'She won't. Not unless I find her.'

'Not unless we find her,' said Polly. 'OK. You go to the police. You go specifically to Cairncross, because presumably your connection with Eddy gives you some cred with him, which might get action quicker. Meanwhile I go round to Fairfax's other place – the vandalized building he's hired you to protect.'

'Why?' I asked.

'Because it's the only address we have. It can't hurt to check it out.'

'But if Nick's being kept there, Fairfax wouldn't have drawn my attention to it.'

'He may not know she's being kept there. Hobbs is Boy, right? You suspect Boy. Hobbs may be using his mate's place with-

321

out his mate knowing.'

'Or it might be a trap,' I said.

'Or it might be a trap,' she agreed.

I looked at her. She was wearing 'rich woman travels to warm climate' clothes, loose cream silk-look but presumably uncrushable trousers and shirt with a coffee-coloured cashmere overcoat slung over her shoulders. 'You can't go poking round a derelict warehouse dressed like that.'

'Of course not,' she said. 'I'll change.'

Lil was waiting in the office, sitting reproachfully upright. When I came in she pointed at a mug of tea on the desk. 'It'll be cold by now,' she said.

'Sorry, Lil. I was held up.'

'I'll go on the assignment straight away, shall I? I've opened a file in the folder *Ongoing Investigations*, called it *Fairfax.1* and backed it up to floppy. You'll find all the details in there, including the rates agreed with the client. Incidentally, I intend to claim expenses for an evening meal, since I've missed supper at the home. I assume you will approve that.'

'You opened a file on the computer?'

'No need to sound so surprised. I am conversant with the use of computers, of course.' She folded her lips together as if they'd been stapled.

She couldn't possibly take the assignment, even if it was absolutely kosher, nothing to do with the Killer. A frail old woman, up against teenage vandals? What could she do? Her sight wasn't good, so she couldn't easily hide and watch. To make a useful identification, she'd have to see them up close, and if she was up close, they'd see her. She couldn't move fast enough to make her escape. She wasn't on a Zimmer frame yet, but her stiff and laboured movements made Fishburn's creaking lumber seem lithe. And her bones must be as brittle as dried flowers. One energetic push, and she'd be in Intensive Care and there'd be an empty bed at the old people's home.

She wouldn't like it, but I braced myself to tell her I'd decided not to let her handle the Fairfax enquiry. I didn't mention Polly: insult to injury.

For a moment she said nothing. Then she launched into her quotation bellow. 'And though/ We are not now that strength which in old days/ Moved earth and heaven; that which we are, we are; /One equal temper of heroic hearts,/ Made weak by time and fate, but strong in will/ To strive, to seek, to find, and not to yield.'

'Who's that?'

'Tennyson.'

'No, I mean who's supposed to be speaking?'

'Ulysses.'

'Another retired librarian, I suppose,' I said unforgivably. I wanted her so annoyed with me that she'd walk away from the whole thing. I didn't want her acting on her own initiative.

'Very well,' she said in a voice tight with resentment. 'Since I'm not wanted, I'll leave you, then.'

It would be best if she left. I could make my peace with her later. 'Right,' I said. 'Thanks. See you.'

She wrapped the scarves round her neck viciously – she was probably, mentally, whipping them round mine – and heaved herself creakily out of the chair.

'Thanks, Lil,' I said again.

'You're out of date,' she said. 'You don't understand the implications of the technological revolution. Just because I'm old, you brush me aside. This–' she pointed to the computer '–with this, my age doesn't matter. Forget guns. These are the equalizers. I have a young lover in Australia, you know.'

'What?'

'Very passionate and virile. We speak over the Net. I've told him all about myself. Some aspects of my information are slightly adapted, of course. We have very similar sexual tastes. Healthy, but robust.'

I didn't point out that her lover in Australia might be a twelve-year-old boy who also adapted his information, and now wasn't the time to start asking whether Nick let her run up bills on my modem.

'You thought *Benbow* was old, because *I* am. He isn't old! He's a YOUNG DOG.' And you think I'm useless because my body's packing up. But THIS ISN'T!' She slapped the palm of her hand against her forehead, dislodging her hat. Lopsided tufts of grey hair made her look disorganized and absurd. She straightened her hat with a powerful downward tug of both arthritic hands and went storming on. 'It's all about knowledge. The knowledge to target information, and retrieve it and co-ordinate it and apply it. Accumulating that knowledge takes YEARS. And I've had years. I've had a LIFETIME. What do you think librarians DO? Whereas you don't even know my name,' she said bitterly.

'What?' I said, losing patience.

'On the telephone. When I gave you my name, you didn't recognize it.'

'I've never heard it,' I said. 'I've always known you as – oh, SHIT! You're Seymour!'

'Please!' she snapped. 'Language! I've never–'

'Leave it out, Lil.' My mind was spinning. 'Come here, look!'

'Well, I–'

I switched on the computer and waited while it clicked and whirred and flashed pointless information and pictures. When it settled down to readiness, I logged on for e-mail and waited again. Every second seemed to stretch and stretch while the whimsical hourglass *wait* icon wobbled about as my hand shook on the mouse. *Read e-mail* click *Internet Cafe* click, flash –

Have collected the following accounts: Lagrange, Atiyah, Leibniz, Ireson, Abel. Do not pursue these clients: debts paid in full. Actively pursue Bourbaki. Consult Seymour.

I moved away from the chair and pointed Lil at it. 'Read,' I said. 'You're Seymour. I'm consulting. Read.'

She read it, her annoyance gone, her

wrinkled face intent. 'And this is?'

'An e-mail that means nothing to me. I thought it was a mistake, or a joke. But it just could be from Nick.'

'Sent from the Internet Cafe on Thursday afternoon,' she said consideringly, 'and she was last seen on Wednesday evening. Yes, it could be.'

'What does it mean?'

'I've no idea, apart from the obvious.'

'What obvious?'

'That it's a coded message of some kind, and probably from Nick.'

'Why?'

'Because of the names.'

'What about the names?'

'They're mathematicians,' she said. 'Famous mathematicians.'

'Famous for what?'

'For work in mathematics. I can't see a pattern,' she said. 'And I don't recognize Ireson. That one's not familiar.'

She took a piece of paper and started doodling, still looking at the screen.

'*Actively pursue Bourbaki*,' I said. 'That's a hint, surely. Is Bourbaki a mathematician too?'

'Yes.'

'What else do you know about him?'

'He's French, I think, and very prolific. His name keeps coming up in catalogues – there's something odd about him, I know there is, but I can't *remember*,' she said, exasperated with herself. 'And I don't understand. If Nick could send a message, why couldn't she express herself clearly?'

'Because she got someone to send it for her?'

'But if she had to disguise the meaning from them, it presumably pertained to them. In other words, they're her kidnappers, in which case, why should they send her message at all?'

'Never mind that. Keep trying to make sense of it. She must have thought you would.'

'Not just me. She could have addressed it to me alone, but she addressed it to you, and advised you to consult me. Presumably the solution requires both of us.'

'Concentrate on the message,' I said, looking at it again myself. What I know about mathematicians could be written on a Rizla paper and leave plenty of room for a rollup. The words meant nothing.

What to do now? Lil could take for ever working out what the message meant, if it did mean anything apart from an appeal for help. Meanwhile the time pressure was building up: I was even surer now that Nick was in danger. 'What's the address of Fairfax's place?' I said.

Without comment, her eyes still fixed on the VDU, Lil fished a piece of paper from her pocket and passed it to me. 'Unit 12, Kensal Industrial Estate.'

'Where's that?' I said.

'Go to Wood Lane, turn right, follow the Scrubs round to the left, that's the industrial estate. I don't know the unit,' she said abstractedly. 'Why include Ireson? Is that a case you've had?'

'No, I've checked that. It doesn't mean a thing.'

'Where d'you keep your CD-ROMs?'

'I don't have any.'

Lil clucked impatiently. 'Yes you do, they came in the package with the PC. Nick told me about them. I need an encyclopedia.' She searched through the desk drawers.

The door opened. 'I'm all set,' said Polly. 'Oh, hi, Lil, how's things with you? How's Benbow?'

'Evening, Polly. We're both well, thank you,' said Lil, her attention only briefly distracted from the CD she'd found and inserted.

'Come on, Alex, give me the address, and I'm off.'

Polly looked quite different, as she so easily could. Old, loose grey jeans, a baggy black sweatshirt, a dark-blue padded waistcoat and charcoal trainers, her short dark hair brushed straight back, no make-up. In the fog and the dark, she'd blend into the background. She wasn't even obviously female. 'Get a move on, Alex,' she said. 'Address?'

'Hang on a minute, Poll. We've got an e-mail from Nick, I think, and we need to work it out first.'

'Dammit,' said Lil explosively, after a flurry of keyboard clicks. 'No Bourbaki in the encyclopedia: too general.'

'What're you trying to find out?' said Polly.

I explained, and she read Nick's message on the screen, over Lil's shoulder. 'Makes no sense to me,' she said. 'Have you tried the Net for Bourbaki?'

'I'm just about to,' said Lil, keying in the password, which she evidently knew better than I did.

I watched her search with a heavy heart. Nick had sent her message two days ago. She knew I was coming back to London on

Thursday: maybe she'd been expecting me to work it out very soon after, expecting rescue every minute since then, and here I was on Saturday evening, no closer. I felt guilty, and stupid.

'Got it!' said Lil, keying in Print. We all watched the paper inch out of the machine, read it as it came, read all of it, only two paragraphs. When it had finished we looked at each other.

The relevant bit was the heading and first line.

Who is N. Bourbaki?

A group of mostly French mathematicians ...

'A group,' Polly said blankly.

'More than one, anyway,' I said. 'Oh, shit.' One had been bad enough, one who was possibly the Notting Hill Killer. But a group – we needed the police. We needed far more than us.

'Tell the police,' said Lil, echoing my thoughts.

'We can't afford the time,' said Polly, echoing my further thoughts. 'We'd have to explain. You call the police and talk to them,

Alex. I'll go round to Fairfax's place, now, in case it's them, which it probably is. That's a group, for heaven's sake. Three of them.'

'I'm coming with you,' I said. 'It'll be much safer with two.'

'And I'll handle the police,' said Lil.

I did what I could to minimize the risks. Very quickly, I told Lil all I knew. About Arthur Fishburn (that upset her – 'oh no! Not Arthur! Poor, poor man!'), about the letters and about James Hobbs being Boy, and about my dealings with Cairncross. She could use his name to get some action from the police. I tried him myself but he wasn't answering, so I left a message with the mobile service telling him where I was going, and that I had reason to believe a woman was being held captive there, possibly by the Killer.

As I said it I was aware how far-fetched my reasoning was. Reasoning was too precise a term for it. Wild guessing, more like. I hoped Cairncross was sensible enough not to scream up with sirens blaring: that way Nick might get killed. If she was there. If, of course, he got the message and bothered to respond to it.

I checked the Kensal Industrial Estate on

the A-Z – Lil's directions were spot-on – and took a torch and the chisel and the wire-cutters which could double as a weapon, and the mobile phone.

'I've brought my phone as well,' said Polly, brandishing it. 'I must remember to cancel the contract, I keep forgetting, it's just been sitting here in London useless, bleeding money–'

Lil interrupted, ignoring Polly. I empathized. 'If I come to any other conclusions, I'll leave a message on your mobile, Alex,' she said. 'I assume you'll keep it switched off.'

'Unless I call 999.'

'Don't forget to check the phone for messages,' said Lil. 'I'll do what I can with the police, and handle things here at GHQ. And the best of luck.'

Chapter Thirty

Polly drove, I navigated.

We began by driving past to take a look. We went north up Wood Lane and into Scrubs Lane with the Scrubs on our left. The fog-screened bonfire party was reaching its climax, the guy just visible as bare sticks and flaring straw-stuffed head on top of a huge blazing pyre. Crowds drifted around the blaze, some children trailed cascades of spitting light from sparklers.

Next came the estate we were scoping out. It seemed completely deserted, but it was hard to tell because it was in almost total darkness: most of the street lights were out. Beyond the estate, the road became a bridge spanning the West London Junction, acres of railway sheds and marshalling yards, with a few trains clattering and shunting and very few people.

'Pull in here,' I said. She stopped in a lay-by. 'Decision time,' I said. 'Do we drive in or do we walk?'

'Walk from where?'

'Not from here. Too far. We could turn round, go back and park on the other side of Scrubs Lane from the Scrubs, then walk casually into the estate and find Unit 12.'

'The advantage being?'

'Surprise. No noise of the car. No warning given to possible kidnappers.'

'Or?'

'We drive in and right up to Unit 12.'

'The advantage being?'

'We're less vulnerable going in, we can sus it out first and we have the car for a getaway.'

'Plan B has my vote,' said Polly.

'OK. Let's do it.'

Back over the bridge, right into the Kensal Rise Industrial Estate. 'Slow down, Poll, I can't read the signs—'

The single road immediately branched into three. 'Take the left,' I said. We crawled along while I tried to get my bearings.

It might not have been outright winner of the Bleakest Place in the Universe Award, but it was in contention. An ill-assorted collection of huts, sheds, outhouses, the common factor being that they looked shabby and seedy, as if they'd been shoddy to start with and abandoned long since. Weeds crept through cracked concrete, corrugated iron roofs were rusted and slipping, and blistered and peeling signs advertised defunct businesses and hopes.

Unit 12 was deep into the estate, up against the high tottering wire fence that bordered the Scrubs. Its name was misleading: it sounded like a dead average unit, another rickety shed. But it was a Victorian factory which must have been there long before the estate proliferated in squalor round it. Built in solid confidence, proud and profitable, with high brick walls, narrow long windows and towering chimneys that once belched smoke and now soared into invisibility in the fog, it was about the size of the red-brick Victorian schools that dotted the London streets.

Compared to the other units, it was huge. But the sign outside was clear, maybe the only clear sign in the place, with a functioning light on it: UNIT 12. It should have been called Satherthwaite's World-Renowned Sanitary Ware or Fuller's Fine Furniture, but its current alias was Unit 12, and it had too much bourgeois self-assurance to be faced down by a label. It was the sign that looked silly.

I didn't point it out to Polly. I let her drive past. All the irrational fears I'd had about Bartlett Close seized me here, only stronger, added to the rational fears that had been solidifying on the drive over as my brain sorted through what I knew.

'Turn right here,' I told her, then, 'right again. Stop on the left.'

When she turned the engine off, the car was in an area with no functioning street lights, well placed for a getaway to Scrubs Lane down the middle road of the three, partially hidden from the factory by intervening sheds, but with a good sight-line from the driver's seat to the main factory door, only about ten yards away and visible through the fog. It was my best shot.

We both got out, into the quiet, and listened. Trains, from the junction. The faint fizz and pop of fireworks from the Scrubs. The murmur of traffic. London is never completely silent.

'Which is Unit 12?' said Folly. 'That ginormous soap factory thingie?'

'Yes.'

'I can only see one door.'

'Me too, but there's probably one round the back.'

'It'd have to be right up against the fence.' Then she gripped my arm. 'Listen!' she hissed. 'Something moved.'

She pointed. I couldn't see movement, but

338

I walked in the direction she'd pointed out, towards a shapeless mound.

There was an explosion, squeals and howls and leaping shapes that streaked away from us and past us.

I jumped. At least a foot in the air, or that's what it felt like. When I landed Polly grabbed my arm and buried her head in my neck. 'OK, Poll, OK, it's only cats. Cats. Feral cats, Poll.' I kept walking towards the mound, and switched on my torch.

'Let's go back to the car, Alex.' She was tugging at my arm.

'In a minute,' I said, and shone the torch on the mound. At first I saw only a tattered black plastic bag with lumps of meat bulging from it. Then I realized what the meat was, switched off the torch, and turned back to the car.

'What was it?' she said. 'Did you see?'

'It's OK, Poll.'

'Tell me. Was it a body?'

'No. Only puppies.'

'Puppies?'

'An unwanted litter, I expect.'

We got back in the car and closed the doors, quietly.

After a moment, she said, 'What sort of puppies?'

'I didn't see.' I had, but the fuzzier her mental picture, the better.

'And the cats were eating them?'

'They have to live,' I said, as neutrally as I could. No point in snapping at her. She needed to get her nerve back.

'I'm sorry,' she said, cleared her throat and squared up her shoulders. 'I'm all right now, really.'

'Of course you are. And we're going home.'

'Why?'

Because you'll be as much use as a Kleenex in a typhoon, I thought. Not blaming her, because I was frightened myself. 'Because I didn't see any vandalism in Unit 12, that's why. No graffiti sprayed on the walls, no broken windows. They're protected by wire screens anyway.'

'No vandalism,' she said. 'Which means?'

'Which means that Fairfax was lying and we're walking straight into a trap. Let's go.'

'No, wait. We only came because we thought it was trap, actually, didn't we? We came to flush them out. And it's also a very good place to keep Nick, isn't it? So she might be in there.'

I looked at the factory. Isolated, well built. A very good place to keep Nick.

'We won't go yet,' said Polly, attempting

firmness through the nervous wobble of her voice. 'Try the mobile, see if Lil's left a message for you.'

I dialled. No message.

'Try Cairncross again.'

I dialled. His mobile service answered. I wished it was a person, not a recorded voice, then I could have asked if he'd picked up my earlier message.

'Listen, Alex, I think we should give it a try.'

'Why?'

'Because if it's a trap we're on the right lines, and Nick might actually be there, and she'll be alive of course.'

'Will she?'

'She bloody well will,' said Polly. 'That's all.' She looked at me. 'I know you think the world's a terrible place—'

'Do I?' She'd never said that before. I couldn't imagine why she thought it.

'Yes, you do. You think if things can go wrong they will, and that people only act out of self-interest, and if they do things to help other people it's because that makes them feel good...'

Thanks for all the hours I spent listening to you chuntering on about your love life, I thought. Thanks for all the foot-sore weary slogs round the shops helping you choose additions to the zillions of clothes already hanging in your cupboards, thanks for the albums full of family photographs I didn't yawn over.

'...and it's like the old story about the economist, the physicist and the engineer on a desert island with a can of beans and no opener. "Heat it till it explodes," says the physicist. "Bash it open with a rock," says the engineer.' She paused. 'What do you think the economist said?'

Stop drivelling, I thought. 'No idea,' I said.

'The economist said, "Assume a can-opener".'

'The point being that economists have no grip on reality?'

'The point being that economists deal with so many variables that they have to start somewhere, so they make an assumption. Like us. We're starting from the assumption that Nick is alive.'

Which doesn't open the tin of beans, I thought. Meanwhile Polly had talked herself into a pause. Then she took a deep breath, and said more calmly, 'If you think I'm not brave enough, just say so.'

'I don't think either of us is stupid enough,' I said.

'We're wasting time. It'll be better if you go in, and I stay here and watch the door. We can have the phones on, an open line, then if anything happens either end we can let the other one know.'

It wasn't such a bad idea. 'You'll stay in the car?'

'No way. I'm a sitting duck here. I'll take cover. In the opposite direction from the mound. Do feral cats eat people?'

'Never,' I said.

She was unconvinced. 'They can't eat live people, anyway. Surely.'

'Of course not.'

'What's your number?' she said, and when I told her, repeated it several times, then dialled.

Brr Brr. I punched the button. 'Hello,' I said into the phone.

'Hi,' she said, giggling. 'What's the signal like?'

'Not bad.'

'Probably be worse inside,' the phone crackled into my ear. 'Never mind. Come on. No, wait, we need the interior light off. Don't want to advertise the car to the bad guys, do we?'

We got out and moved away from the car into the darkness.

'What's that?' she whispered, directly into my car. 'I didn't hear anything.'

'I saw something move. Over there.' She pointed.

'Cat?'

'Bigger.'

We both peered at shadows through the fog. Nothing moved. 'Could be Cairncross's men,' I whispered, not believing it for a moment. But nor did I believe she'd seen anything significant. She was jumpy.

'Yah. Twenty strong policemen.'

'Thirty strong policemen.'

'A hundred strong policemen. We got back-up.'

'We got an army.' We were whispering into each other's ears like lovers, then we giggled like lovers then she squeezed my shoulder like a very frightened but willing woman, well out of her depth, and I set off towards the door, keeping close in to what cover the other buildings offered. When I reached the last building I looked round.

No Polly. She'd vanished. Good girl.

'I'm off,' I whispered into the phone.

'All clear,' she said. 'Go go go.'

This is really, really stupid, I thought as I scurried across open ground towards the blank face of the towering building.

Chapter Thirty-One

Close up the double doors of the factory were enormous, tall enough and wide enough for transport lorries, except it wouldn't have been lorries, it would have been horse-drawn carts when it was built. The doors were solid wood, and smooth, no handles. They must open from the inside. No way I could break through them.

I switched on the torch and flicked it the length of the doors. There was a handle, a small handle. In a wicket-gate.

I jammed the phone in my pocket and tried the handle. It turned, smoothly, and the wicket opened.

Trap, surely. I kicked the door wide open and shone the torch inside.

Nothing that I could see.

I went in, shut the door behind me and moved quite a way down the wall to my right before standing still to get my bearings, far enough from the entrance not to be a complete sitting duck. The floor was stone flagged and mostly clear underfoot. I

345

only had to pick my way round one pile of rusty metal.

No one. Nothing. The darkness wasn't absolute: the pale beams of the street lamp leaked through the tall windows, making the dark darker by contrast. I switched off the torch and listened to the silence.

My eyes gradually accustomed themselves to the dark and the space. I'd expected a derelict industrial museum, but although there were occasional smallish piles of litter or junk metal, there were none of the bulky powerful lumps of Victorian machinery that would once have moulded artefacts proudly stamped MADE IN BRITAIN, tended by workers who took for granted the roar and clatter and the dirt and the heat. Sold for scrap, I supposed, long after they'd stopped making a profit, and with them had gone the heart and muscles of the place.

Now it was effectively an empty rectangular warehouse, with a gallery running round the walls halfway up and what looked like rooms (offices?) off it. There'd probably be stairs up to the gallery at each corner, and judging from the condition of the doors they'd probably still be sound but I couldn't see. I also couldn't see any other doors but there must be some.

I was beginning to relax. I didn't mind the feel of the place. It was damp, of course, and cold and dark, but not menacing.

I stuffed the torch in one pocket and pulled the phone out from another. I listened: just the faint crackle of an open line.

Briefly, I was appalled by the extravagance of the call and tried to remember who had dialled who. 'Polly?' I said quietly.

'All clear,' said her voice in my ear, quite strong. A surprisingly good signal.

'Nothing so far. I'll keep you posted.'

The phone safely in my pocket, I took a last look at the door I'd come through before I set off along the wall, exploring. I felt safeish standing still but didn't like the thought of edging on towards who knew what, with who knew who slipping into the building behind me, and I wasn't going to keep the phone to my ear the whole time, it was too constricting.

There was a bulky object fixed to the wall six feet from the floor, just this side of the door, with thick dark cables snaking down from it. Electricity. Put in long after the place was built. I looked down to the bottom of the wall where the cables ran, and a glint of something paler caught my eye. I bent down, and stared. Nestled among the thick dark cables was a white plastic electric lead. Modern.

Suddenly, I was scared again. The Victorian ghosts of the place were Heritage ghosts, exhausted and exploited and, as resentful as the factory workers had probably been, they'd long slept in Kensal Rise cemetery. The owners had banked their profits and cashed in their chips. None of them cared about me.

But someone had installed this lead, connected it to the mains, and got the mains turned on. Someone was paying London Electricity, month by month, for power in an apparently deserted building. I was intruding on that someone.

At least I had a lead. I followed it, nearly to the corner.

Noise. Little high-pitched noise. I froze.

It was Polly, squeaking from my pocket. 'What?' I said into the phone.

'Someone's coming in now. Small, woman, I think, alone. 999?'

'No. Keep watching.'

I darted away from the wall to the biggest pile of junk I could see and lay face down behind it. If there were overhead lights I was done, but otherwise...

The door opened, someone came in, someone with a deformed and bulbous head and one elongated and bulbous arm. No, wearing a crash helmet and carrying a shopping bag. She walked purposefully, using a torch whose beam came nowhere near me, keeping close to the wall in the same direction I'd been going. Someone familiar with the building. Certainly, from the shape and movements, a young woman, and probably Sam Eyre. She was the only small young woman in the cast of characters to date.

Sam Eyre, part of Bourbaki, the group who'd kidnapped Nick? Why? Especially since I was sure the kidnappers were also the Killers, and the killing had started months before she'd gone to stay at Bartlett Place.

Sam Eyre an intended victim, going willingly to slaughter? Why?

Sam Eyre the housekeeper with a bag of provisions for Nick? I hoped so.

When she reached the corner she stopped, bent down and pulled up a section of the floor. Must be a trapdoor. Then her torch light wobbled, diminished and finally vanished, presumably as she shut the trapdoor behind her.

349

The crash helmet worried me. Was she the Golden Kid's pillion passenger? He'd said she'd liked the Harley. Was he just outside, following her? Or was she wearing the helmet because she rode her own bike? Was the Kid part of the Bourbaki group?

Waste of time speculating. I'd follow her but not immediately, in case she was the bait. There might be someone not far behind her, ready to pounce on me. There might also be someone beneath the trapdoor ready to pounce on me, but it'd stretch their nerves to wait.

'Polly?' I whispered into the phone.

Crackle-crackle of an open line.

'Poll?'

Crackle. I pressed the light button on the phone and looked for the signal strength. It was high. I should be able to hear her.

Squeak from the phone. 'Alex? Alex?'

'I'm here. All well?'

'Thought I heard someone, went to look. Seems all clear.'

'The person who just came in went into a basement place. I'm going to follow. Don't speak unless it's vital.'

'OK. Take care.'

'And you.'

With the phone in my pocket, I went in

the direction of the trapdoor, walking quietly by keeping my weight on the outside of my feet as Barty had once told me stalking soldiers did. It was so quiet I could hear the thumping of my heart, the hiss of the open line and the muffled clanking of the tools in my pocket. I could have done with Barty now. He'd been in the army for years and probably knew a hundred and one deadly uses for torch, chisel and wire-cutters.

A needle-thin line of light marked the rectangle of the trapdoor. I squatted down to listen, but either the place was too solidly built to leak sound, or else there was no sound to hear. A D-shaped brass handle lay flat, flush with the floor.

When I went in, it had to be quick, I knew that. Quick and noisy, to fluster Sam and whoever else might be waiting down there. And I'd go in with my hands free then grab the wire-cutters, the heaviest weapon I had, once I was safely down the steps – there must be steps, or a ladder.

I grasped the brass handle, ready to pull, breathed deeply, and yanked the trapdoor open. Steps, beneath me. 'YAAAAAAA.' I yelled, and scrambled down into the light.

Chapter Thirty-Two

When I landed in the room, I felt seriously stupid. The first thing I saw, in the muted glare of spotlights from the ceiling, was Sam gaping vacantly at me, about five feet away. She looked half-familiar, as people do when you've only seen a photograph of them, but most of all she looked young, and unthreatening, and frightened.

'Oh! Oh!' she squeaked.

I wondered if the SAS had a course in how to behave if you burst into a room in warrior mode in error. I wished I'd taken it, because she was alone, understandably alarmed, and completely non-aggressive. 'Would you like a biscuit?' she offered, fishing in her plastic Tesco bag and producing a packet of chocolate digestives, which she began to open.

I could think of several things she could have said, like 'Who the hell are you' or 'Get out', but according to her parents she was more than a bit dim so perhaps attempted bonding was all she knew. 'I'm Alex,' I said taking a biscuit. 'I'm a private detective. Your mother sent me to find you. She was worried.'

'Oh, she needn't have been,' said Sam breathily. She had a little Marilyn Monroe voice which went well with her little Marilyn Monroe body, curvy in tight jeans and tight pink crop-top exposing a pretty belly button pierced by a gold ring. 'I'm fine. Would you like a cup of tea?'

'That'd be nice,' I said, and she moved to a worktop with a sink in it and fiddled around with a kettle while I looked around the room. It had been refurbished, recently: there were several oil-filled electric radiators, and it was warm and smelt of too sweet air-freshener over an underlying musty damp. There were spotlights in the new ceiling, and CCTV cameras, one in each corner.

The room looked fresh and clean and purpose-equipped, with different usage areas, like a converted loft. There was a bedroom section with a large double bed and two doors in the wall behind it, a little kitchen area, a corner with armchairs and bookcases, and a work area with a large table, tools hanging on the wall, and storage boxes neatly arranged on shelves.

I don't know what I'd expected, but it

hadn't been this. It looked like a display section from IKEA, all the furniture new, or like a show flat. 'So who lives here, then?' I asked.

'Nobody, right now. Rich's just trying it out, as a conversion, then maybe he'll do the whole building, but that'd be expensive, so he just did this bit first, do you take milk and sugar?'

'Just milk, not very much.' And not very much was also what I thought of Rich's chances of selling flats in a building tucked away in the armpit of an industrial estate, not to mention that he'd never get planning permission. Sam seemed to believe what she was saying, though. What I didn't know was whether her reference to Rich by name and without explanation meant that she knew that I knew him, or whether she simply confided, without context, in everyone she met.

'Have a seat,' she said. I took the mug she offered and sat beside her on the sofa.

'So why'd you run away from home?'

'I didn't run away from home,' she said miffily. 'I'm nineteen. I left home. I wanted to get a job and get a life, and I have. And I didn't tell Ma and Pa where I was going because they'd have made a fuss. Pa seems to think I belong to him.'

'So why'd you come to Notting Hill, then?'

'Because of the carnival. I like carnivals.'

That was the first seriously odd thing she'd said, just as I'd started to believe that her parents were the odd ones in this deal. The carnival was only on for two days a year. She could have moved to Scunthorpe and still come down for the carnival. She didn't seem exactly retarded, though. Maybe unusually unsuspicious. She was really very pretty, or she would have been if her huge blue eyes had suggested intelligence or humour or sympathy or warmth or anything whatsoever apart from huge blue eyes. 'How did you hook up with Jack?'

'I didn't. I met Rich and Russell in a pub my very first day, and they said I could stay with them, but Jack insisted I took a room in his place because they have a cleaner and he doesn't and he thought it wasn't fair, and I'm good at cleaning, so I said fine. It didn't matter to me.'

'D'you like Jack?'

'He's OK. Rich and Russell are more fun. They do more exciting things.'

'Like what?'

'Oh, you know.'

I didn't know, but I was beginning to feel creepy again. 'So has there been vandalism here?' That was supposed to be what I was investigating, after all, so I'd better investigate. I got up, moved over to the bedroom area and opened one of the doors. It was a bathroom, neatly fitted out with bath, basin, lavatory and power-shower. Sam followed me. 'That bathroom needed a good going-over,' she said chattily. 'With bleach.'

When? I thought, my muscles tensing. And why? But I wasn't going to ask, not now, not with her so close.

I opened the second door. It opened outwards. Behind it was another door, iron bars, like the front of a cage, fastened with a padlock. Through the bars I saw into the room. About eight feet by six, utterly bare. In the middle of it, Nick, slumped on the floor, asleep or unconscious or pretending to be either. She was breathing, anyway, thank God.

Sam was just behind me. I moved away from her, but she wasn't threatening, she wasn't surprised, she was the same co-operative blank she'd been since I'd arrived. My heart was beating so fast and so loudly I thought she must hear it but she just smiled, and I made a huge effort to sound normal when I spoke. 'What's the matter with Nick?'

'She's been very unhelpful,' said Sam. 'She wouldn't talk to us. She's pulled all her hair out. So we gave her pills to make her sleep. It's time she woke up and went to the bathroom and had a drink of water. She doesn't usually sleep this long. That's what I'm here for, actually. And that's why I brought the chocolate digestives. I think she likes them. She eats them, anyway.'

Questions I wanted to ask flitted and collided like bats inside my head, but first I had to get help for Nick, who was still breathing but whose face was gaunt and grey under its normal yellow and whose scalp was raw and utterly bald. She'd always had the habit of tugging out tufts of her own hair when stressed, but never as badly as this. I refused to imagine the fear and anger she'd felt that had made her do it. She'd been missing coming up for seventy-two hours. How long had she been caged like this?

She was wearing clothes I recognized, an old pair of jeans and a thick black hooded sweatshirt with OFFA'S DYKE on the back. They were crumpled, but I couldn't see any bloodstains. There was no sign of the leather flying jacket she would certainly have been wearing when they caught her, and she was barefoot, but her feet looked undamaged. They'd probably taken away her boots: she'd have kicked.

I wished she'd come round and know that I was here, that she was nearly free. Was she really unconscious, or just pretending to be? If she was pretending, still, now she knew I was in the room with her, was it because there was more danger about than just Sam? Because she knew someone was watching the CCTV?

I took the phone from my pocket with my left hand, keeping a firm grip on the wire-cutters with my right, and keeping my eyes fixed on Sam. Was she only seriously dim and biddable, or actually crazy?

'You won't get a signal down here,' she said. 'I've tried. You'll have to go up to the ground floor. Who do you want to call?'

'A friend who's waiting for me,' I said. 'Sam, did you send an e-mail message for Nick?'

She nodded.

'Why did you do that?'

'Because she asked me. She said she'd get in trouble with her boss, if she didn't. Pa taught me about that. It's very important to do what your boss tells you, always, that way you'll get promoted.'

'I thought you said Nick wouldn't talk? How come she talked to you about the message?'

'She didn't talk, she wrote. She wrote to me that she couldn't talk, she was too frightened.'

'Didn't you feel sorry for her, in the cage?'

She shook her head. 'She needn't have been in the cage. She didn't behave. If she'd behaved, she'd have been all right. I behave. I'm all right. Rich and Russell like me a lot. And Jack.'

'Do you want to come upstairs with me while I make my telephone call?' I said.

She shook her head. 'No, thank you,' she said politely. Her eyes were as empty as ever but there was an element of calculation in her answer, I could feel it. She was beginning to worry me. I wasn't at all sure who was conning who. If she was bright enough to play stupid – if she had any of her father's cruel selfishness, or her mother's obstinacy, come to that – she could be a fully paid-up member of the group, although no girl had been killed since Sam'd left home.

Anyway I wasn't going to take her word for anything. I checked the phone. She was right, the signal strength was very low. I forced myself to look round the room again.

Although it was large, about forty feet long by twenty wide, it obviously occupied no more than a fraction of the factory's under-floor space. There were four wide shallow wire-screened windows high up on the right, in one of the longer walls. They would look out of the side of the factory and I could just see glimmers of street lamp light through them. It was worth trying for a signal.

I moved past Sam, towards the nearest window, and pointed the phone at it. 'Polly, Polly, come in,' I said, watching Sam, who didn't move.

'Alex?'

I could only just hear Polly, but just was enough. Just was just wonderful. 'Call the number we were talking about,' I said. 'Call now.'

'999?' said Polly.

'Yes, now.'

'999, now,' she said. She spoke again but she was fading. She needed her line free to call out, but she'd hesitate to cut me off, so I did it for her. I punched the end-call button, heard the crackly faint intermittent dialling tone, and knew I was alone.

Now was not the time to feel alone. Now was the time to do something. I checked

361

Nick was still breathing, looking for a wink or a twitch or a sign that would show me she knew I was there. Nothing.

I tugged at the padlock on the cage door. 'Do you have a key for this?'

'Oh yes,' said Sam brightly.

'Where is it?'

'In my pocket.'

'Can I have it?'

'I don't think so,' said Sam. 'We need her locked up. Do have a biscuit.'

The missing key itself didn't bother me – my wirecutters or chisel would sort the padlock chain – but Sam's resistance did. I didn't want to threaten her openly, but I was very conscious of my lack of command of the situation, which came mostly because I didn't understand where she stood. Did she realize I'd sent for the police? Did she mind, and if she didn't, was it because she didn't realize that locking people up was illegal, or even unusual?

I forced myself to look round the room again, particularly the work area. The table was spotless but the quarry-tiled floor round it was blotched and stained. I pointed. 'What's that?' I said.

She looked. 'The work table,' she said. 'We mustn't touch.'

'What's it used for?'

'I'm not sure,' she said, her smooth forehead wrinkling in puzzlement. 'Cutting things up, I expect. The floor was very messy there and I gave it a good scrub but the stains didn't all come out. Quarry tiles do stain, and they're hard on the feet. You wouldn't put them in a kitchen now, for instance.'

I glanced at Nick again. She was still breathing, and she hadn't stirred. I wanted to open the cage and check her out properly, but I didn't trust Sam, and I didn't know what fed her eerie self-confidence. Her expression was still lively, open, eager. All of those things, but something else as well, I realized with sudden jolting clarity. Expectant. She looked expectant.

'Look,' said Sam. She pointed above and behind my head. I stepped back and well out of her reach, took a firmer grip on the wire-cutters and glanced up. A red light was glowing beside the trapdoor. 'Pressure pads,' she said smugly. 'There's pressure pads so we know if someone comes in the door or comes down this end of the factory. Isn't that clever?'

'So the light means?'

'Someone's coming,' she said, and smiled.

Chapter Thirty-Three

'Who's coming?' I asked.

She shrugged. 'Don't know.'

I didn't understand Sam's attitude but one thing I did understand, that I was Nick's only protection, and that whichever of Sam's mates was approaching, he'd have a lot more grip on the deep shit kidnapping landed you in than she appeared to, and he'd be a lot stronger besides. I moved back, against the wall, so I was behind the steps.

The trapdoor opened. I pressed myself further against the wall, out of the newcomer's line of sight, and watched Sam's face.

It lit up in welcome. 'Hi." she said, to whoever it was coming down the steps. 'Hi."

It was Jack Hobbs. Before he reached the floor, I swung the wire-cutters in a wide arc and slugged him as hard as I could on the back of the head.

I could tell from the horrid, heavy sound of the blow that it had been accurate, and from the crumpling of his body that it was effective. I checked him over, pulling his body away from the steps. He wasn't dead but he did seem deeply unconscious.

'Why did you do that?' said Sam. She wasn't angry, just mildly curious, and my heartbeat, which had steadied at the sense of danger past, quickened again. Had I knocked out, maybe seriously injured, an innocent man, a possible ally? I thrust away the stab of guilt – I couldn't afford it. When the police came, they could call an ambulance.

'Can you look after him?' I said. 'Have you done any first aid?'

'Oh yes,' she said, moving over to check his airway and put him into the recovery position.

I moved back to one of the windows and dialled Polly. She was outside, alone, and I had no idea who else might be out there. I didn't even know for sure that she'd managed to call the police. I punched the green send button. One ring, then the phone company's recorded voice suggesting I leave a message. Her phone was switched off.

Savagely, I punched the red button, ready to dial 999 myself, and then saw my own phone's digital display flashing at me.

MESSAGE MESSAGE MESSAGE, it said.

The message must be from Lil. I punched in the message-retrieval number, noticing how sweaty my fingers were, slipping on the keys. Fear. Nearly panic.

The message scrolled from right to left.

DOES LALIA MEAN ANYTHING? REPEAT LALIA? GOOD LUCK. LIL.

Lalia. The initials of the list of names in Nick's message. Meant nothing to me – yes it did! Echolalia. Russell Jacobs with his odd habit of repetition. Russell Jacobs? Why was he the only one Nick had tried to name individually? Was he the leader of the group?

I didn't have time to speculate. I cleared the phone, ready to dial 999. No signal. Something was blocking the signal, or it had just faded, as they do.

The phone went back in my pocket, the wirecutters into my right hand, and I darted across to the cage door and started wrestling with the padlock, watching Sam and Jack all the while.

Sam was on her feet in a flash when she saw what I was doing. 'No.' No." she shouted, and started pulling at me and

367

beating me around the head with her fists. She was strong for her size but no street fighter: she didn't pull my hair or go for my eyes or bite or any of the effective things. I stamped hard on her feet with my boot and she screamed in pain and clung to me.

As I pushed her off I felt the chain part and the cage door swung open. Nick didn't stir. She was still breathing, but she looked like death. I hoped she was faking unconsciousness: if so, she'd probably make her move now.

Sam had tumbled backwards onto the floor, where she now squatted, glaring at me. No more Miss Congeniality. I'd have to knock her out, or tie her up. Tie her up what with? Or get Nick out of the cage and lock Sam in it.

I moved towards her and she shrank away, scuttling backwards on her bottom and hands, empty eyes filling with empty tears. Perhaps she thought I couldn't do violence to a pretty, small, young person oozing vulnerability. She was wrong. I could do any amount of violence to a person who'd colluded in torturing Nick, and who had just tried to stop me releasing her.

'Get up,' I said, when she reached the back wall, behind the steps.

She got up, slowly, dusted off her jeans, and smiled at me. Her whole body language had changed. She was confident again: my nerves twitched and my muscles tightened. It was all I could do to keep still.

'Sam?' I said.

She pointed over my shoulder, down to the far end of the room. I stepped back several paces in case it was a trick, turned sideways and gave a quick glance in the direction she was looking, towards the armchair/bookcase corner. A red light was flashing, high up on the wall above the bookcases Someone must be coming in. But where? I couldn't see a door.

'Everything's all right now,' said Sam, gleeful. 'You can't hurt me. My mates are here.'

'Shut up,' I snapped, my fingers itching to slam the wire-cutters right into her gloating face, my eyes switching back and forth from her to the light to her to the light to her again – one of the bookcases was moving. It creaked as it moved, opening like a door into the room, but towards me so I couldn't see who was behind the door.

Then it stopped moving, half-open, and the creaking stopped and in the silence I could just hear the cheers and whoops from the firework party in the Scrubs. Normal people. A crowd of normal people that I couldn't reach.

'Rich?' said Sam.

Fairfax stepped into the room, relaxed, smiling. He looked pleased with his little trick and with himself, but as far as I could see he wasn't armed. He was wearing the same pseudo-country-gentleman clothes he'd worn when I met him that morning, and looked just as bland and ordinary. My heart jumped and thudded.

'Surprise, Alex,' said Fairfax

'Not really,' I said. 'This is your place and you're the one who kept Nick in that cage. Are you the Notting Hill Killer, by any chance?'

'That's right,' he said. 'Clever girl. You worked it out. And I'm afraid I'll have to punish you. Then kill you, actually.' He looked pleased at the prospect. He nodded at Hobbs's unconscious body. 'Thanks for your help with Jack. I think I'm going to blame it all on him. Bit odd, Jack. All those stuffed animals, not normal, d'you think?'

He was standing in the direct glare of one of the ceiling spots and in the centre of one of the camera sweeps. His blond hair glowed like a halo in the light, and he was aware of it and enjoying it, I was sure.

He could hardly kill me from there. Sam, on the other hand – I flicked my eyes back to her. She'd moved to block me off from the steps and a way out, not that I was going to take it because I had to guard Nick. Sam was only about four feet from me, much too close. She was poised lightly on the balls of her feet, ready to jump.

I weighed the options. She wasn't much of a fighter and one good crack with the wire-cutters would sort her out, but if I did that Fairfax would surely move to help her, and what I needed was time, because Polly must have called the police and they must be coming.

'You can't get away with it,' I said to Fairfax. 'How can you blame it on Jack? You own this place–'

'Jack's my friend. He knew it was here. He could have furnished and equipped it, couldn't he? Nobody can trace it back to me, I promise you. Do you want me to tell you all about it?'

He was prepared to talk. Probably I should keep him talking, until the police came. But his self-satisfied tone annoyed me. More than annoyed me, I realized. I was angry, furiously angry, at what he had done to Nick, to the murdered girls.

'You'll want me to tell you all about it,' he said again.

'No, thanks,' I said. 'I'm not interested. Save it for the police psychiatrist.'

A flicker of doubt crossed his face, then it settled back to complacency. 'You'll want to know how I found the girls, of course, specially since I gave you a clue, and you didn't get it. I'll tell you the clue again, then see if you can work it out...'

He seemed pleased with his kid's game, and he was standing still. So far, so good. I glanced at Sam, who'd settled down to listening, no longer poised to jump, and Nick, who was in exactly the same position, and Jack Hobbs who had shifted a bit and was quietly groaning. Then I felt a wave of anger, but not mine. Where from? Sam? Was there someone else in the room?

Fairfax was talking on. 'Listen now, concentrate, here's the clue. My job. I'm a civil servant. And I'll give you another clue. I work in the Passport Office.'

'Rich,' said Sam. Her voice had an attention-claiming, warning note, like a child's while it tugged at a parent's sleeve.

'What is it?' he said.

'They might be coming. Soon.'

'Who?' he said impatiently.

'The police, maybe. Someone. *She* came, didn't she?' – pointing at me – 'And she spoke to someone on the phone. We'd be in trouble, wouldn't we? I don't want to be in trouble.'

She was, sensibly, telling him to get on with it, and he wasn't happy with her intervention. 'Leave it to me,' he snapped. 'I know what's best.'

'But Rich–'

'I'm talking to Alex. Passport Office, you see? Height, address, photograph. I've always had very high standards in women.'

'Rich–'

'Yes, Sam, women like you. I like women like you,' he said soothingly.

She flashed him a white-toothed smile, but it had the mechanical emptiness of a lighthouse beam. 'I'm glad you like me,' she said, 'but shouldn't we–'

'Quiet,' he snapped. 'I'm in charge.'

He clearly wasn't. I've never known anyone who really was in charge having to state it. This man has a reality problem, I thought. He had to know best, he wouldn't accept evidence. Maybe that was how the killing had started. When the girls, normal girls he met socially who'd reached his 'high

373

standards' of looks, hadn't responded to him as he wanted, he'd created his own world down here and brought strangers to a place where he made all the rules. He had fantasies but he wasn't effective. Or maybe–

'Rich,' said Sam, more urgently this time, 'I really think–'

'Quiet, Sam,' said Fairfax. 'I don't want to hear from you again, do you understand?'

'Yes, Rich,' she said, sulky-meek, shuffling her feet and hanging her head.

'Alex wants to know,' he went on explaining to her. 'Alex wants to know and I think it's fair to tell her... You'll want to know why we kept Nick,' he said to me.

'No I don't,' I said, feeling the wave of anger again, trying to trace it to source. Not Fairfax, not Sam, not me – who? Where?

'She wasn't frightened,' said Sam. 'Rich didn't like it because she wasn't frightened. He likes people to respect him, don't you, Rich?'

There was an element of needle in this, I was pleased to hear. They weren't arguing exactly, but they weren't singing the same song either, and she wasn't obeying his direct order to shut up.

'It's time,' said Fairfax. He sounded different: purposeful, not gloating. He was looking up, over my head.

I looked up too, as Sam skittered round me and ran down the room to Fairfax. No red light had flashed, but the trapdoor was open and someone was hurtling down the steps – Polly! She landed in a heap at the bottom and scrabbled to get up, one arm clearly useless – broken? 'Omigod,' she squealed, then 'look out Alex, he's coming. Look out!'

Russell Jacobs was on the steps, standing still and assessing the situation. He was even bigger than I remembered and his ugly awkwardness had crystallized into pure menace.

'Is it time?' said Fairfax.

'Time, yeah,' echoed Jacobs, but now his echo was an order. He was the boss, I should go for him, but Polly was there and could delay him and Fairfax must be eliminated.

'Look out,' squawked Polly again but even before she'd spoken, urgency kicked in. I saw Fairfax heading towards the work corner with its shining ranks of tools, presumably to use on us, and I concentrated everything in me on the back of his head. Fear fuelled me down the room, the wire-cutters clutched in my hand. As he reached up for an axe, I swung at him, twice, three times. He crumpled at the first blow. After that, I was hitting a body, unconscious or perhaps dead, but I didn't care.

Then Sam was on me, clutching and screaming. I shoved her off with a punch meanly aimed straight at one of her nipples, her hysterical screaming changed to a screech of pain and she crawled under the operating table and curled up like a foetus.

'No no no!' shouted Polly. I turned to see Jacobs, knife in hand, just about to reach Nick. Polly was sprawled on the floor, her good arm scrabbling for something in her jeans pocket, pulling it out. She hurled herself towards Jacobs, fingers working at the small gleaming object she held in her hand. He checked and stumbled, but then kicked Polly away and kept on going, towards Nick.

Before I could move to her defence, the room was filled with howling.

I knew it was Nick who got up and grabbed Jacobs by the throat and threw him out of the cage room, knife spinning uselessly away, and followed him and seized his hair with her left hand and jammed the thumb and two fingers of her right hand into his eyes and kept jabbing into the bloody pulp, howling all the while, but Nick didn't look like Nick, she looked possessed, demonic. I wanted to stop her before she tore his face off – not for his sake – but I was frozen by the horror of the sight, which I wanted to stop watching, and by the terrible noises filling the room. Sam's screeches, Nick's howl, and louder than either, Jacobs's bellows of agony and rage.

It was Polly who moved first and stopped it. She scrambled up and threw her functional arm around Nick and pulled her, still howling, away.

After a moment Nick stopped struggling and fell silent. She looked with disgust at the blood and pulp on her right hand, and began wiping it on her jeans. I forced myself to focus on Nick and Polly, because what I'd already seen of Jacobs's ruined face was going to be hard enough to forget, but his bellows were increasing in volume and turning into tortured wails which blended with another, familiar, approaching wail. Police sirens.

Sam heard them. She crawled out from under the table, stepped over Fairfax's immobile body without glancing down at it, and said to everyone and no one, 'It wasn't my fault. I didn't do it. It's not fair.'

'When the police come, don't say anything,' I said.

'But it wasn't–' she began, and I cut across her.

'You're in shock. Don't say anything,' I repeated. Much as I loathed the girl, her mother was my client, after all.

Then the police came.

Chapter Thirty-Four

They were uniformed police, ordinary patrol coppers, well out of their depth. They stepped down into Fairfax's factory basement and at first stared, bemused, at the carnage it contained.

The older one was a heavy-set beef-faced East Ender in his forties who looked as if he supported the local football team, devoted much of his off-duty time to home improvements and believed that the country was going to the dogs. His eager-to-please twentyish constable looked as if he spent his time trying to prove to the older one that he wasn't one of the dogs the country was going to.

The East Ender phoned for ambulances. Sam approached the young constable, crying. He still looked bemused, but with a trace of 'Poor little thing' sympathy, and took her name and address.

Russell Jacobs had stopped howling. I kept my eyes averted from him but hoped he'd fainted. I went up to Nick and patted her on the shoulder. 'Sorry I took so long to find you,' I said.

''Sall right,' she said. 'I was stupid to get caught.'

That was a handsome admission from Nick, who never apologized. I'd been afraid she might have been traumatized, might have lapsed back into her elective silence. I'd been wrong.

'But it was a bloody stupid message you sent. Clever-clever. How'd you know I'd even get to hear Russell Jacobs talk?'

'I didn't, but I thought it'd help if you did. He's the scary one.'

'Not any longer,' I said. We both looked at him and looked away.

'I didn't know what Sam could work out and what she couldn't,' said Nick, justifying herself. 'Sometimes she was half-witted, but other times – I couldn't say anything obvious at all.'

'It was a brilliant message,' said Polly soothingly.

Nick looked at her. 'Don't just stand there,' she said to me, bossily. 'I need water. Get me some.'

I went to the bathroom to fetch her water. When I came back, she'd moved Polly over to the work area and was splinting her fore-

380

arm with knives and torn towels. Polly looked very white and once her arm was in a sling Nick sat her on the floor with her head between her knees and hugged her. 'You did good,' she said. 'Yuck Polly, you stink though.' She gulped down the water I'd brought. I sniffed and for the first time noticed a miasma of pungent, expensive perfume. Nick smiled. 'Yeah, she sprayed his face, held him up for a moment, gave me time.'

'Shouldn't we do something to help him?' I said. Jacobs had started moaning again.

Nick smiled again, without amusement. 'I don't think so,' she said.

While the older policeman listened to Polly's account of why she had dialled 999 and the younger one checked the casualties I took Nick aside. 'Did Jack Hobbs have anything to do with it?'

'Who?' she said blankly. I pointed him out, realizing, worried, that he'd been unconscious for some time now.

'Nah. It was three of them. That shit–' she pointed to Jacobs and my eyes didn't follow her finger – 'the posh blond git and the tasty little robot.'

'Bourbaki,' I said.

'You don't want to hear what they did to

those girls.'

'But Sam wasn't involved in that, was she? Did she even know about it?'

Nick shrugged. 'I didn't hear them talk about it in front of her, if that's what you mean, and I never knew what she understood and didn't understand about anything. She just liked attention and flattery and control. Fairfax was all over her. And she sucked up to him by jerking me around, and she enjoyed that plenty, trust me. *You must do what Rich says, Nick, Rich isn't pleased with you, Nick, that's why he's punishing you.* Yuck.'

'But maybe Fairfax was all over her because she was due to be the next victim.'

'Could be. Or could be she was his dream woman, so he didn't have to get rid of her. But Russell would have. Very practical, our Russell. Don't you worry about him. He deserves what I gave him, and more.'

'I'm not worried about Russell, but about you,' I said gently. She was shaking, with fear or anger or reaction, I didn't know.

I squeezed her arm and she pulled it away. 'You can stop worrying. I'm a public benefactor, acting in self-defence. He was going to kill me. Listen, did you take the phone off charge? I forgot it. I was pissed off at Laverne. I'm really sorry about that.'

I passed her the phone. 'It's working fine,'
I said.

The older policeman called Andy Cairncross, at my suggestion. When he got
through, he said 'Sergeant Cairncross says
he knows all about you,' his tone of voice
suggesting Cairncross wasn't pleased with
me.

I had tangible evidence of this when
Cairncross arrived at the same time as the
third ambulance crew. By that time Jacobs
and Hobbs had gone in the first ambulance,
Fairfax, still unconscious, and Sam,
claiming to have broken ribs, in the second.
Cairncross wouldn't allow me to go to the
hospital with Nick and Polly but sent me
back with the patrol officers to Notting Hill
police station, where I was put into an interview room, by myself, and ignored.

I supposed someone would come and take
a statement, eventually. Very eventually. I
was the least of their concerns, a very minor
player. The SOCO people would be swarm-
ing all over Fairfax's basement, senior
officers on the Killer investigation would be
pouring into Hammersmith Hospital to talk
to Fairfax and Jacobs and Sam and Jack

383

Hobbs, if he was conscious yet. I hoped he was and that he'd make a full recovery. But most of all the detectives must be drooling over Nick, alive and intelligent and a witness, especially since her captors had obviously talked openly in front of her. And since none of the police yet knew that I'd been the one who found Fishburn's body I'd be lucky if they took my statement by Christmas.

Or midnight, anyway.

I looked at my watch. Eight o'clock. Only two hours since Polly and I had set off to the industrial estate. It had seemed much, much longer and I wondered how long Nick's seventy-two hours of captivity had felt.

Then I stopped thinking about it, because it upset me and didn't help her. I fiddled with the knobs on the big old rusty radiator, trying to coax it into giving me enough heat to take the arctic chill out of the air. When that failed, I kicked the radiator until it clanked into a semblance of life. Then I made myself as comfortable as the upright chair allowed, tried not to think about how much I wanted a cup of coffee, reflected that, though it said INTERVIEW ROOM on the door, the dump I was in reminded me of an ill-equipped broom cupboard, propped my feet on the scarred wooden table, and rang my office. I hoped Lil was still manning GHQ. I had work to do.

She answered on the second ring, and I talked over her anxious questions, re-assuring her that Nick was safe and mostly unharmed, though I wondered as I said it how true that was, remembering the wreck of her scalp and what she'd done to Jacobs. I told Lil what I needed: for her to give me the Eyres's telephone number from the files, and then bring me my notebook. Further chat could wait till she came. I knew Lil wanted to pick over what had happened, and I'd have to go along, but not till Pauline Eyre knew the mess her daughter was in. Pauline was still my client however much her fault it was for conspiring in the family sickness, whatever Sam had done. Fairfax hadn't created Sam, he'd merely adapted her. Her desire for attention and control, no matter what it cost anyone else, had curdled in a pot cooked by both Eyres. Dr Eyre because that was how he functioned, and Pauline because she hadn't stopped him. And she'd suspected something about Sam. What'd she said about her, in my office? Something about *she has her own ways.*

The Eyres's number rang and rang. Finally he answered. 'Dr Eyre? Alex Tanner. I need to speak to your wife, urgently. Is she there?'

'I'm not accepting calls from you, Miss Tanner. Not now, or at any other time. We can manage perfectly well without your rude and amateurish assistance–'

'Dr Eyre, your daughter is currently in hospital, shortly to be charged with a serious crime. Do you or do you not want your wife to know the details? Sam needs a lawyer, urgently.'

I heard Pauline Eyre's voice protesting in the background, then she was on the line. 'Miss Tanner?'

'I have bad news, I'm afraid.'

Her response was bizarre, but it betrayed what I had suspected. Instead of asking what had happened to Sam or if she was all right, she said, 'What has she done?'

For a moment, the words hung and crackled on the line. I didn't want to receive them: she wanted to swallow them back. Then she said, lamely, 'Has she been in an accident?'

I told her what I knew. She didn't waste time discussing it. She was repeating the name of the hospital when her husband took over. 'My wife is distraught,' he snapped. 'Distraught as a result of your exaggeration and interference, as a result of your intrusive trouble-making–'

I punched the end-call button before he could get further into his blame-shifting stride. I blew on my chilly fingers and watched my breath curl up and dissipate in the freezing air, and wondered what Pauline had expected, and how much she'd known, and exactly why Sam had been educated at home, and what that education had been.

The conversation, and the thought of Sam herself, left me with a bitter taste. I realized that all my muscles were knotted up. It was as if I'd been holding myself tense for hours, not knowing that I was doing it. I rolled my head around, slowly, and did some stretches. That was better.

But not completely better. My body was more relaxed but my mind kept going back to the bright light-flooded basement room, the brutality of Nick's imprisonment, and the stains on the tiled floor around the work table. I kept pushing the pictures away. Evil doesn't interest me and I can never understand why people find it so enthralling and gobble up books and films about it, and manage to be so continually surprised when it erupts in real life. Surely anyone who's been to school must know how vile children can be. Some of them never grow out of it, that's all. The police would sort out what they'd done and the courts would sentence them and then the shrinks would get on to it and try to explain why they'd done what they'd done, which is much easier of course in retrospect. What they never explained was why other children with as near as dammit the same influences had grown up to be criminals of a different type, or not to be criminals at all.

Enough. I focused on the tattered posters still warning against infestations of the Colorado beetle which, if it had any sense, would have long ago retreated to Colorado before it froze solid. I kicked the radiator; it died into silence. Then I heard Lil, bellowing.

'I know not whether Laws be right/ Or whether Laws be wrong;/ All that we know who lie in gaol/ Is that the wall is strong;/ And that each day is like a year,/ A year whose days are long.'

The jaded WPC who let her in to the Interview Room rolled her eyes at me and slammed the door behind her, which shocked the radiator into gurgling life. 'I'm not in jail, Lil,' I said, 'just waiting to give a statement.'

'Since Oscar Wilde didn't see fit to write "The ballad of waiting to give a statement in Notting Hill Police Station", you'll just have to take what you're given,' she said tartly. 'For each man kills the thing he loves,/ By each let this be heard... I brought you coffee.'

She plonked two takeaway plastic cups on the table and herself in the other chair; pulled off her woollen cap and tugged at her flattened mop of grey curls. 'Hat-hair,' she said. 'A cross I have to bear, in winter. Here's your notebook. And there hasn't been...' her voice tailed away into silence, then she changed tack. 'Both those coffees are for you.'

'There hasn't been...' I prompted, feeling that on several occasions already I hadn't listened to Lil when I should have, and resolved not to make the same mistake again.

'Any answer from Cairncross,' she said, dodging an issue, I thought. Presumably she'd come back to it. 'I kept trying his number but I never got an answer. And I did talk to the police. They said they'd check it out, but I didn't believe them.'

'Never mind. Good work on Nick's message: Lalia did mean something to me – Russell Jacobs, the big man you saw in the pizza place having lunch with Fairfax and Sam, has echolalia.'

'Did Nick name him specifically because he was the most dangerous of them?'

'Could be. Or could just be that he was the easiest to point out in a coded message. Echolalia was part of a private joke between Nick and me. She got Sam to send the e-mail on the pretext that it was part of her job...' I stopped talking. Lil wasn't listening.

'How long are you likely to be kept here?' she said.

'No idea. You don't have to stay, though, I just needed the notebook.' I was surprised she wasn't full of questions about what had happened.

'It isn't that,' she said, looking at me with a kind of peering intensity. 'How do you feel?'

'Cold. Tired. Worried about Nick and about a perfectly innocent young man who's unconscious in hospital because of me. Better for the coffee. How do you feel?'

'Worried about you,' she said. 'There hasn't been a further e-mail from Africa–'

'Never mind,' I said repressively. I absolutely wasn't going to talk to her, or anyone, about Barty. Not yet. Nor was I going to think about it myself.

'And I am also concerned,' she went on remorselessly, 'about your physical condition.'

'I'm fine—'

'Because I believe you are pregnant,' she said defiantly.

'None of your business,' I said. 'None of your bloody business.'

'And I want you to know that I have every intention of looking after you.'

That was too much. 'Shut up, Lil,' I shouted.

She patted my hand. 'Have a good cry,' she suggested, and to my own horrified surprise, I did.

Chapter Thirty-Five

Embarrassingly, once I'd started crying, I couldn't stop for what seemed like an age but was probably only about five minutes while Lil kept the Kleenexes coming. Finally she said briskly, 'Finish your coffee, then you can tell me what happened earlier this evening.'

So, with a few snuffles, I did. She kept asking questions so she got the full detail. I wasn't sure whether this was all curiosity or partly tact, but anyway she deserved to hear. Eventually she said, 'What very unpleasant young people. And you think that Fairfax and Jacobs, together, were the Killer initially? And they selected Sam as a victim, for physical reasons, but she then became part of the group?'

'Yes.'

'And Arthur Fishburn was killed by one of them?'

'Probably Jacobs. The first time I met them, noonish today, Jacobs was late. I think he did it then. The time fits.'

'And you think he did it because Fishburn had found something out?'

'Yes. I'd pointed Arthur in their direction, Arthur was obsessed with the case; he may even have confronted them. Maybe Nick can tell us.'

'And you also suspect them of killing Philip Gein?'

'Yes.'

'Why?'

'Gein was asked to talk to Jack Hobbs about his mother's suspicions that Jack was the Killer. He may very well have told his mate Fairfax, thinking it was funny or annoyed by it. Fairfax wouldn't want any suspicion even of someone sharing a house with him.'

'And Jack Hobbs wasn't part of Bourbaki?'

'No, Nick said he definitely wasn't, and Fairfax talked about putting the blame on him.'

'If he wasn't part of it, why did he go to the industrial estate at all? Do you think he suspected them?'

'He could have. Does it matter?'

Lil looked at me anxiously. 'Alex, there's something wrong—'

But I didn't get to hear it, because Andy

Cairncross came in and chucked her out. 'Who's your lawyer?' she shouted from the corridor.

'Don't need one,' I called back.

'Alex – Alex, listen–' Her protesting voice receded down the corridor. She did fuss.

The first thing Cairncross told me was that Jack Hobbs had recovered consciousness. The hospital were keeping him in for observation, but they reckoned he'd be OK. Ditto Fairfax, but I didn't care about him. Polly was waiting at the hospital to get her arm properly set, and Nick was, apparently, in terrific form, though again the hospital were keeping her and she had police in her room in case she remembered anything further.

After that, the statement procedure was quite quick. It would have been quicker if any of the electric sockets in the Interview Room had worked so he could use a cassette recorder. As it was he had to find a spare constable to take it down in longhand, and few constables were spare that night.

I'd already decided not to volunteer the fact that I'd found Fishburn's body, and Cairncross didn't ask me. Apart from that I had nothing to hide. He was abrupt but not hostile. I got the impression that he'd spoken at length to Polly and that my statement was something of a formality. I could feel, lurking behind his businesslike manner, an enormous satisfaction and relief, which I could well understand.

When I'd read through the statement, signed it and the constable had taken it away, I stood up and Cairncross said, 'Where are you off to?'

I hadn't thought, I looked at my watch. Nearly ten. 'Hammersmith Hospital, to see Nick and Polly,' I said.

'You might have to wait to see Nick. She'll probably still be talking to us.'

I shrugged. 'Whatever. I'll wait.'

'D'you want a ride over? I'm going in that direction.'

'No, thanks, I'll walk. I need some fresh air.' I also, needed to pick up some food on the way: I couldn't remember when I'd last eaten, and the baby probably needed zinc or protein or calcium – I'd have to get a pregnancy book to find out what. First thing tomorrow.

I stepped out of the police station and breathed in the damp air. The fog had gone; I almost missed it. I didn't like change, at the moment. Now, it was raining. Hard. Plastering my hair to my head, running down into my eyes, dripping inside my collar and soaking my jeans.

I walked up the Grove, back to my flat, for a quick bath and a change of clothes. On the way I bought milk and smoked mackerel and french bread and fresh orange juice, which I ate and drank in the bath, and thought about Barty. I comforted myself that he was sharp and wily and experienced, and if he came out at all he'd probably come out with great footage. He didn't seem far away, either: it felt almost as if he was in the living room downstairs, and would answer if I called.

I fell asleep in the bath, briefly. A soggy floating lump of bread bumped into my face and woke me. I got out feeling more tired rather than less, dressed, shoved some things in a bag for Nick, and drove Polly's car over to Hammersmith Hospital.

I was directed to a small corner waiting room on the third floor. It was a bleak light-green box with the exhausted air of a disregarded public space used round the clock by unhappy or anxious people. Polly was in there alone, her arm plastered, flicking through, a tattered supermarket lifestyle magazine aimed at followers of a lifestyle light-years removed from her own. The corridor outside was full of policemen: some of them uniformed, guarding doorways; some in plain clothes with a 'We've got 'em' glint in their eyes and, a spring in their steps, bustling about.

We hugged. A hug of relief on both sides and thanks on mine. 'You were brilliant,' I said.

'So were you. And lucky. We were both lucky. Let's talk about it some other time, OK?'

I looked at her blankly. Was she sedated? Why wasn't she gabbling away as usual, telling me all the details, swamping me with words? 'You've had painkillers?' I said.

'Of course.'

'Tranquillizers?'

'No, why? I'm OK, apart from the arm and it's a clean break. It's you I'm worried about.'

'Me?'

'Yeah, Lil came by, she's in with Nick now. She said you were off with the fairies. She said you didn't even get a solicitor before you gave your statement, and your brain wasn't working.'

'Did *you* get a solicitor?'

'I hadn't hit anyone. Jack Hobbs could have died – maybe he still could – and how can you call that self-defence?'

'He's all right,' I said huffily, 'and my brain's just fine.'

Polly was looking at me with the same anxious protective expression that Lil'd had earlier, and I was equally irritated. 'Lil told me about Barty,' she said.

'He'll be OK,' I said. My tone warned her off. 'Why don't you take a cab home, Polly? You should be in bed. I brought your car but you can't drive with that arm, and you shouldn't hang around here. I want to see Nick.'

'I'll wait for you,' she said firmly.

There was a policeman outside Nick's room, a WPC sitting inside on a chair in the corner, a nurse taking Nick's pulse, and Lil yammering.

Nick looked good. Her head was bandaged, her colour was better, her face was as animated as I've ever seen it, and she was talking more than I've ever heard her talk to strangers. She was even responding to the WPC's feeble jokes.

When the nurse had left and Lil had gone

to wait with Polly (why wouldn't she just go home?) and the WPC was tactfully studying a magazine with exaggerated interest, I sat down on a chair by the bed.

'You look terrible,' she said.

'I'm tired,' I said. 'And I'm worried about Barty.'

'Lil said. He'll be fine, you know.' She sounded suddenly older, trying to look after me. 'Go home and get some sleep. We can talk tomorrow.'

That course of action was powerfully appealing. Not just rest, but oblivion, for a while. But I couldn't. I had to pretend some interest, first, in what had happened to Nick, so I asked.

'I'll make it short,' she said. 'I wanted to get out of town for a while because I was pissed off at Laverne. On the way to the station I dropped by Bartlett Close because there'd been a sighting of Sam there and I wanted to confirm it before I left. I was poking around when Fairfax spotted me, overreacted and hit me. Then Jacobs decided they had to get rid of me because they didn't want a complaint to the police which might attract attention to them, but Fairfax wanted to torture me first, so I was put in the cage at the industrial estate. I managed to con Sam into sending the e-mail to you. I had to keep it obscure so she couldn't understand, and I just hoped if you took over the Eyre case you'd meet them and I knew you'd remember echolalia.'

'Sorry it took me so long,' I said again. 'D'you want me to ask how they treated you?'

'Not really,' she said. 'Let's leave it.'

'It's good for you to talk,' said the WPC. She was young, fresh, plump with blonde frizzy hair and eager, slightly dim blue eyes.

'I know, thanks, maybe later,' said Nick, more obliging than I'd ever heard her. Maybe what'd happened would hit her later, or maybe the best cure for a period of captivity was to put your captor's eyes out. 'So anyway because they were going to kill me they talked quite freely in front of me. Fairfax was the pervert, Jacobs the practical one. He didn't mind a bit of rape and torture and murder, but actually I think he was planning to blame it all on Fairfax and rip him off somehow, because Fairfax is the rich one. Hobbs – is that his name? I never met him – had absolutely nothing to do with it, and I don't know why he turned up in the basement when he did. Then they set the trap for you, mostly because of someone called Arthur Fishburn who they thought was working for you and had got onto them.'

With the WPC's ears flapping, I couldn't enlighten her about Fishburn. 'What about Sam?' I said.

'I couldn't make her out. Sometimes she seemed half-witted, other times she enjoyed keeping me locked up. Something seriously wrong there. She doted on Fairfax. Called him *Daddy*. Have you been in touch with Pauline Eyre?'

'Yeah, I called her from the police station.'

'She's here with Sam, you know.'

'I'm in no hurry to see her,' I said, 'but I ought to see Jack Hobbs, say I'm sorry for knocking him out.'

'It'll keep till tomorrow. Go home, Alex.'

'Have you seen a doctor?' said the WPC.

'No. I don't need one.'

'Go home, Alex. Now,' Nick said again. 'Ring me tomorrow. I've got the mobile.' She waved it at me. 'See?'

I wasn't responding to her enough, I knew, but I was exhausted. So I went home.

Sunday 6 November

Chapter Thirty-Six

I slept dreamlessly and deeply, and woke up at seven feeling terrific. Terrific lasted until I remembered about Barty, and being pregnant, when I downshifted to anxious. As I showered and ran through the events of the previous evening, I downshifted still further, to worried as hell. What was pregnancy doing to me? Lil, Polly and Nick – they'd all seen that something was wrong and they couldn't see the half of it, because it was inside my head.

I'd lost my sense of reality. How could I *possibly* have given a statement to Cairncross without even consulting a solicitor? I could have been, might still be, in, all kinds of trouble, depending on what attitude to me the police took.

I'd also lost my curiosity. Now, this morning, I was bubbling over with questions, about what had happened to Nick, about what Bourbaki had done and why and how, about Fishburn and Philip Gein, but yesterday I'd been sleepwalking. All I'd wanted was to get home to bed, presumably because my baby needed me to sleep and didn't want his/her resources squandered on my self-indulgences. If the whole pregnancy was going to be like this I'd better fix myself up with seriously undemanding work, specially if I was going to have to support us without Barty. And I'd also better seize this window of access to my normal self to get things done.

As soon as I was dressed and on my second cup of coffee I called Eddy in Florida. OK, it was two thirty in the morning over there, but at least I'd be sure to get him.

After he answered it took five minutes to pacify him, ten minutes to explain what had happened, still leaving out my discovery of Fishburn's body, five minutes to endure his well-deserved bollocking, and a minute to apologize. Then he said he'd talk to Cairncross, get a picture of my situation, and ring me back with advice.

By this time it was as light as it ever gets in London in November. Clear sky, watery sun, pavements still puddled from last night's rain but no trace of fog. I made more coffee and drank it looking out at the empty Sunday-morning street, listening to Mozart, thinking about Barty.

Then I played the messages on my answering machine. The only relevant one was a ring-back from Barbara Gottlieb, the professor from NCL. She'd left the message last night and said she'd be in all Sunday morning.

That decided my next move for me: while I was still firing on all cylinders I'd better finish up the Hilary Lucas case. I rang Nick on the mobile. She answered perkily. 'Hi,' I said. 'Are you alone?'

'Hi. I'm fine and being well looked after. I've still got the police with me. Not Jenny from last night, though, she went off-shift. It's Caroline now. Say hi to Caroline.'

'Hi, Caroline,' I shouted and heard a muffled response. When the acoustics told me that the phone was safely back at Nick's ear I said, 'Listen carefully but don't let her know what I'm talking about. This is another case I'm working on, might be connected. Jack Hobbs's father was a guy called Philip Gein. He was killed in a mugging last summer. Did you hear anything to suggest that Bourbaki did it?'

'No,' she said airily, 'nothing like that at all.'

'No mention of Jack's father?'

'Absolutely not, and I got every detail, believe it. You can rely on me.'

I signed off, promising to come round and fetch her in an hour or two, and bring the clothes I'd brought and forgotten to leave for her the night before.

Then I took the DESTROY UN-OPENED envelope to my desk and looked at the last letter again.

Now I'm really worried. I thought he was pretending, to annoy me. You know he likes to annoy me. He always has. But he really likes that place he's living in – I didn't know why. It was built over that dreadful murderer's house, where he killed those sad women and buried them or bricked them in. 10 Rillington Place. He chose to live there, and he likes it, and he says some women deserve to die. Our own Boy. He was such a beautiful child. I'm now seriously afraid. He talks so oddly about the Notting Hill Killer Please speak to him, One. He listens to you.

Now I knew a little more about Jack Hobbs the letter made no sense to me. I'd liked him ever since I'd seen his stuffed animals. A hard-working creative artist who'd been nothing to do with the Bourbaki

408

conspiracy, who'd treated me well and tried to help me when I said I was fainting...

I rang Nick again. 'Hi. Look, I really want to talk to Jack Hobbs, apologize to him. Is he near you? Is there any way you can get the phone to him?'

'Hang on.' Muffled conversation, movement, then Nick once more. 'Yeah, he's just down the corridor, I'm on the way there now. With Caroline.' Inaudible conversation, then, 'Here he is. Talk to you later.'

'Jack Hobbs here.'

'Jack, this is Alex Tanner. How are you?'

'Bit of a headache, otherwise OK.' Same flat pragmatic voice. 'What can I do for you?'

'I'm really sorry I hit you. Did the police tell you why? I was frightened, and I didn't know what was going on.'

'Ah, forget it. Made sense at the time. You did the right thing. How were you to know?'

'What were you doing there?'

Hesitation. 'Hard to say. Don't want to say, really. Let's leave it that I wondered what Rich and Russell were up to, all right? I'd been worried for some time. I actually thought of hiring you, would you believe it? When I found you in my studio.'

That's right, I remembered. He'd started

409

to say something and I'd brushed him off. No point in going over my mistakes on this case, though, it'd take all day. 'It's a terrible thing,' I said, fishing. 'Those girls.'

'Yeah,' he said unhesitatingly.

'Though some might say they deserved what they got.'

'Who'd say that? How could they?' His voice was incredulous. 'Did I hear you right?'

'I've heard people say it.'

'I haven't. Look, Rich was my friend for years. He's still my friend, I suppose. But there's no way, absolutely no way, that I'd ever defend what he's done.'

He sounded genuine and angry. I believed him and did my best to soothe him down. Eventually, half-mollified, he said, 'Ah, forget it. And hitting me on the head. You can forget that too. You like my animals, yeah? I'll forgive you anything for that. Right?'

'Right,' I said. 'Maybe I'll see you later this morning. I'm coming in to fetch Nick.'

'She's a great woman, isn't she?'

'Yeah. How do you know that?'

'We had a long talk last night. See you later, if you're here before ten. My ma's coming for me then, taking me home for a bit of tlc. Fussing, more like. Want me to hand you back to Nick?'

'Don't bother.' I rang off and looked again at the letter. What was the woman up to? Her son never would've said anything favourable about the Killer; he sounded affectionate when he spoke of his mother. So why had she claimed she was seriously *afraid?* Was she lying, to get her lover's attention? Did she actually believe what she said? And what kind of internal pressure was she under, either way?

I rang Barbara Gottlieb, not sure even as I dialled how I'd get what I wanted from her. 'Alex Tanner here. Thanks for returning my call.'

'How can I help you?' She sounded as cool and intelligent as I remembered her, and I decided to go as near the truth as Hilary Lucas's confidentiality would allow.

'It's difficult,' I said. 'When I called you yesterday, the position was very different. I needed information for an urgent situation then.'

Pause. 'And now?'

'Now, I'm just tidying up loose ends.'

'For your research into lifestyle for a television programme on heart attacks.'

'Yes,' I said.

411

Silence. She went in for them. But she didn't ring off. 'Can I put a hypothetical situation to you?' I said.

'You can try.'

'Suppose there was a man, rather like Philip Gein – call him the Professor – who had an affair which went on for years, and suppose he had a close friend like you.'

'I'm listening.'

'He might tell you about it.'

'He might,' she said, rather wistfully, I thought.

'And suppose, after his wife died, he found someone else.'

'Yes?'

'He might tell you about that too.'

'He might indeed,' she said. Definitely wistful now.

'And he might tell you about his mistress's feelings. The long-standing mistress, I mean. She'd feel very hurt, surely. Betrayed, even.'

'Wouldn't you?' There was anger in her voice now, either for the woman of the letters or for herself. Maybe both. Maybe she'd been waiting on the sidelines for his wife to die, when she could step into her rightful place in Gein's life. No, that was unfair, she was more intelligent than that.

Maybe she'd dreamed it, knowing it was only a dream. Either way, I was on the right lines.

'And the Professor might be finding it difficult to break off the long-standing relationship.'

'To break it off gracefully, I imagine he would.'

'It would all depend what his mistress was like, I suppose. Would you care to guess at that, at all?'

Silence. Eventually, 'She might be a very passionate woman. Even hysterical, at times.'

'Manipulative?'

'Oh certainly.'

'Capable of distorting situations, even lying, if it suited her?'

'If it got her what she wanted, yes.'

'Capable of violence?'

'Physical violence?' She was more doubtful, this time. 'I don't know...' Then, more strongly, and with the beginnings of suspicion, 'Yes. Yes.'

After two slices of toast to stave off morning sickness I went for a run, to take advantage of the good weather while it lasted, and to fill in the time until ten o'clock, when I needed to be at the hospital to meet Jack Hobbs's mother. An added advantage was that it got me out of the flat. Polly hadn't surfaced yet and I wanted solitary thinking-time before she tackled me about my odd behaviour. I wasn't going to tell her I was pregnant. More than ever now that he was missing, I felt Barty had the right to be told before I told anyone else.

As I set off for the Scrubs, past my office, I considered dropping in to check the e-mail for a message from Inge Ericsson in Nairobi, then decided against it. I didn't want to hear bad news, not now. Good news could wait until I'd finished up Hilary Lucas's case to my own satisfaction.

Getting on for nine o'clock on a Sunday morning, the Scrubs were almost deserted. Two dog walkers, an old man doing those slow Chinese exercise movements, some leaden-footed middle-aged male joggers. The fog had vanished as if it had never been. I could see clear across the flat common land to the prison on one side and the industrial estate on the other. I could even make out the outlines of Unit I2, towering solidly over the shacks around it. I ran past the firework party site, strewn with burnt-out fireworks, food wrappings, and the blackened acrid-smelling bonfire-patch, towards Fairfax's factory. When I got closer I could see the yellow police tape marking it off, some constables guarding it, dark dull middle-range cars parked outside. Scenes of crime people still working, I supposed.

After the first mile, movement felt easier and I could stop forcing myself to keep going, let my body do the running, and just think. Jumbled, floating thoughts, with jealous Janey Protheroe mixed up with Polly's model friend's mother who'd Been There and my own pregnancy and the likely age of Hobbs's mother and Lil quoting at me in Notting Hill Police station last night.

Each piece fitted into place, eventually. Too neatly, perhaps. In my experience neat is often facile and wrong, when you deal with people. Nick says that's why she likes mathematics.

By now I'd run the perimeter of the Scrubs and I slowed down for the street-jog home. It was time for forward planning. What could I possibly get out of a meeting with Hobbs's mother? Hilary Lucas was still my client, and Hilary had made it very clear that she wanted confidentiality about the letters. And if I couldn't refer to the letters, how could I bring the subject up? 'Good morning Mrs Hobbs, any lovers died on you lately?' But I wanted to see her, if only from curiosity, to see what sort of a woman sustained a love affair for that length of time. I'd never even been in love myself, not as an adult, not since Peter. I wasn't sure love wasn't just self-delusion rebranded.

But I wasn't sure it wasn't possible, either, which was one of the reasons I had been dragging my heels with Barty. Barty knew he loved me. I *thought* Barty knew he loved me. Or perhaps I only thought Barty thought he knew he loved me. But I was pretty darn sure I didn't love him, though I liked him a whole lot and I desired him, and *was* there any more to love than that?

Anyway, if he came back from Zaire, it would be too late for heel-dragging. It was straight-to-the-registry-office time, if he came back, so that at least our child would be provided for by its father as well as its mother. Especially since its mother was on the hormonal blink.

And if he didn't come back, should I go ahead and have the baby anyway? Money would be tight. Life would be hard. What kind of a start would the baby have?

My mother had gone ahead and had me in far less favourable circumstances. On the other hand she'd also effectively gone off her head as a result. First depression, then schizophrenia, then Alzheimer's. Could that happen to me? Well, of course it could, but was it likely to? And did I have any right to consider killing the baby in the first place?

Destroy unopened. Whatever spin you put on it, that's what I was considering. The more I thought about it, the less I liked it. My mother had done her best for me. At the very least, she'd given me a chance. My chance had effectively destroyed hers. But I was tougher than she was, and my baby might well be tougher than me.

And besides, I thought collapsing exhausted on the front steps, it wasn't only my decision to make, and I didn't have to make it until I knew about Barty, for sure.

Chapter Thirty-Seven

Polly still hadn't emerged from her flat when I left for the hospital, so I borrowed her car, which got me there at a quarter to ten.

The hospital, like the Scrubs, was Sunday-morning deserted, though when I got up to Nick's corridor police were still on duty guarding doors. I asked my way to Jack Hobbs's room, but the constable outside wouldn't let me in. Only one visitor at a time was allowed, he said, and Hobbs's mother was in there. If I went to the waiting room he'd ask her to come along and tell me when Hobbs was free.

That suited me fine since it was her I wanted to speak to, so I didn't argue. I took myself off to the empty waiting room which looked even more shabby and exhausted in daylight, scanned the battered outdated lifestyle magazine Polly had been reading the night before, and tried to imagine under what circumstances anyone would want to cook a four-course dinner for eight and then spend hours pissing around with table decorations. I kept flicking through. My husband's affair – how I coped. Six delightful desserts using summer fruits. Things to do for kids in the long August days. Keep your hands lovely on only thirty minutes a week. I looked at my hands: short nails, square-cut. Perhaps if I let the nails grow, shaped and buffed them, I'd fall in love. Or perhaps not. How could women read this stuff? They told me my baby was deaf – bit near the knuckle, that. 'You're not deaf, are you?' I said to my stomach. I really must get a book on nutrition in pregnancy.

'Hello. Are you the person waiting to see Jack?'

She was in her fifties, medium height, medium build, well preserved, plenty of greying black hair in a loose top-knot, arty clothes: expensive materials, rich dark colours, several layers. A good-looking strong-boned rather lined face, no make-up, dark burning eyes. Nothing about her reminded me of her son, except her hands, big, strong, square and work-roughened.

I got up and introduced myself. 'Alex Tanner.'

'Antonia Hobbs,' she replied, without making a move to shake hands.

I explained who I was and what I'd done

to her son. 'I'm sorry,' I concluded.

'Never mind,' she said. 'You must have been frightened, I suppose. It's quite understandable. Would you like to go in now? I need to take him home.'

There was something wrong with her voice. It sounded mechanical, as if she wasn't listening to herself. Tranquillizers? Or just shocked by what had happened to her son?

I had to keep the conversation going, couldn't think how. 'Jack does terrific work, doesn't he,' I said. Couldn't miss with a mother, surely.

'Do you think so?' she said.

'I like them a lot. I hope to buy one. Depends on his prices, of course.'

'Oh, good,' she said. There was something wrong with her posture, as well. She hadn't moved at all since I first saw her. She was standing locked, like a statue, one large hand clasping the other, her eyes fixed at a point somewhere out beyond the window, somewhere in the London sky. 'Will you go in now?'

I wasn't going to get anywhere at all, chatting. It had been stupid to think I could. I took a deep breath, and said, 'Did you kill Philip Gein?'

She didn't move her body, only her eyes.

They focused on me, then refocused beyond the window. 'No,' she said, in the same mechanical voice. 'He was killed by muggers, poor Philip. Did you know him?'

'We never met.'

'He was an old friend,' she said. 'Will you go in now?'

Hilary Lucas made excellent coffee, I remembered as she handed me a cup, and this time there was no problem getting her to the point.

She sat down in the same place on the same sofa three days almost to the minute since she hired me, looked me square in the face, and said, 'You said this was urgent so I presume you've discovered something.'

'Yes.' I pulled the DESTROY UNOPENED envelope out from my squashy leather bag and put it back on the coffee table between us.

'Will this be painful?' she said, and bristled her eyebrows at me. She was frightened. The quicker the better.

'Absolutely not,' I said. 'The most important thing for you to know is that I'm convinced those letters weren't written to your husband.'

She stared at me in astonishment. 'To

whom, then?'

'Philip Gein.'

'Philip?' She let out a great breath of air. 'Of course. Philip. Of course.'

'But I can't actually prove it unless you'll let me use them to show someone.'

She'd got up and was pacing up and down. The size of the room gave plenty of scope for pacing. 'Who do you propose to show them to?' she said.

'The woman who wrote them.'

'And that is?'

I shook my head. 'I'm not going to tell you,' I said. 'You shouldn't actually have seen those letters at all, I don't think. Your husband should have destroyed them. He didn't. Maybe he never saw the envelope. Was Professor Gein's office sorted and cleared before your husband died?'

She was still pacing. 'It may well not have been,' she said precisely.

'If I can use the letters I can get definite confirmation for you, but I'm sure I'm right.'

'Let us be clear about this. Are you guessing about the identity of the writer of those letters?'

'No. I'm sure about that. From internal evidence. I'm nearly sure about who they were written to – beyond reasonable doubt sure – but if you want absolute confirmation, I need the letters.'

'That won't be necessary,' she said. She looked quite different: relieved, radiant, vigorous. 'I'm sure you're right. Of course! I was so stupid... Oh, thank God! I'll write you a cheque... What do I owe you?'

'Hang on a minute,' I said. 'There's something else I think you should know. It may be a police matter.'

'Police? Why?'

'Because I think she killed him.'

'Killed *Robbie?*'

It took me a few seconds to remember who Robbie was, then I caught on. 'No, not your husband. Philip Gein. Her lover.'

'Do you have any evidence for that serious allegation?' she snapped.

'No,' I said. 'But I'm sure–'

'If you have no evidence, then you will be very ill-advised to repeat it,' she said. 'And I have no intention of allowing you to use the letters. Is that clear?'

She was as intimidating as a hungry alligator. If I had an international contract pending, she'd be my chosen legal adviser. 'Right,' I said, and told her my final fee, doubling it. She wrote the cheque, handed it over, then looked at me consideringly.

'Alex,' she said. 'Perhaps it would be only fair... Yes, it would.'

Silence. She was sticking again. I put the cheque away and waited.

Eventually she said, 'You've done a good job on this.'

'Thank you.'

'So perhaps you should know that I was nearly certain in my own mind, before I hired you, who wrote those letters.'

'Did you read them all, then?'

'No. I told you. I didn't want to. But the letter I did read in full – the last one – made it quite clear. And I was angry. No. Not just angry. Furious.'

She looked at me defiantly and I could feel her rage. 'Which is why you said you ate the letter.'

'Did I say that? Lord, so I did.' She clicked her teeth together, reminiscently. 'I wanted to bite someone or something, that's true.'

'Then why hire me?'

'Because I didn't *believe* it. I couldn't. It couldn't be true. I'd have known.'

'Known because of your husband?'

'Partly. And partly because Antonia Hobbs is my sister.'

Our eyes met. Now I was angry. She'd well and truly jerked me about, and I wasn't going to tiptoe round her sensibilities any more. 'If she's your sister, then Jack is your nephew.'

'Of course.'

'So you must have known that the last letter was a complete lie. Jack's a sweetie. He'd never have said those things about Christie and Rillington Place and women.'

'Of course not.'

'Knowing your – *sister* – as you do, you can help me out. If Jack had told her he was worried about the men he was living with and their attitude to women and the Notting Hill Killer, would she have used that idea, only put it on Jack? Told Jack's father all that stuff as if it had come from Jack, just to keep her lover's interest and keep his involvement going?'

'No!' she said. Pause. I reckoned she was weighing up how badly she'd treated me, how much she owed me. Then, reluctantly, 'She might have done.'

'I think she did. And I think when all her manipulations weren't working any more, she stabbed him to death. That's what I think.'

'No evidence,' she snapped, but I saw the evidence in her eyes. That's what she thought too.

Chapter Thirty-Eight

We were in Polly's living room because she has two sofas. She wanted to lie on one and nurse her broken arm; Nick wanted to lie on the other and get some mileage out of being an invalid, and I got to sit on the upright chair and run around after them. They'd been nagging me to go round to the office and check for an e-mail about Barty, but I wouldn't, and they'd given up and were nagging me about Antonia Hobbs instead.

'But why do you think she killed him?' said Nick. 'I don't get it. Why shouldn't it just have been muggers, like the police thought?'

'I think she killed him because she was menopausal and desperate,' I said.

'That's not very PC,' said Polly. 'Meno-pausal.'

'I think hormones make a difference,' I said, nibbling a dry biscuit.

'Of course they do,' said Nick. 'But not every fiftyish woman kills someone.'

'She'd had a lover for over twenty years. She'd spent all that time and effort and passion on him. Then he was going, and she knew it, and she tried everything, even lying about her son, and it wasn't working. I just feel it, all right?'

'Did you know she was a sculptor?'

'What's that got to do with it?'

'Strength. Familiarity with tools, knives,' said Nick. 'When did Gein die?'

'August.'

'Jack said she's been more or less off her head since August,' she said. 'Neither of us could sleep last night. We talked for hours. He's OK. Actually, Alex, I think you could be right.'

'But you've got no proof,' said Polly. 'And she could just have gone off her head because her lover had died.'

'It doesn't matter either way,' said Nick, 'because she's not likely to do it again, is she? She doesn't have another twenty years in her and she's not likely to get another lover, not at her age.'

'Well, I can sort of understand it if she did. What I can't understand is Fairfax and Jacobs,' said Polly. 'That whole thing.'

'I can,' said Nick. 'They're men.'

'That's not an explanation,' said Polly.

'OK, try this. Fairfax is spoilt rotten by all the money, and he likes things his own way, and he's fixated on little blonde blue-eyed girls, but maybe they don't come through for him as quickly as he thinks they should because all he ever talks about is himself and maybe also they think he's gay, because actually I do, and then he meets the real love of his life, a big strong man, and the big strong man sees easy pickings...'

'But the *violence*. The *killing*,' protested Polly.

'They liked it,' said Nick flatly. 'Believe me. That's the bit they liked.'

Polly looked at Nick, who was beginning to sweat and said 'What do you think, Alex?'

Obviously she wanted me to take the weight off Nick. I didn't think anything, much, because all that mattered to me at the moment was Barty, so I rambled. 'Odd, what people like. Football, for instance. Anyhow I agree with Eddy.'

'Eddy Barstow? Your sweaty policeman?' said Polly.

'Yeah. He said not to worry about what people could or should or might have done, or why. He said to find out what they did do, and Nick has. What I'd like to know is why they didn't get rid of me earlier. They picked Nick up straight away.'

'I really got up Fairfax's nose,' said, Nick.

'Right from the start. And I mentioned the Killer because I said Sam was Killer-bait, and he thought I knew more than I did. I knew sod-all about–'

'Listen,' interrupted Polly.

'What?' I said.

She flapped a silencing hand in my direction and opened the window, on to the street. Then I could hear, too. A dog barking. A woman bellowing.

'O! stay and hear! your true love's coming,/ That can sing both high and low:/ Trip no further, pretty sweeting;/ Journeys end in lovers meeting,/ Every wise man's son doth know.'

'Yer what?' said Nick.

'Alex? Alex?' Lil was bellowing even louder now, to be heard over Benbow's frenzied barks. 'Alex? I went to check at the office. There's an e-mail for you, I've printed it out, I've got it with me. Alex?'

This Large Print Book for the partially sighted, who cannot read normal print, is published under the auspices of

THE ULVERSCROFT FOUNDATION